Gilmore House Mysteries

Old Bones

Brian R Lindsay

Printed in Canada

ISBN 978-0-9948042-0-4

Fifth Iteration

FIN 14 07 2017

Disclaimer

This is a work of fiction.
The town of Westport is a real place as are some of the local businesses mentioned in the story but I have taken the liberty of rearranging some of its geography and adding people, buildings and businesses. All else is fiction, as are all the characters.

Acknowledgements

Thanks are due to a great many people.

Thanks to Jennifer Sallans of Volumes Publishing for helping me through the process.

Thanks to Susan and John and to Tom and Carol in Calgary who allowed me the use, undisturbed, of their respective backyard patio tables a few years ago, to pursue my folly. It was there that I finished the first draft. Thanks to Bruce for boat and boating information and to Mary for the loan of information books.

It seems as if the book has quite suddenly come together. In fact it was several years in the making, and I am grateful for the encouragement of several early readers: people who read an unfinished manuscript and who, without exception, pronounced it okay and worth pursuing.

Thanks to early readers Bruce and Terrilynn in Mission, Marg and Bruce in North Gower, Grace in Thornhill, Erin and Chase and Mike in Waterloo.

Other early readers were later conscripted as editors and looked at the ongoing work more times than I had any right to ask them to, but they helped out without complaint, at least none that I heard.

Thanks for editorial assistance to Mike Lindsay for editing and some law-related information and Marg Penniston, who put in a great deal of time and effort on my behalf. She also provided Rideau Lakes and Canal information and a photograph which appears on the back cover of the book.

Then there are Nikki Everts-Hammond and Mavis Fenn. We three are a "critique group", most recently known among ourselves as The KWG (Kitchener, Waterloo, Guelph) Writers Collective. We have been meeting once a month, more or less, for several years, sharing and critiquing our writings. Mavis and Nikki, both published writers themselves, have been listeners, readers, editors and critics. They are both friends and mentors and their value to the completion of this book is incalculable.

And thanks to Jane, who was and is computer teacher, early reader, sounding board, editor, researcher and more. Hopefully the dedication of this book says all that is needed.

Dedication

For Jane, with love.
Without you this book would not ever have been finished.

And for Grace

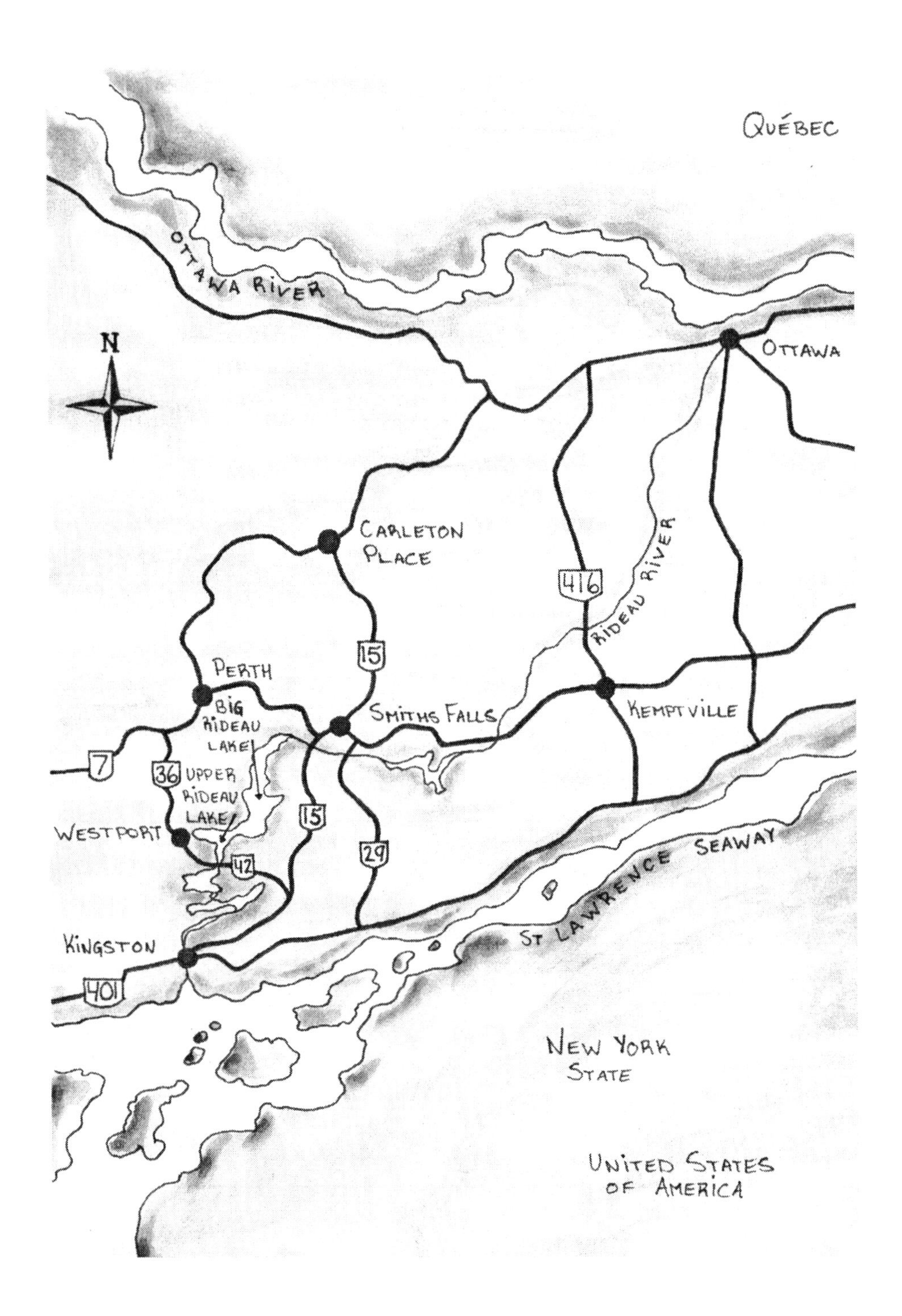
QUÉBEC
OTTAWA RIVER
N
OTTAWA
CARLETON
PLACE
416
RIDEAU RIVER
15
PERTH
BIG
RIDEAU
LAKE
SMITHS FALLS
KEMPTVILLE
7
36
UPPER
RIDEAU
LAKE
15
WESTPORT
42
29
SEAWAY
ST LAWRENCE
KINGSTON
401
NEW YORK
STATE
UNITED STATES
OF AMERICA

This is a copy of a topographical map found among the stored Gilmore family items at the Westport museum. It is thought to have been made by Alexander Gilmore, the youngest son of the Gilmore family. There is however, no way to verify this.

It is a very accurate representation of Gilmore Island.

Landmarks and labels have been added as none were found on the original. RJH.

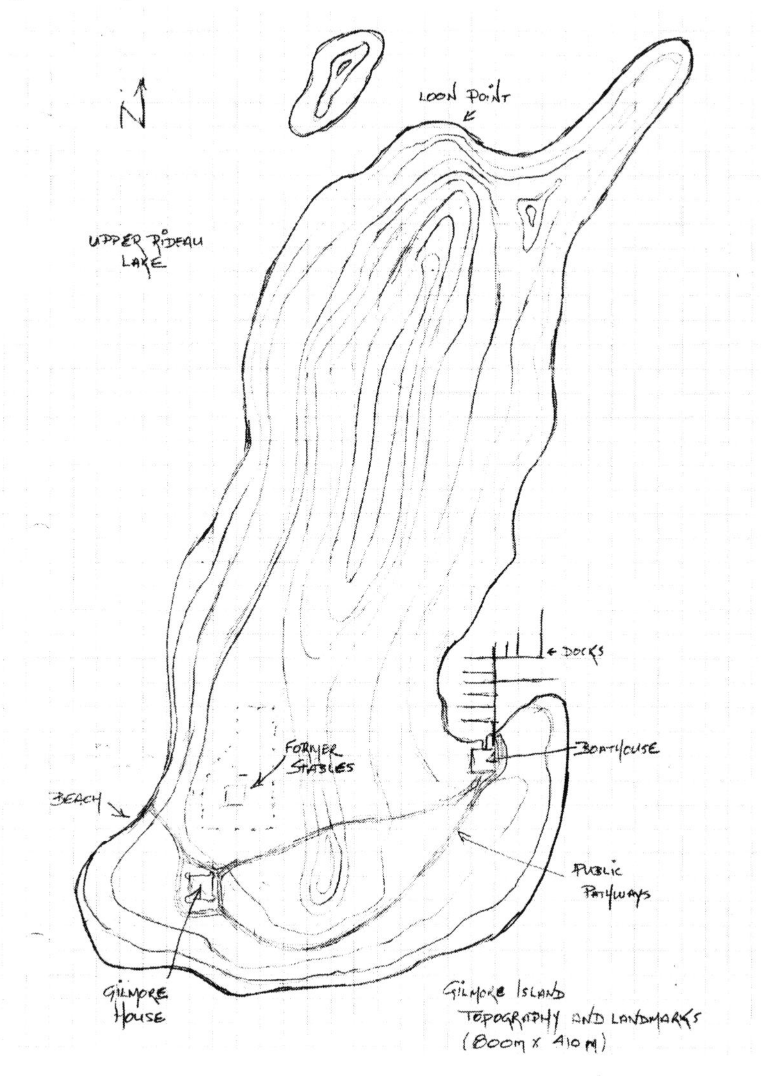

Gilmore House Floorplans

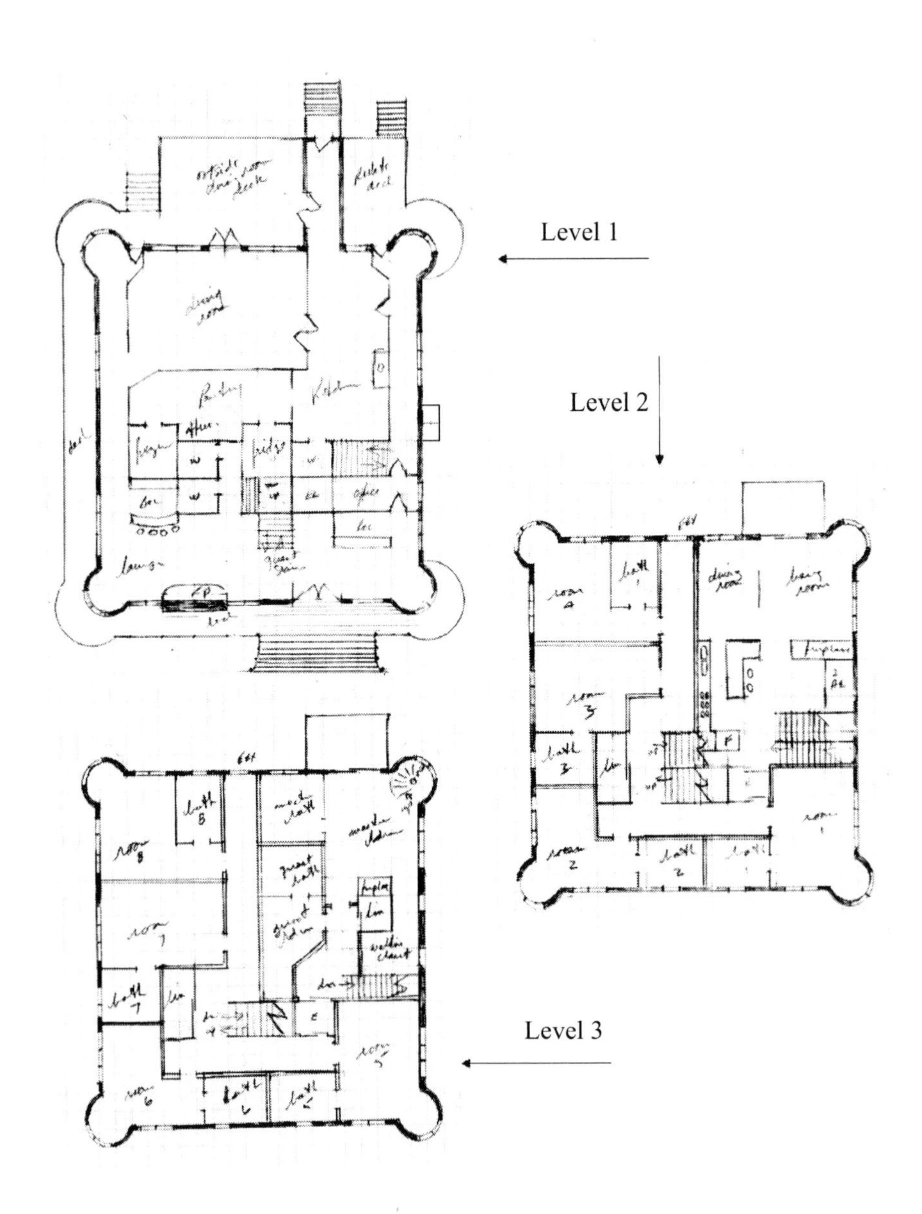

Chapter 1

My name is Robert James Harrison. Most people call me RJ.

For about 100 years before I arrived here, Gilmore Island had been collecting mysteries.

I'm told the first began on an August morning in 1916.

Mrs. Gilmore, matriarch of the Gilmore family, noticed that her eldest daughter, Victoria, had not appeared for breakfast. Nor had one of the guests, Albert Greenwood.

She had their rooms checked and did not find them. Thinking something might be amiss, Mrs. Gilmore required that Simpson, the butler, gather some of the staff and begin a complete search of the house and grounds. Any guests currently on the island were to have their rooms discreetly checked by the maids and housekeeper. Other staff would look at the boathouse, the bathing change area and the stable. Still others were sent out to explore the rugged northern end of the island.

The room searches revealed that some of Victoria's belongings and all of Greenwood's were gone.

A short while later the gardener arrived, breathless from running, to announce that one of the rowing-boats was missing. He said that he had been assured by the boatman, Morrison, that all had been accounted for the previous evening.

The Gilmores had been trying to end what they saw as an unsatisfactory relationship between their daughter and Albert

Greenwood, a business man from Kingston, but now the wilful Victoria seemed to have done the unthinkable: she had gone away with him. Mrs. Gilmore debated notifying the police, but decided to wait for her husband, George, to return the following day.

After being told by his wife about the events of the past few days he immediately began questioning the guests, the staff and the children. By the next afternoon Mr. Gilmore was convinced that his daughter Victoria had indeed run away with Albert Greenwood. There seemed no other explanation.

There was no police involvement and no stories appeared in the press.

The consensus among those in the house was that what George Gilmore really wanted was to prevent his own name and family from being associated with a scandal.

Whatever his reasoning, the effect was the same.

Any possibility of locating Victoria Gilmore and Albert Greenwood slipped away and was lost.

Since no-one outside the mansion ever knew with certainty why or how Victoria Gilmore had disappeared, the mystery grew. Rumours of Victoria's absence, and occasionally her presence, drifted around the surrounding community, and lingered through the years.

I first saw the Gilmore Island property advertised in the out-of-town Real Estate section of the *Waterloo Region Record* about a year and a half ago. The ad read something to the effect of: "Small, rustic, semi-Victorian Hotel on Private Island. Needs repair."

The agency was apparently in need of some better copy-writers. This was not what I would have called a glowing recommendation. Still, it stirred something in the recesses of my mind; one of those hazy ideas, half considered, half dreamed, of a long buried desire and a new future. I had occasionally thought of the idea of a small Hotel or Bed and Breakfast as appealing but had never pursued it. I wasn't actively looking for such a place but, well, I was always looking, if you know what I mean. I liked my job – mostly - but I was restless.

After a lifetime of working for other people, at jobs I didn't really love but didn't hate enough to get off my butt and find something else, I was drifting. Fifty-odd years old and going nowhere. Then the final straw.

"RJ, there's a message on your desk but I can relay it if you like."

Suze was the ever efficient sixty-something secretary to all the Investigators at our branch of Mediterranean Rock Insurance. She called us her boys. There were six of us in the Waterloo Region office and Suze handled all the calls, mail, messages and whatever else happened along that might keep us in the office instead of out in the field. She was great.

I was in no great rush to get to my desk. "Okay Suze. Shoot." I leaned my elbows on the low wall that made up one side of her workspace and prepared to listen.

"Mr. Maxwell wants a change in tactics in handling the Carson case. He says you should take a more direct approach; get in his face a bit and see if that shakes anything loose."

I raised my eyebrows just as Suze looked up.

"His words, not mine. He says Eric got new information over the weekend and this is how he thinks we should proceed. Mr. Maxwell thinks so, that is."

"Do you have the file? I'd like to see what Eric came up with before I go rousting this guy. I've always thought Carson could be a problem if he was cornered."

"The file is locked in Mr. Maxwell's office and he's at a meeting in Toronto today."

"What about the computer?"

"Not entered yet."

"So Maxwell left the file in his office instead of giving it to you to enter and left me a message to go act on information I haven't even seen? Great. What about Eric?"

Suze checked her watch. "Right about now he's at 35,000 feet over the Atlantic, on his way to London. Vacation."

"Right. I'd forgotten he was headed out early today. All right, what the hell. You only live once, right? I have a couple of phone calls to make then I'll go visit Mr. Carson."

I went to my office and fired up my computer. As I waited for it to boot up I read the message Maxwell had left. It was not even in his own writing – strange in itself but not unheard-of. He'd obviously told Suze what it was about and she'd written it out.

The note said that there were new developments in the Carson case which suggested that we were right in our assessment that he was healthier than he was letting on and that, if prodded, he might give the game away. All pretty vague. It sure would have been nice to have Eric's notes – see what was actually happening. Oh well.

I made a couple of follow up calls and checked email. All my other cases were under control and there was nothing to keep me in the office, so I closed down my computer again and left the building.

By now the day was hot though it was still early – the sun bright and low in the morning sky and not much breeze.

I drove to Carson's address and parked half a block away on the opposite side of the street. This was nuts. All I could do was go knock on his door and try to piss him off enough to take a run at me? What was Maxwell thinking? Sure we'd been on this, Eric and I, for quite a while with no results to speak of. Hopefully Eric had made some serious progress over the weekend which would turn the tide. But this was still stupid.

I was thinking all these things as I approached the Carson house and went up the walk.

The house was an older bungalow with cream siding and a dark shingled roof, a double garage with windows in the doors and several flower beds, nicely tended.

I heard banging as I approached so I diverted my line from the front door of the house to the garage and looked through one of the dirty windows.

There on the garage floor was Harve Carson, wrench in one hand and rag in the other sliding out from under a car on a wheeled dolly. He rolled off the dolly and hopped up, reached for the handle of a chain fall hoist and began lifting the engine out of the car.

Not bad for someone with a damaged back and partial paralysis on the right side – the side he was using to crank up the engine.

I knocked on the glass. He looked around at the sound. I waved. He threw the wrench at the window. I ducked. The wrench broke through the window and I beat a hasty retreat down the driveway, passing the wrench as it skidded to a halt on the asphalt.

As I ran I heard the garage door open and the sound of footsteps running. Carson's voice called out.

"Can't you just leave me alone?"

A pistol shot rang out over the quiet neighbourhood.

"I hate insurance companies!"

Another shot. This bullet embedded itself in the trunk of a tree, sending up a spray of bark chips and moisture. The tree was only half a metre from where I'd been at the time. I kept running, hoping to make it to my car before his aim got any better. No such luck.

The third shot found its mark. It hit the back of my left knee and pushed the whole leg out in front of me. I fell in a twisted heap on the concrete sidewalk, stunned briefly as my head bounced off the hard surface.

I sat up quickly. There was blood all over the sidewalk. I couldn't see the extent of the damage because of the pant leg of my Chinos but it hurt like hell.

While I gripped the wound with both hands, trying to slow the bleeding I was aware of Carson still approaching behind me.

His pace had slowed to a walk which, although I couldn't see it, no doubt included his usual swagger. His face surely held the self-satisfied smirk I'd often seen before.

I didn't look around. "Where'd you get the gun, Harve? I thought even you had more brains than to do something like this."

"Shut up asshole. I'm the one in control here. You're the one bleeding out on the ground."

"It's a big step from insurance fraud to murder, Harve. Have you thought about what's going to happen to you if I do bleed out? The price you're going to pay is going way up, Harve."

Carson was quiet but he kept on walking toward me.

"Want to guess how many 911 calls have been made from around here in the last minute, Harve? I bet they're swamped. Cops'll be here soon." My breathing was now in short sharp gasps.

"Shut up."

"When they get here you'd better be sitting quietly on the lawn there with the gun several feet away, and your hands in plain sight."

"I said shut up." He walked around me, on the grass to avoid stepping in the blood on the sidewalk, and stopped a little further along, turned and looked down at me. Now I noticed the gun for the first time. A Beretta, 9mm, nine shots at least, maybe thirteen depending on the model. He'd only fired three. At least six left. Even if I could have rushed him, the odds were not exactly favourable.

The gun was gripped so tightly that his knuckles were white but it was pointed at the sidewalk.

I kept hold of my knee. I was starting to feel lightheaded from the blood loss.

"So now what, Harve? You thought this through yet? You really want me dead bad enough to spend the rest of your sorry life in jail?"

He just stared at me briefly. "Maybe I do asshole. Yeah, I do. But I'm not so sure I'll be going to jail. I can finish you off and get in the car and drive away before the cops even get here. You'll be dead and I'll be gone. What do you think of that?"

I have to admit it was not the response I was expecting or hoping for.

"You won't escape, Harve. There are too many witnesses. You have to know that every window on this street has someone looking out at what's happening here." My head was spinning more now and I was having trouble keeping a grip on the wounds in my knee.

Carson walked around behind me again, back in the direction of his house. "Time for us both to be going, I guess."

He was still close. The midmorning sun cast a long shadow. He had stopped only a metre or two behind me. He raised his arm and pointed the gun at me once again. I expected the shot that would end my life any second, though at the same time I wasn't sure Carson was either crazy enough or strong enough to just outright murder me. My vision was starting to blur and I was sweating.

At that second a prowl car from the Waterloo Regional Police rolled to a stop about fifteen metres along the road. It drew up at forty five degrees to the roadway, silently – no siren – no lights – and almost before it stopped fully the passenger door burst open and an officer stepped out, drawing her weapon as she did so.

The street was silent – no kids – no dogs or birds or mowers – no breeze. I heard the safety click off. Maybe Carson heard it too.

The officer braced against the roof of the car and took aim.

"You there, with the gun. I know you can hear me. I need you to lower the weapon and toss it on the grass. Do it now."

Carson's shadow didn't move.

The officer's partner had by now slid across from the driver's seat and out the open door. He took up a position a little further along the car's roof, also now ready to fire if necessary.

"Please throw down the gun, sir. We don't want this situation to get any worse than it already is."

I can't begin to imagine the thought process that goes into the decision to try to shoot two cops who already have their sidearms aimed at you. Maybe there isn't one.

I no longer had the energy to both sit up and hold my knee. I toppled slowly onto my left side staying bent at the waist, still holding closed the ragged holes in my knee.

As I was going over, the shadow of Carson's arm moved and I anticipated the final shot. I found out later that Carson had not been attempting to aim at me but rather at the police officers.

As soon as they saw the gun begin to move in their direction they fired, one time each. There was a sound like two ripe peaches thrown hard against a concrete wall and a half-surprised grunt, then Carson's body, pushed backward by the force of the impacts, slammed down onto the sidewalk.

I didn't see or hear any more.

I came to briefly in the ambulance, peering around an oxygen mask at the worried-looking paramedic leaning over me. He acknowledged my consciousness with a smile and a gentle pat on the shoulder.

Many hours later I surfaced briefly again. This time, when I turned my head to relieve the stiffness in my neck, it was to see Suze, sitting in a chair beside the window. I was hooked up to an IV but there were no other tubes and no monitors – a good sign. Suze must have heard me move and came over to stand by the bed. I was groggy – still only partly there.

"Welcome back, RJ. You had quite a day."

"Yeah. I think I only remember part of it and that not exactly fondly."

I was feeling no pain in my knee so I raised my head just a little so I could see if I still had two whole legs. The sight of a huge bulge in the covers about half way down and two sets of toes moving around set my mind at ease a little. As if she sensed my thoughts, Suze spoke up again.

"Your knee is a mess, RJ. No sense saying anything else. The bullet went in the side and at an angle so it was not as bad as it might have been. They rebuilt it as well as they could – there was some sort of specialist available here today and he pitched in. It will heal and you'll be able to walk. It could be a long hard recovery. That's all they're saying for now. Maybe you'll need a new knee sometime – or not. You'll have to wait and see. That may not be the best news you ever got but it's not too bad, considering the alternatives."

That was all I heard from her as I drifted off to sleep again.

The next time I awoke it was quite dark and very quiet. I remembered my eventful day in vivid detail and reflected on what Suze had said. She was right. I was lucky to be alive.

Mid-morning the next day Suze was back but she was a different person. Anxious and unsure, she poured out the events of her morning.

Since she expected there would be a lot of upset around the office because of what had happened to me the previous day, she came in very early to get a start on the day's work before things got too crazy.

"RJ, the overnight cleaning crew was just finishing up. Of course they have a key to Maxwell's office.

"Since the door was open I went in and took a couple of files from the basket on the credenza, same as I do every day. When I reached for the files I saw there was one shoved under the basket – just a corner peeking out. I figured Mr. Maxwell had just missed the basket; you know – shoved it back without really looking. I took it with the rest. When I got back to my desk that file was on top so I opened it first.

"I knew what it was as soon as I saw the first line. It was Eric's writing so I was sure it was his notes from the weekend, ready to be entered in the computer. I opened a standard form for case notes and started typing."

Suze stopped talking and lowered her head to her chest, as though she was too tired to continue. Tears rolled unchecked down her cheeks and puddled briefly in the folds of the flowered, summery scarf around her neck.

"What's got you so upset, Suze? What's wrong?"

"Everything, RJ. Everything is wrong. None of this should have happened – the shooting – the hospital - ." She gave a kind of helpless wave in my general direction.

I began to have a bad feeling – a coldness in my core that warned me that I was not going to like what was coming.

"What did you find in the file, Suze? What did Eric write that I should have seen before I went out to visit Carson?"

Suze took out a tissue from her purse. She dried her eyes and wiped her nose and generally collected herself.

"Eric knew, RJ. Eric found out that Carson had acquired a handgun. There's no indication in the notes of where he got it. Eric doesn't say he saw the gun himself but says he talked to a neighbour who definitely did see it. The neighbour's name and address are in the notes.

"Eric stated very clearly that he thought we, the company, had to rethink the approach to Carson in light of this new development. He said he thought Carson was dangerous and that we needed a meeting to discuss ideas before anyone went out in the field on that case again. He also said the police should be notified about the gun even though he hadn't actually seen it. Better safe than sorry."

This time Suze didn't look away when she stopped talking.

"That's incredible, Suze. Are you saying Maxwell hid that file on purpose? I knew he didn't like me. We've butted heads lots of times. He did that with all the investigators. We may not have said it out loud, but I'm sure he knew we were aware that he had no background in investigation and that we believed he had no business running a department like this."

I paused.

"That bastard sent me out there knowing that Carson had a gun and, given what I remember from the file on him, knew how to use it. I think he was training to be an armoured truck guard but washed out for being too aggressive."

I thought a moment.

"Where's the file now, Suze?"

She actually smiled.

"Well, RJ, you know how conscientious and efficient I am. I did my job exactly as I was supposed to. I entered the notes from Eric into the computer, then as per procedure, since you guys like to work from paper while an investigation is ongoing, I copied Eric's notes for your folder and I copied some of your notes from last week into Eric's folder. I put Eric's folder on his desk and, since there are no rules about taking folders from the office, I brought yours here."

She reached down beside her chair and came up with my well worn folder of the investigation of Harve Carson, deceased.

"You're sticking your neck out here, Suze. Maxwell isn't going to be happy about any of this."

Suze smiled again. "It's my neck to stick out if I want to. Besides, I have less than no interest any longer in what does or does not make the great toad happy."

I'd never before heard Suze speak of anyone in derogatory terms. I laughed.

"Why are you so disinterested in Maxwell's feelings suddenly?"

Suze was now very serious.

"I'm never going back to that place, RJ. It was a good job for a long time but it will never be the same. My letter of resignation, effective immediately, is already in the HR office, along with a full accounting of my reasons for leaving. I've had my own problems with Maxwell over the years – harassment if you like – but this was the end. I cleaned out my desk of all personal stuff before I left there this morning. I'm going to miss you boys but I don't feel as though I have any other alternative."

"What will you do?"

"For the short term, I'm going to visit my sister in Seattle. She's been at me for years to come for a visit. Now she'll get her wish. You're the only one I'm telling that to. I don't want there to be any chance the toad might be able to find me. I know you and Eric won't say anything but I can't say as much for some others. After Seattle, who knows? I'll be in touch anyway."

Several weeks later, after an extended period of first hospitalization, then convalescent care and numerous varieties of therapy, I was ready to return to Mediterranean Rock, if only briefly.

I'd spent most of my down-time doing what I do: investigating. I collected all the information I could and accumulated a significant amount of evidence for my lawyer to work with.

I spent some time relating the truth of the Carson incident to the Investigators who were there that day and left some notes for the others. I said hello to Suze's replacement then went upstairs to the executive offices.

I entered Maxwell's office with a better feeling than I'd ever had doing it before.

Maxwell sat behind a giant, highly polished and absolutely empty desk, a huge, nearly bald, fat-faced toad of a man with bulging eyes and no neck. The greenish-brown colour of the suit he wore added to the image.

"This is for you, RJ. Now you've finally decided to quit milking your little injury for all it's worth and come back to work."

As usual Maxwell tossed the file he'd been holding across the desk, not exactly at me but close enough that I'd be able to catch it before it hit the floor if I moved fast enough. I didn't even try. The sudden shift of weight to my left leg would probably have sent me crashing to the floor and, since Maxwell knew that and it was probably what he wanted, I refused to play. The manila folder slid off the desk, hit the carpeted floor and stopped dead, the contents continuing on for another metre or so. I just looked at him, not speaking.

Maxwell's face reddened. He stared at me, not immediately processing the change in the game. He glanced at the spilled file on the floor, then back to me. When I made no move to pick it up, he spoke again.

"So? What's going on, RJ? You used to be quicker than that."

"I used to be a lot of things. I used to be someone who cared what you thought of me but that ended a few months ago. I also used to be someone who worked for you but that ends now."

Maxwell's breathing had become shallower and his face redder. He sat bolt upright on the front edge of his chair, both hands palm down on the surface of his pristine desk, his large and ugly head thrust forward – the toad ready to spring at its prey. Before he could interrupt, I went on.

"I'm not sure how you kept your job after what you did – well, maybe I do know. You lied. You lied to the company brass and lawyers after the shooting just as you lied to me before. They bought it, for now. I know you tried to convince them that it was all my fault that I got shot - that I mishandled it. Maybe they even believed it up to a point. The payout they offered to get me to quit while I was still in the hospital had you written all over it. But I couldn't quit, not without coming back here to say goodbye to you and to make very sure all the other investigators working here know, if they don't already, what a devious, slimy, corrupt bastard you are. Oh, and also to let you know that I'm suing you and the company. See you in court."

The case never made it to court.

When my lawyer and I met with the company's lawyers and senior management the meeting only lasted a half hour. We'd provided the company with our evidence and our requirements several days in advance so that they could be prepared. It was easier than I'd thought it would be.

By now the company had figured out that there was much more to be gained than lost by settling.

We had decided to sue for $25 million, knowing full well that they would not agree and that we would end up in court. That would mean that all the stuff that Med. Rock would rather not have made public, would be.

Med. Rock knew that they had the wrong person managing the investigations department. He had no experience. That in itself wouldn't have made them much different from a lot of other companies. But they also knew that Maxwell had a history of erratic behaviour, causing him to be moved around the company.

My investigation turned up many other damning pieces of information about Maxwell and his behaviour, some of which cast a poor light on other employees of the company, particularly some executives.

The end result was this.

The company settled for a sum of $10 million – half up front and the rest over ten years. This was a big settlement for Canada, but I think they went for it in the hope that I would go away and not come back.

There was never any mention of my returning to work.

As I limped to my car after the meeting I realized how much my life had changed in the past few months. I opened the door and tossed my cane across to the passenger seat and carefully manoeuvred my way into the vehicle.

I should have been elated by the thought of all that money. Don't get me wrong. I was glad to have the money but there was something else. I had a long hard recovery ahead still and I was far from sure I would make it back to what I had once thought of as normal.

For many months I made only half-hearted efforts at rehab. My work life, hell, my whole life, was on hold. Maybe it was some sort of a midlife crisis thing. Although it never took on crisis proportions, the symptoms were there, I guess.

I had decided that I would not be returning to the Insurance Investigation business and I think my former associates were relieved. Even if I'd been with another company my presence would have been a constant reminder of what had happened to me – something that isn't supposed to happen to Insurance Investigators, not in Canada at least.

The serious on-the-job injury and the subsequent settlement left me without work but with a significant amount of cash; enough to retire on if I was ready for that and certainly enough to work with if I could find a good way to spend it.

That was when I found the newspaper ad that changed my life again.

When I thought about it I found that the idea of owning an Inn was appealing when nothing else was. I had had some food service experience before and during college. I liked the work, but the killer hours and lousy pay had pushed me out of food service. I knocked around Europe for a while, travelling and working. Some of those jobs were way more memorable than others – not necessarily all in a good way. I then returned to Canada and moved into the oh-so-glamorous life of an insurance investigator. Yeah, right. Perhaps if I could be my own boss, the hours and the pay would be better. Or maybe the lousy hours and lousy pay wouldn't matter so much. Maybe.

So I made an initial inquiry, a phone call to a realtor in Barrhaven, a suburb of Ottawa. I was passed on to Sarah Marshall, the primary associate trying to move the Gilmore Island property. We talked briefly on the phone and I decided to go and meet her and see the place. I had nothing to lose, right?

Chapter 2

Thinking back on it now, I realize that there were some things that I hadn't grasped at the time. The place had been up for sale for a long time. What I still don't understand is why the right person didn't walk through the front door and see the place for what it was long before I did. Okay, the front door was boarded up and there was trash all over. These things were all cosmetic. I really didn't have to do too much with it at all. All the hard stuff was done before I took over.

But I'm getting ahead of the story.

I met Sarah at her office in Barrhaven and we drove to the village of Westport, on the west end of Upper Rideau Lake, a drive of about an hour, and the closest town to the Island. Sarah had arranged for a local Real Estate affiliate to have a boat ready for us and together we crossed nearly a kilometre of water to the Island. Fred, a local agent for the same realty company as Sarah, was the resident expert and he gave a running commentary as he piloted his small Doral Cruiser across the water. His topics ranged from yearly weather and water conditions and local sights and activities to hints about past and present residents of Gilmore Island. When I tried to enquire about "present residents" I was distracted by Sarah's excited pointing at a family of loons we were passing at that moment and by the time I was able to return to the topic we had arrived.

I found out later from Sarah that her present resident was nothing more than a wide assortment of birds and animals that live all over the island but not, remarkably, in the building itself.

The large and elaborately laid-out dock comprising several long and short sections seemed to be in pretty good shape as we tied up the Doral. Fred remained aboard the boat with his newspaper and the remains of an extra-large Tim's double-double while Sarah and I hiked along the flagstone pathway, around a wooded area and along the eastern shoreline toward the house. I had the feeling that Fred did not expect us to be gone long.

As we walked I realized that I would, if I was going to consider living in a place like this, have to get into better shape. My injured leg had healed well but the recovery had been tempered with more self-pity and apathy than I had cared to acknowledge and had left me far less fit than I had been before the shooting.

I think Sarah had been expecting a seriously negative reaction when I first saw the place. On the ride to Westport she had mentioned some less than enthusiastic reactions from other clients and had heard some horror stories from other Realtors when they had shown their clients this very old, very shabby-looking, weather-worn and water-bound almost-Victorian house with weeds and rocks and broken trees, and litter all over the place.

My first sight of the house when we rounded the last trees was eye opening to say the least.

My initial impression was that it was huge. Three and a half stories high – the basement was partly above ground but hidden on three sides by a wide deck – it was built of square-cut limestone blocks with carved granite lintels over the doors and windows, and a vertical row of squared granite blocks at each side of each turret. The basement walls were also of granite blocks. A deck surrounded three sides of the building and the fourth was grown over entirely with ivy which threatened to cover all the windows on the east wall. There were four turrets, three of which rose three floors and the last climbed higher yet, one story above the roof. The roof itself was of aged cedar shakes and was in four sections, two larger and two smaller. A cone-shaped roof topped each of the turrets.

The house had shuttered windows and boarded-up doors. The porch had broken railings and missing boards. Two chairs from some previous owner lay smashed in a heap at the side of the door. A small circle of campfire stones sat cold and desolate a couple of metres from the front steps.

Well, that's enough to give you the idea. What a disaster.

Fortunately I've never been one to form solid impressions from first appearances.

In fact, even though it looked like something out of an Alfred Hitchcock film, I found the place strangely appealing. Well, a little.

When I didn't attempt to strangle her amid the rubble of the front entry, Sarah gained a new enthusiasm for the place.

The sun shone brightly, casting dappled shadows on the flagstone pathway and now that I was away from the fast moving boat, I was quite warm. My leg hurt.

As we went around the west side of the building I noticed a slight breeze and I was quite suddenly reminded of the proximity to the water. I had momentarily forgotten we were on an Island. Because of a fairly thick screen of trees near the shoreline it's easy to forget Upper Rideau Lake is only 40 or 50 metres from the house at the southwest curve of the island.

The warm, moist breeze was welcome. Its freshness filled my nostrils and cooled the perspiration on my forehead as we picked our way through the rubbish and broken branches to the back veranda and door.

As soon as I rounded the corner I began to see possibilities for the back area: a spot for a beach shower to rinse off the sand before coming inside; a raised place near the porch that could be used as a kitchen garden and what looked to be a natural spring which could form the basis of a pond were the first things that came to mind.

Sarah was way ahead of me now, and talking rapidly. I had to get her to stop and go over part of the story again. My train of thought and hers had diverged and suddenly I was lost.

She was saying something about someone who had previously lived here and how they had never really found out what happened to her.

Great. Was she trying to sell me a haunted house? Was there a body in the basement? That had definitely not been in the Real Estate paper.

Before I could ask her what she was on about she fell through the porch and was protesting loudly. Fortunately she was wearing jeans and boots and though she had gone through one of the rotted deck boards up to the knee she was not injured. I'd have hollered too if the floor had disappeared from under me. I did in fact, later, and more than once, but there was no one around to hear.

Sarah was mostly up from between the broken boards by the time I got to her. I held out a hand to help her up if she wanted it. She accepted with good grace and brushed the dead leaves and dirt from her jeans and jacket. Neither of us commented on the incident and we carried on, both now more wary of further pitfalls, careful to avoid the rotted planks.

"This is the farthest I ever got with a prospective buyer," she said as she took out the keys to the back door. "Most people, in fact everyone else I've brought here, have run for it before now."

I looked at her for a moment, and then said, "I signed up for the full tour. Wouldn't be fair to bail out half way through."

She smiled briefly then turned her attention to the double lock. I watched quietly as she worked first the deadbolt then the door lock. First one satisfying click, then another, and then the door swung open. Good locks. Hopefully they had done their job adequately.

After the brightness of the afternoon sun the hallway seemed totally black. You might almost have expected a cloud of bats to come pouring out, but none did.

Sarah made for the breaker box at the far end of the passage, pulled up the main switch and returned to the door. She reached behind me, to the wall next to the door and flipped the switch there. The hallway lit up and we moved on.

Sarah hit more switches - overhead lights and wall lights came on and we entered the kitchen. And what a kitchen it was, even then. You should understand as I start to gush about the kitchen that I am a cook. When I worked in restaurants all through High School and College I got to be pretty good at working with food. Everyone, myself included, expected me to carry on in that line of work but when I got sick of the hours I decided to try 'something completely different' as they say in Monty Python and I ended up in Law and Security at Conestoga College and a while later wound up as an Insurance Investigator. As you know, that didn't end well. I hoped my return to the Hospitality Industry would work out better.

Anyway, I like kitchens, some better than others. This one was amazing. A lot of good-sized city restaurants I'd seen didn't have cooking facilities that were up to this standard. Every piece of food equipment I could have thought of for this kind of business was here and it was all brand new, most with protective plastic film and some even still in boxes.

"This would be one of the highlights of the place for someone who liked to cook," said Sarah, giving me a sidelong glance as she headed for the nearest door. In our few brief conversations about the place I had found out that Sarah was not much for cooking and she knew that I was. I opened several cupboards and drawers as I passed, finding still more, smaller, items of food gear hidden away within. I was like the proverbial kid in a candy store. Reluctantly I followed Sarah out the door opposite the one by which we'd entered.

Sarah had already switched the light on in what I found to be the dining room.

The dining room was about six metres by eight and had warm beige paint above Cherry wainscoting and a medium-dark hardwood floor. I knew that outside the large and currently boarded-up windows was the deck we'd just crossed, roughly the same size as the dining room. The tables and chairs I saw inside were maple, evenly spaced, in places for two and for four, all bare of accessories, naturally, and all covered with a thick coating of dust. From what I'd seen, the outside furniture was probably in storage somewhere inside the building so it could not be stolen or ruined by weather. I wondered why the inside tables were spread around as if waiting for diners who were not going to arrive any time soon. I'd need to ask Sarah.

"I'm sure you can envision two or twelve satisfied guests happily enjoying one of your superb breakfasts before heading out for a day of touristing among the Rideau Lakes," said Sarah.

Without waiting for an answer she was gone, out of the dining room and around the corner, with me close behind.

Yes. I could envision that - and a whole lot more.

The next stop on the tour was the bar – un-stocked of course – and a lounge area with a nice large stone fireplace in one corner and several big, soft-looking chairs and some low tables, all covered with dust covers – again spread out - waiting.

Sarah pointed to the bar wall. "There's a cable hook-up to the Island and there's a satellite dish on a rocky ridge somewhere. They didn't want the dish on the roof. Aesthetics or something, maybe? All the rooms have cable and the satellite is for the bar here.

"The reception area is around here."

We were now at the front of the building and I saw, for the first time, the inside of the huge double doors which I had seen boarded over from the outside. I hoped whoever had done that job had been careful with the placement of the nails.

The doors were of solid oak panels, both doors each a metre wide and nearly three metres high, each constructed from three panels. These doors were probably worth more than most of the cars I'd owned in recent years.

I turned slowly from my ruminations to find Sarah, an excited smile on her face, standing in front of an ornate old elevator.

"This is another of the highlights," she said.

The outer door was an opaque panel of some material I didn't immediately recognize. Sarah lifted the lever handle and pushed gently. The opaque panel accordioned back against the framework. Inside was a black metal grid, hinged at every joint, which simply folded upon itself against the wall of the car on the same side as the outer door. The floor was carpeted to match the stairs and part of the lobby and the walls were wainscoted in dark wood and painted a sort of dusty rose above.

"From what I understand one of the previous owners or a family member was in a wheelchair," said Sarah, "and because the stair layout didn't allow for a wheelchair lift they opted for the elevator. Some closet space was lost on each floor but it was worth it as far as I'm concerned. Too bad the renovations were never completed. Whoever this was built for never got a chance to use it. Come on." She gestured for me to follow as she stepped into the now open elevator.

Once we were both inside Sarah pulled both doors closed and pushed the button marked "2". "Back in the day, when this was installed it would have been specifically called an Automatic Elevator. It was the latest thing."

First there was one little shudder then, smooth as silk, the old car moved up, very slowly, and came to rest at the second floor.

"You try it this time," said Sarah, indicating the door handle. I opened the doors without difficulty and we disembarked into a neat and plain hallway.

"Always remember to close the doors when you leave the elevator," said Sarah, "otherwise you won't be able to call the car from another floor." She walked on.

"All the guest suites are on this floor and the one above," said Sarah as we quickly toured the four sets of rooms on that level, then went up the stairs to the third floor. Each guest room consisted of a large bedroom – sitting room and a private bathroom. Three of the four rooms on each floor were corners that had a window nook created by the shape of the turret.

It was almost identical to the floor below, the only real differences being in paint and paper, large portions of which were peeling off.

"Okay, now for the really good part," said Sarah as she led the way back to the elevator.

Sarah pushed the call button. Soon the car arrived from the second floor. After we were inside, with the doors closed, Sarah turned and stepped to the rear of the car. For the first time I realized that the rear of the car was covered floor to ceiling by fabric – more like an old-fashioned wall-hanging. Sarah drew back the curtain to reveal that this side of the elevator was not a wall but rather another set of doors, identical to those on the other side but with no floor indicator above.

Sarah reached up to a point above the decorative moulding around the door and slid a recessed lever.

"This switch allows these doors to be locked so that the guests can only use the ones at the front of the car," said Sarah as she pulled open the rear doors.

"This area of the building is the private quarters of the owner – it's a two-storey suite," said my guide as we exited the elevator into yet another hallway, this one significantly more modern looking than those below.

"This floor has the owner's master bedroom and bath, and a small guest suite. The master bathroom is terrific; big tub - shower with hundreds of jets – and there's a fireplace – well not in the bathroom but in the bedroom. There's a spiral staircase in that curved area in the corner. It goes up to the turret. It's a neat little space and the view is pretty good too."

Silence followed briefly as we walked and looked.

"This is great," I said as we passed through the master suite. It was indeed terrific.

"Let's go downstairs. You're going to love the rest of the place too."

Sarah was now in high gear, talking constantly about various aspects as we went down one floor, this time by way of the suite's own private staircase.

Immediately outside the elevator and at the stair head was the suite's private kitchen, much smaller than the Inn's main one below, but similarly well equipped. Then came the dining room and adjoining living room, both spacious with lots of windows. The living room had a wall that curved out at the corner. This was the second floor portion of the turret.

"Both of these upper floors have balconies, did you notice?"

"Yes, I saw the balconies," I answered.

"Should we go down and have a look at the office behind the reception area? We missed that before."

We went back to the elevator and down one floor, more for the opportunity of using it again than from any desire to not use the stairs.

As we travelled Sarah filled in more details about Gilmore Island.

"A guy named Smythe was the most recent owner of the island. I met him once, a few years ago when I was just starting out. He's quite old; seventy or so. He gave the impression that he was very rich and powerful. He had all the recent work done on what he said would be the most beautiful hotel in the area. I guess he wasn't as rich and powerful as he led us to believe 'cause apparently he went broke and then just packed up and left."

"All the water used on the Island is from the lake, taken in through a large pipe on the open water side of the island and treated by ultra violet light and some other fancy equipment I don't know anything about. He also put in a state-of-the-art micro water treatment unit so none of the used water goes back into the lake without being cleaned."

"I'll bet the fish and birds would he happy to hear about that," I said as we exited the elevator.

"I think there's an information package on it in a box we have in storage at our office in Barrhaven. There's also some building drawings – from the current renovation I think - and a topographical map of the island."

Sarah pointed to the right.

"Those are the guest stairs, and," indicating the other direction, "the office is here."

We circled the reception area and entered a large office with a big old desk, some chairs, a credenza and shelf units and file cabinets.

Sarah had said that the office contents were in storage so I would not have expected to find any papers of any kind, but I was wrong.

Right in the middle of the desk was a large manila envelope, somewhat tattered looking and with what appeared to be oily finger marks all over it.

I walked over to the desk and reached down and turned the envelope slowly around so that I could read what was printed, in stiff block letters, on it.

TO WHOEVER THINKS THEY WANT TO BE
THE NEXT OWNER OF GILMORE ISLAND

"What's in here?" I asked.

Sarah hesitated briefly, then said, "I don't know. I've never seen it before. I wonder who put it there. Should we open it?"

I thought about it, maybe not for long enough in retrospect, and then quite surprised myself with my answer. I handed the envelope to Sarah.

"I think you should hold onto this for a while."

"Aren't you going to see what it says?"

"I guess I'll find out when I buy the place."

I couldn't believe I'd made the decision so quickly. I wasn't even aware of having made it until the words came out.

Sarah was staring at me in disbelief.

"What did you say? Are you really going to buy my white elephant?" she asked finally. Suddenly she was very serious. "Are you sure you don't want to open the envelope?"

"Do you think there might be something in there that will make me reconsider?"

"I don't know. Maybe. Are you really going to buy Gilmore Island?"

I considered again briefly then said,

"I guess I am."

That was that.

Probably I should have read what was in the envelope. Not that it matters now. I was decided and I would go ahead with it.

Besides, I was beginning to think I might like the inn-keeping business.

As to the letter – I didn't get a chance to look at it for a while. We decided to leave it there on the desk in the office and I didn't see it again until after I'd made the purchase.

one of those real estate agents was showing the island again. She's been here before. Nice Most of'm aren't so young and cute. Keep comin' to look but so far none have had the guts to take the challenge. Hope noone ever does. My note'l persuade'm to get lost.

Chapter 3

Sarah's reaction had been predictably enthusiastic. I don't think she stopped talking all the way back to the city.

At the Barrhaven office we took care of the preliminary paperwork and then I headed back to Kitchener, by way of Kingston where I spent the night with friends. All the way home I thought about the decision I'd made and wondered if I was crazy. By the time I got home I had decided that the decision was a good one and put it to rest.

I had also decided to make the move right away after signing the final papers, even though it was getting on for fall.

I'd been assured that the place was suitably sealed, powered and heated for winter habitation and I hoped they were right. This would soon be my only place to live.

The condo in Kitchener was easy to sell and since there was no-one living where I wanted to move to, there was no waiting for someone else to vacate before I could move in.

There were few local ties to contact. I realized as I packed that my life as a loner who lived to work was a mixed blessing now – no family and few friends to leave behind.

I went with a mover from the Kitchener / Waterloo area and the move was done with no unwanted side effects.

At Westport my possessions were put into storage and would be taken out a little at a time. Everything would eventually have to be taken across to the Island by boat and that would take a while once the building was ready for me.

One of the first things I did when I had access to the building was go to the office and read the note that had been left there. I had supposed that it was probably from Mr. Smythe, the most recent owner, wishing me, or whoever, luck with the place.

I was sure wrong about that.

On a piece of plain printer paper was a note, in the same stiff block capitals as on the envelope:

IF YOU VALUE YOUR LIFE DO NOT EVEN THINK ABOUT BUYING THIS PLACE. IF YOU DO YOU WILL REGRET IT

I put the note back into the envelope and left it on the desk, wondering as I did whether or not I would end up needing to show it to the police at some point. I wished the writer had been as direct on the outside of the envelope as on the note inside. Would I be standing here now if I'd read it when I first had the chance? Maybe not. Somehow though I felt I probably would be. I don't like being threatened and it made me angry. It would have had the same effect two weeks ago. Only difference is that I'd have had two weeks to worry about it. Too late for that now. Let somebody try to get me out. See how far they get.

During the initial weeks at my new place I lived on a houseboat tied up at the Gilmore Island dock. On one of the earlier trips to the area I had stopped at an outfit called Big Rideau Lake Houseboat Rentals in Portland. I found a good, comfortable-sized one, ready to go, and with the help of a couple of associates from the rental company, took it through the locks and into Upper Rideau Lake to Gilmore Island. I expected to only need it for a few weeks while the worst of the clean up was going on, then I could move into my own rooms. For sure I had to be out of the houseboat and have it returned to Portland before winter. It was a good thing I had lots of help with the houseboat. While most of the locks on the Rideau system are tall and sheltered, with ropes up the sides to steady the assent or descent, the lock at Upper Rideau Lake is very short, only about one metre deep, and is open and subject to wind. There was a stiff breeze the day we took the houseboat from Portland to Gilmore Island and because of the unusually low stone walls, the ropes couldn't hold the boat in place; it was all we could do to keep the craft from slamming into the sides of the lock.

I hired a contingent from a local office cleaning firm, and we spent a few weeks cleaning, scrubbing, debugging and painting my new home. You never saw so many spiders – more varieties than I knew existed. Not among my favourite things either.

Nearly six full weeks from my initial and propitious trip to Gilmore Island I moved the bulk of my personal possessions into my new home. I enlisted some local help to move furniture and other larger items out to the island and to help me return the houseboat to Portland before the Rideau Canal closed for the season. That trip was made on a clear and windless fall day and was less stressful than the one *from* Portland had been.

As a business owner the big question was still to be answered. When could I open the Inn?

I would have liked to open right away but there was no possibility of that happening.

Even though I had cleaned up my personal space there was still the rest of the house to get in order before guests could be considered. Lots of finishing construction, painting and cleaning were still to be done.

There was also the approach of winter, not a trivial thing in this part of Canada. Eventually the whole lake would freeze over (hence one of the reasons for my determination to be done with the houseboat as soon as possible) and until then the water would potentially be treacherous. Ice cold rains, wind and snow would surely make travel to and from the island an uncomfortable proposition as the pleasant fall turned to winter.

I thought it best to use the rest of the fall and early winter to complete the clean up, hire some professional construction workers, and start looking for people I would need to help run the place. I would also use the time to set up local and regional suppliers.

My idea was to be the owner/operator and the chief cook and kitchen manager. These were the only jobs I wanted to hold officially. I knew, of course, that I would end up doing some part of everything else involved with the operation but I hoped not to have to do it all alone. If that happened I would not last long.

During the time I was moving in I had been using a very small boat with a trolling motor, borrowed from a friend who lived in Kingston, to get to and from the island. It seemed to take ages to travel the kilometre or so to and from the mainland and I was getting wet more often than I liked.

Now I thought it was time to get something a little more substantial for everyday running around. I was never comfortable going that far in a very small boat and with winter approaching it was time to trade up in size. I would also have to look into renting a snow machine to use once the lake froze.

Having left the small boat tied up at the public dock I collected my Lexus Hybrid and drove into the main part of town to get a few groceries and some wine, then took an alternate route back so I would pass the boatyards and marinas.

There was one seriously large marina and a few smaller ones to choose from. The larger advertised short and long term rentals so I decided to try that one first.

I parked on the street and approached the main entrance.

It was a quiet October morning, clear and warm, and what I took to be the owner of the marina was sitting in a chair on the porch, eyes closed, collar up against the faint breeze, enjoying the sunshine.

His sleepy manner quickly disappeared when he heard the Lexus door close and he was on his feet and ready for business by the time I got to the steps.

He was neatly and casually dressed, aged somewhere between 70 and 80 years and had the look of someone who had spent most of his life in the sun and wind and water.

"Mornin'" he said as I topped the stairs. "You're not from around here, are ya?" It was a question and it wasn't.

"Well, yes and no actually." I hesitated then added, "I just moved into the area to live and run a business," hoping that was enough information to keep my initial response from sounding too glib.

Apparently it was.

"I know who you are right enough now," he said. "You're the fella bought the Gilmore place."

"That's right. My name is Harrison," I said as we shook hands. "Call me RJ."

"Wil Bascome. Saw ya a couppla times in town here but I didn't make the connection til just now." He went on.

"What brings ya here?"

"I'd like to rent a power boat," I said. "Nothing too big, but bigger than I'm using now; just enough to get around in, take supplies over, that sort of thing. Something with a covered cabin and a decent sized motor."

"Could rent you a boat if you like but it hardly seems necessary when you have boats of your own over at Morrison's wait'n for ya."

I felt my eyebrows rise involuntarily and I must have looked as puzzled as I felt because he launched into an explanation before I could speak.

"Morrison Boat Works, over there," he said gesturing along the harbour, "has a few power boats, some row boats and I think, a few canoes belonging to Gilmore Island."

He paused for effect, and then carried on.

"Old Morrison was the Gilmores' boatman back at the turn of the century – that is the last century, not this recent one, and the company's kept up a relationship with most of the successive owners of the island. Some of them bought or rented boats from him and those that were bought he maintained, wintered, whatnot. As the owners came and went so did the boats. Some of course have been owned by individuals. Some have paperwork sayin' they belong to Gilmore Island. You should go see 'im."

In retrospect I think that was possibly the longest speech I ever heard him make.

I was only partly recovered from my surprise when he finished his story.

"I guess I'd better do that," I managed to say. "Thank you for the information. I see you run a water taxi service from here. Perhaps we could still do some business."

He was interested.

"Well lad, if you can spare a few more minutes before you head off to see Morrison, I've a pot of coffee on and we could discuss your ideas over a cup."

I hadn't been called "lad" in a long time.

"Sounds like a fine idea," I said, gesturing for him to lead the way into the shop.

About twenty minutes later I emerged with the basis of a contract for water taxi service and with a new friend.

"By the way," he said from the doorway, "you should be warned that Morrison won't likely want to part with the boats without some kind of an agreement to pay for storage and maintenance."

"Maintenance?" I asked.

"Yep." said Bascome. "Morrison's the best boat mechanic in this area. I wouldn't be surprised if you find those boats runnin' as well as they did the day they were built. Maybe better."

I was shaking my head as I walked away from Bascome's Marina. There was no point driving that short distance so I left the Lexus where it was. The walk would do me good and I needed the time to think over what Bascome had said.

On the way from Bascome's to Morrison's I passed a hardware store, a bakery, a drugstore and a water sports outlet. These small businesses all backed up toward the water and the marina used the water behind them all.

Between the buildings I could see a large number of boats of all shapes and sizes, tied up to row after row of docks.

I made a mental note to stop at the bakery on the way back. I had heard they made a great Chelsea Bun. Okay so I have a weakness for really good baked goods. Not my only weakness I assure you.

Near the top of the cul-du-sac I reached Morrison's Boat Works. I wondered what I would find here.

Wil Bascome had said "old Morrison" had been the Gilmore's boatman at the turn of the last century. Surely it could not be the same person running the place now who had been in charge one hundred odd years ago. Fresh air and clean living not withstanding, I could not see this being a possibility.

No sleepy old man adorned the front entry of Morrison's.

The building was very old but seemed well maintained, and the main door was propped open with an ancient anchor.

Inside was dark. Old wood and poor lighting.

A small assortment of for-sale boating accessories covered the few shelves on one side of the shop, but it was easy to tell that these sales were not the main focus of the business.

Three of the four walls were covered with photographs of boats.

Most were before-and-after groupings, some of whole boats, some of various parts, all showing damage and degradation and the subsequent renewals.

As I entered I had crossed through an old "electric eye" which caused a rather caustic buzzing sound in a remote area of the building.

Within a minute or so someone came out of the back area, moving very quietly. Since I had been entirely absorbed in looking at the pictures, I wasn't aware of his approach until he spoke.

"Good morning," he said, coming to a halt behind the big old counter.

Startled by the sudden break in the silence I turned abruptly toward the voice and found myself facing a youngish, dark haired man in T-shirt and jeans.

"Good morning," I breathed again. "You do move quietly," I said.

"Sorry if I startled you. It's these shoes," he said glancing down briefly. "I wear them so I don't get marks on the boats. What can I do for you?"

"My name is Harrison. I'm the new owner of Gilmore Island."

I waited briefly while he digested my statement.

"Damn!" he said quietly. "I had hoped to get to you before you came here to see me, but I've been so busy these last few weeks...damn! I wouldn't want you to think I was trying to keep your boats a secret from you," he continued, visibly annoyed by the situation.

"I hadn't thought that at all actually," I said. "I didn't even know the boats existed until a few minutes ago and besides, I haven't exactly publicized my takeover of the island. No need for you to be concerned at all."

"Okay, thanks for that. Let me put my sign up on the counter here and we'll go have a look at your boats."

As he spoke he reached to a shelf behind the counter and withdrew a tall, brightly painted sign which he stood on the counter top.

The sign read "If you're in a hurry ring the bell. If you're not, come back later." There was a large arrow pointing toward a brass boat bell with a pull cord, mounted on the counter.

"That'll do for now," he said, turning to the door at the rear of the shop. "Let's go. Oh, by the way, I'm Andy Morrison." We shook hands.

We left the shop and entered the maintenance area where several boats of varying sizes were in process of being repaired. I told him of my conversation with Wil Bascome.

"The Morrison Bascome spoke of was my grandfather," he said.

At the far end of the repair area there was a door marked "Storage".

My guide took out a key and opened the door.

The storage area was dark and smelled somewhat of damp and disuse.

When the lights came on I saw a room about twice the size of the repair shop housing perhaps thirty or forty boats, none very large and all arranged in neat rows, covered and labelled. There were a few old cars; antiques and classics I guessed from the shapes of the tarps and sheets that covered them. An occasional bumper or fender peeked out from beneath the coverings. A chrome bumper and rear trunk and luggage rack of a vintage MG and a tail light of a Corvair caught my eye.

I was led down the centre aisle to the far end of the room, not unexpectedly since the Gilmore boats would have been stored the longest.

"There you go," said Andy with a sweep of his hand. "Fourteen boats in all, and they're all in pretty good shape. Haven't had any engines running since the spring so they'll need a little tinkering, being as old as they are."

He had begun to take the covers off the larger boats as he spoke.

"No speed here, compared with newer craft but lots of class and character. Some of them were considered pretty fast in their day".

With this last comment he took the covers off the largest boats. The flourish was unmistakable.

I stood in silence and disbelief. No doubt my mouth was open too.

Andy let the silence grow as I recovered my wits and was able to put words together, moderately coherently I hope.

"These are - amazing," I said. "They look new."

"Most of them were among the best boats built in their day and we've tried to keep them up."

"It sure looks like you've succeeded," I said. "Tell me about them."

For the next hour or so I listened to Andy Morrison talk about the boats he had kept here, and how he, and his father and uncle, and their father before had maintained them for the various owners of Gilmore Island, whoever they might have been. There were launches, utilities and runabouts in various lengths and styles as well as row boats and canoes from makers such as Chris Craft, Greavette, Lymans, Elco, Century and others.

I was completely astonished, not only at the array of watercraft I saw there but also that anyone would continue taking responsibility for someone else's property for all these years.

Andy said it was something he liked to do – it wasn't just a job – and he often had the help of his uncle who, though a bit odd, sure knew his way around a boat. The uncle had been the one who'd done most of the upkeep on the Gilmore boats.

It was late when I left there, having made a plan to reclaim the boats and pay off the long overdue storage and maintenance charges owed. Andy Morrison's terms were very reasonable.

words getting around some guys actually bought the island damn it – shoulda been paying closer attention to the ones lookin – maybe I coulda prevented this. My note didn't scare him off may have to take more drastic action with this one like I did with Smythe and the ones before him. I've had lotsa practice dealing with troublemakers. I don't give up easy.

Chapter 4

I do pretty well as a cook generally speaking but baking is not something that has ever been a strong point. I had decided that if possible I would leave the baking in the hands, so to speak, of a professional.

I decided that before the weather closed in for the winter it would be necessary for me to start making the rounds of all the bakeries in and around the Westport area and sample their wares. There weren't all that many to choose from in the town and the surrounding area so I had to test each a few times to be sure I was making the right decision.

As they say, it was a dirty job but someone had to do it. After a week of testing and tasting I made my choice.

The Osgoode bakery, which to my distress I had found closed by the time I left Morrison's that day I'd found out I had boats, is run by the Osgoode sisters, Elizabeth and Sandra. They were both of young middle age; that is to say, somewhat younger than I, married, with kids and firmly rooted in the area, and not likely to be going anywhere in the near future. Perfect for a long term contract. As it happens they had the largest and busiest shop in the area and were quite able to handle the addition of my business without much trouble.

The Osgoode sisters were also twins and it was a constant annoyance to me that I could not distinguish one from the other. Actually I think they sometimes tried to mess me up by telling me I was wrong even when I'd managed to get their names right.

After many visits and many cinnamon rolls, donuts, bear claws and honey buns we came to an agreement that the Osgoode Bakery would provide all the breads and pastries for The Gilmore House Inn.

One of my visits yielded a tidbit of a non-edible variety.

Liz, or was it Sandi, asked me as I was trying to choose one delightful bear claw from among many, "Now that you've settled in on the island I suppose you've been hearing about the Gilmore Island mystery?"

Without lifting my head I looked over the top of my glasses at – whoever it was - and said, "Mystery? What mystery?"

Now I straightened up and looked at the two women. "I'd like to hear more details, if you know any."

Sandi, or Liz, glanced at her sister at the other end of the counter and apparently receiving some sort of confirmation which I could not decipher, took in a slow breath and began to tell what she knew of the story.

"I, that is to say, we, we do not gossip, but we thought, ... we," gesturing to her sister who had now moved closer, "felt you should have the background of the place. I don't guess it can really be gossip since all the people who were involved are long dead."

"I," I said, "will consider it a lesson in local history. Please go on."

Their story took well over an hour to tell, between the twins who took it in turns to carry on the tale, interrupted briefly at intervals by customers needing attention, phones ringing and yet further batches of delicious morsels entering and exiting the ovens.

Sandi, I think it was, began the tale with accounts of the Gilmores' arrival at Westport. Some of these I had heard before. Others I had not.

Complications had begun very soon after their instalment on the island.

"The family had consisted of eight members and there were another half dozen or so support people – servants to be specific."

Mr. and Mrs. Gilmore were both in their mid to late forties and seemed healthy and robust and ready to take on the wilderness lifestyle, as did their children.

George Gilmore Senior was head of a large conglomerate of mostly manufacturing and real estate which he had inherited from his father and to which he had added substantially. He was at the time semi-retired, meaning he controlled his empire from the island instead of from Kingston. He travelled reluctantly to Kingston every few months. Some of his executives travelled even more reluctantly by train, coach and boat to Gilmore Island every few weeks.

The trek into the wilderness was not always a pleasant one for those used to the comforts, such as they were, of city living. The best way to make the trip was by steamboat, a two to three day voyage aboard such steamships as the Rideau King, through the newly built Rideau Canal. This was also the most expensive way to go. Gilmore would not often pay the price for such luxury, for himself or those in his employ. Rough transportation, insects, excessive heat or cold and not infrequent encounters with unsavoury characters made some of these trips unpleasant if highly memorable. There was however no point in complaining to the boss. George Gilmore had little tolerance for what today would be called wimps. 'Deal with it or go away' might have been one of his mottos.

"Seems a really likeable fellow," I said. "He must have been a real joy to work for. I suppose in those days you expected that though."

One of the sisters agreed and continued on.

"Mrs. Gilmore gave all indications that she supported her husband in his desire to leave the city. Some even thought she might have instigated it."

There was a feeling in some circles, though, that she was not happy with the move. No-one seemed to know for sure whether or not this was true but the speculation remained.

Certainly there were fewer occasions for socializing, fewer opportunities to have large parties and there were only infrequent visits by her friends to the island.

There were six children who came to the island. Word was that there had been eight but two had died in infancy or early childhood. Not an unusual occurrence in the late 19th and early 20th centuries.

The oldest, George Gilmore Junior, had moved officially with the family to the island but had already been to university, had his own residence in Kingston and was employed in his father's business.

The next child, also a son, was named Nicolas. He was, at the time of the move, a student at Queen's University and was seen around the county more than his older brother, mostly during summers and other school breaks.

Victoria Agnes was the oldest of the daughters and the primary focus of the mystery.

She was in her late teens when the family moved north and was thought to be rapidly passing marriageable age. Victoria Gilmore apparently did not see it that way.

She brought along with her a number of young people, both male and female. They did not of course move there but seemed to follow in Victoria's wake, coming and going at will. One thing was certain. Her parents did not approve of most of them though for some reason they allowed the traffic to continue.

"Her lifestyle must have been a trial to her parents," said one of the women.

"There were apparently some incidents of wilfulness, talk about becoming a suffragette, and about votes for women," said the other. "I think maybe the parents thought the move would put an end to those things. Perhaps they allowed the constant parade of acquaintances to continue as a diversion from other, more dangerous things. Or perhaps they hoped that one suitor or another would finally take her off their hands."

"That may well be true," I said. "I can't think of many better reasons for them to put up with that sort of thing."

"Before you continue," I said, "perhaps you could tell me how it is that you know all these things about the Gilmore family."

"Sandi used to be a librarian before she was married," said Liz. "The village archives are in the same building as the library and we would look through them now and then, not looking for anything in particular; just looking. We found old letters written to and by family members and there were diaries and notebooks from the youngest boy."

"I thought you said it was Sandi who was the librarian," I asked. "Then you said "we" would look."

The twins looked at each other a moment then Sandi spoke.

"Well sometimes we would kind of cover for one another a bit. It never did any harm and we each got to do things we might not have otherwise." She paused then added, "You won't tell anyone will you? It would only cause trouble and we really never would want that, not for ourselves or anyone else."

"No, I won't tell," I said. "Please, go on with the story."

Next of the children was Nathaniel. "Nathanial Jacob, I think?" said one. "A free spirit he was called. A trouble maker is what he was, who enjoyed nothing better than terrorizing his younger brother and sister and the family's live-in tutor (who eventually quit) and the servants who were unable to do anything about it.

His behaviour went from bad to worse and finally his father enrolled him in a military college. His time at Springfield Academy was undistinguished and when he finished there he immediately became part of the Canadian force being shipped off to Europe to fight in World War I, which was half over by then.

He lasted as a soldier only until his first leave (a day pass from an assembly point in eastern England) at which time he deserted and disappeared, never to be heard from again.

A brief silence followed; then the story continued.

Rosemary Gwyneth was the younger daughter, bright but vague and wistful. Always dreaming, reading, and wandering the island, she had little interest in what education the tutor provided and even less in the running, Victorian style, of a home. As such her prospects for an eventual marriage into a respectable family were remote.

"Another one they were not likely to unload," said the other sister. "The parents must have wondered what they had done to deserve two daughters whose prospects were so bleak."

"I wonder if all these family oddities weren't at least part of the reason the Gilmores decided to move to such a remote location."

"Maybe," said Liz, "but not all of the kids were problems."

Alexander Everett, the youngest of the children, was five or six at the time of the move. Shy, quiet and bookish, though not absentminded as was his sister Rosemary, he learned everything the tutor could teach and read every book in the Gilmores' not inconsiderable library. Not long after the family's arrival Alex developed an interest in his new surroundings, and soon became the only member of the family who really knew about the island and the surrounding waters and mainland. For one so young he accomplished a lot in a short time. He compiled large amounts of notes, drawings and maps of the area, with the intention of eventually publishing a book. Sadly that was not to be.

The severe outbreak of influenza in 1918 wiped out all but two of the family members who had remained on the island and most of the servants.

George Gilmore and his younger daughter, Rosemary, finally gave up and moved back to Kingston in 1920, leaving the island in the hands of a caretaker.

For many years the Gilmores had been the centre of local society, such as it was. The island had hosted a few memorably elaborate parties and summer socials; there had been tennis matches and lawn bowling, sailing regattas, motor launch races and fishing derbies. It was true that most of those participating in these events were guests from the south and that few locals were ever present as anything but suppliers of goods or as supplement to the Gilmores' staff, but when the Gilmores departed they left something of a void.

And, because Victoria, who, along with a man who was a guest on the island, had vanished abruptly in the night, they also left one enduring mystery.

bastard's moved right in lived on that damned houseboat all fall, never left for any length of time then moved into the house. I keep watchin for chances to mess him up but there aren't many so far. thinks he's going to open his little Inn when the spring is here. We'll see.

He's been all over town, talking to every body, learning the history, making friends, finding locals to work on the fix-up. haven't come up with a good plan to get rid of him yet and it's getting to be almost too late. thought he'd pack up and go before now.

Chapter 5

All too soon winter arrived.

With it came wind and rain, and then snow – lots of snow. There were days when I could not have gone to the mainland even if I had wanted to, even before the lake froze. Though I now had a few very reliable, if rather antique looking, boats at my disposal, the water was often far too rough for a novice such as I am to even attempt a crossing.

Fortunately it was not like that all the time and I was able to go across now and then to stock up on provisions. I also had the regular shuttle of a small number of tradesmen commuting to the island to work.

My plan was to spend part of the time over the winter finalizing my service contracts, permits and licenses. Bascome's Marina was all set to haul my food and beverages to the island and ferry any guests who required transportation.

Eventually all outside work ended. The lake froze, temperatures plummeted to minus 30° Celsius and lower and snow fell for days at a time. Icy winds pummelled the old building, rattling windows and banging tree branches against the walls and roof. Some days the sun was so bright on the snow that it was blinding – some days it seemed the sun had hardly any strength at all.

Most of the tradesmen stopped coming over the winter. Some came on snow machines when the weather was suitable and continued some of the inside work. I, also using a snow machine, got into Westport from time to time to stock up on necessities and to visit new friends. Some of the trades guys even brought their ice huts to set up around the island so they could go ice fishing in their free time. Not I, thanks.

It was a long four months.

With spring the pace of work gradually increased and it began to look as though I might make my June opening deadline after all. Local tradesmen were in the house almost every day now and some even stayed on in the guest rooms so as to spend less time travelling and more time working. This had the added benefit of allowing me to test out the kitchen equipment and practice making food for larger groups of people. The food must have been not too bad. They sure ate enough of it.

Climate change has had its impact world-wide and in Canada it is no different. Extremes of weather and unusual occurrences have become the rule rather than the exception. Seasons overlap and are unpredictable, temperatures range higher and lower than in years past and storms are often more fierce and destructive.

Late one day in May, when we should have been expecting some warmer weather and sunshine, a huge storm front approached the Rideau Lakes district, bringing with it damaging winds and ice-cold driving rain. Lightning flashed across the darkening sky and thunder shook the old house.

All afternoon the construction workers and I had been busy covering and securing any building materials still outside and we finished none too soon. By early evening the rain beat so hard against the walls and window glass that it almost drowned out the crashing thunder. Broken branches battered the walls and roof and the rooms were frequently lit up like daylight as the lightning flashed over and over again.

We didn't have to worry about power failure because the electricity for the island comes by underwater cable from the mainland. Unless the storm was very bad and very widespread we'd be all right.

Inside the Inn it was life as usual. By early evening the construction guys who had decided to stay over rather than spend so much time travelling to and from the island had all been fed and some were in the lounge watching hockey on the big screen television. I'd cleaned up the kitchen and set out some things for the morning and was preparing to go watch the game with the others when there was a brighter than usual lightning flash and a tremendous crash overhead.

The entire three storey structure shuddered with the impact, skewing all of what few pictures I'd already hung and rattling the few bottles I'd put in the bar. In the near distance I could hear some of my hanging pots and pans banging together.

Needless to say the crash got all our attention.

It seemed obvious to all of us that something had hit the side or the roof of the house. Very quickly all the resident construction workers gathered in the lounge, some with their outdoor gear - raincoats and hats and boots.

Three of the hardier souls went out through the main door to see if there was any way to get a look at the damage from the ground. I took some of the others with me up to the third level to where I knew the hatch to the attic was.

Right above the top of the third flight of stairs was a trapdoor, and hidden in the closest linen closet a pole with a hook to turn the latch. There was a set of spring-loaded folding stairs immediately above the trapdoor. Once the door is out of the way the same pole and hook is used to pull the steps. These unfolded in three sections and planted themselves firmly on the floor ten feet below.

I snapped on a flashlight I'd picked up from the linen closet and mounted the steps, followed closely by the others.

This is a one hundred plus year old house and the attic is, though not high-peaked, fairly high and spacious, high enough to stand up in comfortably. We climbed the stairs and walked upright onto the attic floor. The storm crashed on, even louder from this much closer proximity and we expected to see windblown rain streaming in but there was nothing. The attic was dark and cold but absolutely dry.

As we started to discuss the matter, rethinking our original idea of something having hit the roof, someone called from the steps. A head poked through from below and the new arrival gave the message he'd been sent to deliver.

"One of the guys who went out to look came back and said there's the top ten feet of a pine tree broken off, struck by lightning from the look of it 'cause the part that's now the top is still smoking from the strike, and come right through the roof. Says there's a hole five or six feet long near as he can figure from the ground."

He stopped suddenly, realizing what he was saying and seeing that there was obviously not a tree in the attic.

A moment of shocked silence followed and then everyone began to talk at once. Numerous theories were voiced as we headed back toward the hatch, most of which had to do with the poor sense of humour of the fellows outside.

But the man who had delivered the message was adamant that there was a real problem.

"Jake's gone to his crib to get some harnesses and a big tarp and Mark and Tom are getting some tall ladders set up," he said. "They wouldn't be doing that in this weather if they were joking. Besides, something happened. We all heard it."

One by one we descended the ladder steps, agreeing grudgingly that what he said made sense and trying to figure out what was really happening.

I was last down and still had my flashlight on as I dipped below the level of the floor. Something was odd. I went up a step and then down again. I couldn't get it. I repeated the up and down routine a couple more times, then the penny dropped.

"Hold on a minute," I called. "I think I see something strange here."

The guys who were half way down the stairs came back up and asked what I was on about.

"One of you please come up the stairs partway – just so your head is at ceiling level and look down the length of the floor of the attic to where the slope of the roof meets it," I said, moving out of the way.

Harry Smithson, the painter foreman, climbed back up and looked as instructed.

"What am I looking for now that I'm here?" he asked.

"Now duck down a bit and look along the length of the hallway ceiling," I said.

Again Harry did as I asked. Then he did it again and yet a third time.

"Anybody got a long tape measure on them?" he called, head still up in the attic. "If not, somebody go get one."

It was quickly established that no-one had a tape so the guy with the nearest room went off at a trot to retrieve one.

Looking down at me Harry said, "I think you may be on to something. It really looks like the hallway is longer than the attic, but they both should end at *that* outside wall."

By now the tape measure had arrived and was passed up to Harry, who immediately played it out across the attic floor.

"Twenty two feet four," said Harry as he retracted the tape and passed it down to me.

I held the housing and handed the other end to the nearest person, who walked toward the end of the hall.

The twenty five foot tape ran out when he was still about ten feet from the wall.

"There seems to be a discrepancy of fifteen feet or more between the attic and the hall," I said to no-one in particular.

"This makes no sense," said Harry as he returned to floor level.

"It almost looks as though there are two separate attics up there. There are no deviations in the roof to account for that space so there must be something there," I went on.

"And now that space has a tree in it and is taking in a lot of rain," said one of the others.

Harry headed for the end of the hall. As he went he called back, "See if one of the insulation guys has a heat imaging rig here. Maybe we can see a point of difference in the ceiling somewhere along here."

"Wait a minute," said one of the other painters. "I remember a day or two ago when I was painting this hall ceiling I noticed a rectangular shaped discolouration in the old paint – almost like different paint somehow. It didn't mean anything at the time but now I wonder if it's not a proper insulated ceiling and had been discoloured by heat fluctuations in the attic."

As we all stood around looking up at the ceiling, trying to find invisible trapdoors, there was a bump against the outside wall. Looking out the window I saw that a ladder had been placed against the roof.

At that same moment one of the insulation guys came along with a heat imaging machine. It would look through the ceiling and detect warm or cold spots indicating the presence or lack of proper insulation. Almost as soon as it was fired up and pointed at the ceiling the imager's screen showed a rectangular space where the cooler attic space was.

"We're going to have to make a mess here'" said Harry as he looked at me for permission.

"Nothing you guys can't put right again I'm sure. Do it."

"I'm going to need a big hammer and a stepladder. Maybe some goggles too," said Harry.

We could now hear the other group on the roof. There were more sounds of wood breaking and some scraping noises.

The tools and the stepladder arrived and Harry started to break away what we believed was the false cover over another entry to the attic.

We were right. There was drywall, not plaster, covering another attic hatch opening. We broke it away. Above that was another set of those spring-loaded folding stairs. As soon as he had all the loose material out of the way Harry pulled on the hook attached to the stairs. They were reluctant to move but slowly and with considerable squeaking and groaning they lowered to a point where some of the rest of us could lend a hand. There was also a torrent of cold, wet wind flowing through the hole in the roof and out the attic hatch.

When the steps finally came to rest on the floor I was nearest to the bottom and, since it was my house after all, I took the lead.

The wind and rain rushed through the hole in the roof as, flashlight in hand, I topped the steps. I had often been in the attic before, during the construction, but this was obviously the first time I had been in this part.

It was dark and even with the vicious wind blowing through at the moment it smelled musty. There was some old furniture at the end opposite from where the hole was and I was about to go that way when one of the guys on the roof poked his head through the hole and asked for help moving the tree.

By now some of the others had come up and we all leant a hand to shift the top twelve feet of a pine tree back out onto the roof and over the edge. Fortunately the still smouldering trunk had stayed outside the attic so there was no fire or smoke damage to contend with. As soon as the tree was gone those outside threw a large tarp over the hole and began to secure it to the roof.

Immediately the wind and rain ceased, inside at least.

Some of the construction workers had already started down the stairs but a couple were looking at the construction of what we now knew to be a false roof. Sloped exactly as the real one was but fifteen feet in from the edge of the wall, creating a separate little attic, the common wall looked odd from this side but would look perfectly normal from the other.

While the others were attending to the roof I went to the other end of the attic to have a look at the furniture and as I approached a peculiar scene began to take shape.

There was a wardrobe, a trunk, a dressing table, a bed and a small oval rug. Nearer the wall was a big, old galvanized wash tub, now pitted with corrosion.

The trunk was open and a lot of moth eaten clothes were visible inside and laid out on the edge. On the rug was a pair of slippers. There was a man's suit and shirt hanging in the wardrobe, shoes on the bottom.

The dressing table was set up as what seemed to be a combination shrine and dresser. A long crocheted runner covered it from side to side and there were two silver candlesticks, the candles long ago guttered out, and a large silver cross. All these things were placed among the mirrors and brushes and powder boxes one might have more readily expected to find there.

At first the bed appeared to be quite ordinary, with a brass head and foot board and a thick down comforter and a pillow. The covering of dust swirled slightly as I approached. Something else moved as well.

At the junction of the pillow and the comforter a fine thread stirred briefly and was still.

Quite suddenly I began to feel as though I was about to step into a very large mess, but I couldn't have said what or why. One more step and I knew.

"Oh shit," I said aloud.

The fine thread was a hair, one of very few still attached to a skull which lay deeply nestled in the down pillow. The rest of the skeleton was covered with the comforter.

Repelled though I was at the sight I could not move away. Quite the contrary in fact.

I moved closer and gently turned back the top of the comforter.

The dress had been blue with some sort of embroidery around the high neck. The woman's arms were folded neatly across her abdomen and in her sleeve was a handkerchief with the initials V.A.G. Around her neck was a fine gold chain from which hung a medallion. I replaced the comforter and turned to go and found myself almost bumping into Harry and a couple of the other tradesmen.

None of them spoke – only stared at the bed.

"Some of you are probably familiar with the Gilmore Island mystery?" I asked. "Well I think maybe we just found out where Victoria Gilmore has been all these years."

local grapevine was working overtime tonight. soon as the guys got off the roof they were on their cell phones telling ther friends. Now the word is spreadin around town.

Damn it my worst fear He found her. I hate this. No-one was ever supposed to disturb her. She was at peace. Now it's all ruined. Of all the places for a tree to fall. Now that interfering clown who can hardly drive a boat has ruined everything. I should have moved her while I had the chance. No. I should have got rid of him before he had a chance to spoil everything.

Chapter 6

I went to my kitchen office and called the Ontario Provincial Police.

"Wait a minute. Hold it. Did you say you have a dead body in your attic?"

I took a slow breath and quickly considered how best to rephrase my statement.

"What I said was," I said, "I have discovered what appears to be a very old skeleton in my attic, yes."

"Okay. Go on," said the voice from the police station.

"Would I be correct in assuming that you are at the Smiths Falls detachment?" I asked. "Sometimes telephone systems forward calls to a central location. You could be in Ottawa for all I know."

"Yes, I am at Smiths Falls. My name is Grant." said the voice. "Sergeant Mike Grant."

"Sergeant Grant, my name is RJ Harrison. I think we might know one-another. Are you the Grant who worked out of Rainy River a few years back?"

There was silence for a moment then Grant spoke again.

"RJ Harrison. The name is familiar. You'd be the Harrison who worked for Mediterranean Rock?"

"Right. We compared notes on a case I was working and you laid some charges after I uncovered the fraud."

"Yes. I remember you being very thorough. I didn't need much more than you gave me to get the conviction. You put together a good case. Are you still with Med. Rock?"

"No. I'm not working a case here. I'm the owner of the – or what will be, the Gilmore House Inn."

"Okay. So now you're an Innkeeper. So what's this about a body?"

"During the storm tonight a treetop came through the roof and in the process of finding and fixing the hole we, that is to say I and some of the construction workers, found a skeleton."

I paused for reaction but was rewarded only by silence so I carried on.

"This is no recently warm corpse, Sergeant," I said bluntly. "She has been very dead for a very long time." More silence.

"I won't presume to tell you how to do your job but I will suggest, if I may, that it would seem rather foolish to rush out here tonight. You'd have to wake up the marine guys because you can't get here except by water and in this storm I don't think even they will want to be out in a boat tonight; not for something that isn't exactly urgent."

"Hm. Yes, that seems like a reasonable enough suggestion," said the Sergeant. "What's the situation with the body right now, Mr. Harrison?"

"The roof has been patched up with a tarp and there's no weather getting in. I closed the trapdoor from the upper floor hallway to the attic. I don't think any of the construction workers here will have any reason to go back up there. We're all a bit rattled by what we found."

"All right Mr. Harrison." said Grant. "We'll leave it like that for now. I go off shift in … well about ten minutes ago. I'm going to write up what we've talked about so far then go home to bed. I'll see you early in the morning."

"Sounds good," I said. "I'm for some sleep too. Good night."

"All right then. Good night."

We both hung up. By the time we had finished talking I had a better fix on Sergeant Grant than I had had when we started. The longer we talked the better I remembered him - he was a reasonable and composed sort of guy. I hoped we'd get along as well this time as we had at our last meeting.

I had hired on several people but at that time only one was working on the island every day. My business manager, Kim Sinclair, was looking after most of the actual operating system setup and was hiring other staff. Kim was a rare find.

She was in her early thirties, five-eight, slim and fine-featured with short dark hair and was a recent business grad from Queen's. She had spent a few years after high school travelling and working in various service businesses, including a couple of small hotels. She decided she liked the business so did a hospitality management course at St. Lawrence College, then the Queen's degree. She'd been home in Westport, winding down and visiting family before heading out to find a job when she heard about the new Inn that was to open in the spring.

Kim wasted no time in coming to see me and we hit it off immediately. I hired her on the spot. She worked from home on the mainland while the weather was at its worst then, later, moved into her office at the Inn, to which she commuted daily.

By the time Sergeant Grant arrived at the Gilmore Island dock at 8:15 the next morning, I was up and working on my opening menus for the restaurant. The work crews had been fed breakfast and I was at the kitchen computer organizing a quick reference for multiple quantities of marinade for my International Salmon when Kim came in. I glanced briefly at her as she came to a halt beside the kitchen desk. Her usually pleasant expression was marred by a frown as she came jogging through the dining room door and into the kitchen.

"RJ," she said, "there are policemen here."

"Oh good," I said without looking up from my monitor. "I was hoping they would get here early and get things rolling."

Silence. I looked up now only to see a deepening of the frown.

"Oh. Sorry. I didn't see you when you came in to work this morning and I forgot to come and tell you they were coming. We had a little excitement here last night." I gave Kim a very quick rundown of the previous evening. Her look was of shock and dismay but her attempt to ask questions was quickly interrupted.

Almost as soon as I had finished my brief story two very large men came into the kitchen. They had apparently followed Kim from the office area. As I rose from my desk it occurred to me that these two, even had they not been wearing police uniforms, would have appeared well suited to their profession.

"Hello again, Mr. Harrison?" asked the one in the lead.

I instantly recognized Mike Grant, the OPP Sergeant I'd met in Rainy River and the person I'd spoken to on the phone the previous night. The voice was unmistakable: moderately deep and clear and with a tone of quiet authority and a slight hint of Ottawa Valley accent. I guessed he must have been raised around here somewhere.

"Good to see you again," I said extending my hand to him. "I run the place, or will if it ever opens."

"This is Constable Brooks – Marine Unit. He and his partner brought me over this morning."

I shook hands with Brooks and indicated my associate.

"This is Ms. Sinclair. She's Gilmore's Business Manager. I may be the owner and chief cook and bottle washer but she is the one who will do all the real work of running the Inn once we actually get open."

Both officers shook hands with Kim.

Grant looked back to me and said, "Well, maybe we should see what we came here for."

As I turned to leave, Kim gave me a look and a body language that said she wanted to know more about what was going on.

"I'll tell you more about it later," I said quietly.

"You'd better."

We left Kim in the kitchen and went up two flights to the top floor and along the hallway to near the back of the house.

I opened the cupboard and retrieved the hooked pole to open the attic trapdoor.

Once the ladder was securely on the floor all of us went up into the attic; first Grant, then me, and Brooks last. Both of the others had oversized flashlights which they snapped on as we entered the darkened attic.

It was a quiet procession.

I'm not sure whether or not they had actually, up to this point, believed me about the skeleton. Now there could be no doubt.

We formed a semi-circle around the bed and looked at the occupant and her trappings. I was at the foot of the bed with Grant on one side and Brooks on the other. After about thirty seconds Grant looked up at Brooks and nodded once.

Brooks backed away from the bed a short way and spoke into his shoulder mounted radio. "We'll need the coroner out here; probably no need for detectives at this point, or Crime Scene guys, but report in and see how the brass feel."

A female voice came back.

"Roger that. I'll go back to the mainland and wait for the suits."

Sergeant Grant spoke for the first time since arriving in the attic.

"Well this sure isn't something you see everyday. I wonder who she was."

I looked again at the figure in the bed and said, "Well, as to that, I think I have a fair idea who it might be."

Grant made no comment but simply looked at me and raised his eyebrows.

"I believe this may be Victoria Gilmore, daughter of the original owners of this house. She disappeared in the early 20th century under somewhat mysterious circumstances."

"I'm not from around here so I'm not familiar with the local history," said Grant. "Identification is necessary of course, but I have to say I'm more interested in the circumstances of her death; how and why she ended up here."

He paused a moment and looked around again at the scene.

"One thing is for sure: she didn't seal herself up in this attic. This is a very well planned and carefully orchestrated setup here. Whoever put her here went to a lot of trouble – the false attic space – the furniture. A lot of work. Also she was put here by someone who didn't want her to ever be found. But was she left here alive or dead, I wonder?"

I had nothing to say to that so I remained silent.

My cell phone buzzed. I pressed the button and Kim's voice came through.

"The rep from Fairfield Cheese is here for your meeting. Do you want me to tell him to come back another time?"

"No," I said, "that won't be necessary. Set him up in the lounge please, and I'll be there in a few minutes."

I looked over the bed at Grant.

"I hope you don't mind my deserting you but I have what will someday be a business to run and I'd like to get on with it. I may not be opening until June – that's only next month isn't it – yikes - but there are still a lot of things to do."

"No problem," said Grant. "We'll stay here and you can

bring up the coroner when he arrives if you don't mind. In the meantime we'll poke around a bit and see if we can turn up anything interesting. Any chance of getting some decent light up here?"

"Sure. I'll round up some extension cords and trouble lights for you."

"That's great. Thanks. By the way, did you touch anything – move anything?"

"Yes. I was so shocked I didn't think. I very carefully peeled down the top of the duvet, then put it right back."

"I guess you know you shouldn't have done that?" It was more a statement than a question.

I nodded once and headed for the ladder.

After I asked Kim to get one of the construction team to take up some lights to the attic hatch where the police were, I took coffee with me to the lounge.

The rep from Fairfield was laying out his materials in readiness to make his pitch. What he didn't know was that unless there was a serious problem with either pricing or delivery there was no way I would not use Fairfield. Besides the fact that they're close by, only twenty minutes by road from Westport, they provide a very wide variety of good quality products.

I let him make his pitch and asked a few questions. We worked out the payment and delivery aspects and I gave him an initial order but we didn't set a delivery date. Who knew what might happen in the next few weeks. I told him the date I planned to open and asked him to call a week ahead of that, to be sure that everything was still on schedule.

He went away an hour later well pleased with his call.

During the last five minutes of the meeting Kim had appeared a couple of times in the doorway between the reception area and the lounge. After I sent the Fairfield rep on his way I went to see what was up.

Kim looked up from her desk as I entered the office.

"I just got a call from Sandi Osgoode. She says she's just seen a coroner's van down by the dock. They were loading equipment into a police boat."

I told Kim some more of the story, much as I had told it to Sergeant Grant the night before and included my theory about the person's identity and about Grant's observations. Kim listened quietly to the end then said. "That poor woman. What must she have gone through? Why would anyone do that to her?"

I had no good answer for that.

"I'm going down to the dock and meet the coroner," I said.

As I turned to leave Kim asked, "RJ, do you think this will interfere with our opening?"

I stopped and looked back. "I wouldn't think so Kim. There's not a lot of investigating that's doable here on site. We'll probably have a parade of people through and likely we'll have to seal up that portion of the attic so it won't be disturbed in case they need to look at it again. Besides, there's what - three weeks still? I don't see any reason why we shouldn't open on time. Speaking of which, we need to get together soon so you can fill me in on the promotional stuff you've been working on. We'll need some guests when we open.

"Okay. Good," said Kim. "See you later, RJ." She turned back to her keyboard but as I left the office she called after me again.

"Oh, sorry. Two quick things before you go. We do already have some bookings for the opening so you don't need to worry about that. And there was a call for you yesterday from the sales manager of the Corbett Gallery in Westport. She said that there's a reception at the gallery coming up soon and she knew you'd been trying to meet with Cameron Alexander, the owner, to get the finishing pieces for the rooms. The manager thought this might be a good time to meet and talk about what you need for the Inn."

"Sounds like a fine idea. I've been trying to arrange a meeting for a month now but things keep happening. Call back and get the details please and say I'll be there. Thanks, Kim."

I stopped briefly at the kitchen office and wrote in the date of the reception at the Corbett Gallery and a doctor's appointment I'd have to go back to Kitchener for. Hopefully a last check up on the knee where I'd been shot during what had proved to be my final outing as an insurance investigator.

I went out the main doors and around to the left toward the dock area. The sun was bright and there was only an occasional cloud drifting lazily across the sky. A soft warm breeze met me as I neared the water's edge and a loon disappeared amid dozens of glittering rings. Except for some broken branches and other light debris there was little evidence that there had been a major storm not so many hours ago.

As I made the short walk to the boathouse and dock I saw the OPP marine unit boat.

It approached the dock and was turned around and expertly reversed beside the longest slip and was about ready to tie up when I arrived.

"I can take one of your lines," I said to the back of the person nearest to me, who was crouched low to the deck.

"Thanks," she said rising from behind the gunwale and throwing the heavy line all in one smooth motion.

I managed to catch the line and pull a little as the marine officer moved to the bow of the craft, took up the forward line and jumped to the dock.

So this was the owner of the voice on the radio with Brooks.

As she hauled the boat to the dock, the fenders were already over the side. I tied my line to the nearest bollard. She did the same. I found myself remembering my impressions of Grant and Brooks and realised that I had been wrong. Their size was not what made them police officers.

I introduced myself to the Marine Constable whose name was Allard, and to the Coroner and his assistant, Dr. Joseph Morgan and Mark Styles. I helped get the gear off the boat and, leaving behind Constable Allard, guided the Coroner and his assistant to the house and then up to the attic.

By the time we arrived the lighting supplies were already there and set up.

I called up to Sergeant Grant and he responded immediately, came over from across the room and looked down. "One of the guys brought the lights – big guy – heavy beard – blue overalls? – but I didn't let him up, though he seemed to want to come up. Brooks went down and plugged in and strung up the lights."

I gestured the coroner, a small slim, grey-haired man, to the ladder which he ascended smoothly, with me to follow behind, less smoothly. Wonky knees and ladders don't mix well. When we reached the top we took hold of the stretcher which was being held up to us by the assistant, Styles, a tall fellow who looked as though he might be able to reach the attic without the ladder. He then followed us up.

"Mornin' Michael," said the coroner. "What have we here?"

"Morning Joseph," replied Grant. They shook hands. "Bit of a change of pace. Don't guess you've had to take too many hundred-year-old skeletons out of attics."

"First time for everything I guess," said the coroner. "You'll be wanting to preserve as much of this scene as possible?"

"Yes please, Joseph. If you can just take her out of the bed gently and not disturb the covers too much I'd appreciate it. Not likely there will be much to see after all this time but you never know. The forensic team will want to look it over anyway."

"No problem. After I do a preliminary examination we'll just slip a blanket under her – no weight left there to speak of – and lift the blanket onto the stretcher. I saw the flash as we were coming along the hall down there. You can keep taking pictures as we go along."

With that he went to work. The comforter and sheet were drawn back to reveal the folded arms, the necklace and pendant and the monogrammed handkerchief. Dr. Morgan and his assistant folded the sheet and comforter carefully and handed them to Constable Brooks to hold. The long-faded blue dress looked as fragile as the bones it surrounded.

Morgan looked up from his work and said to Grant, "Not much I'm going to be able to tell you here, but you probably guessed that. All I can say for certain is that there is no head trauma. The rest will have to wait."

"Fine," said Grant. "Would your initial impression be that she has been here as long as she appears to have been?"

Morgan thought a moment. "Yes. I would say it's – definitely possible. Is that an oxymoron? Certainly indications are that she could have been here for a hundred years or so. No commitments though until after I've done a more thorough examination. As always, Michael."

Grant nodded. "So, for the record Joseph, she is dead?"

"Yes, Michael, she is very much dead," replied the older man.

Morgan carefully removed the pillow from under the skeleton's head and handed it to Constable Brooks who was standing by with various sizes of evidence bags, while Styles started to unfold the blanket from the stretcher. They slowly and gently worked the blanket under the folds of the faded blue dress.

"All right," said Morgan. "We're going to hold her in place while you two – can you assist Mr. Harrison? – while you two pull that side of the blanket through. I'll tell you when to stop."

Constable Brooks came over to the bed and he and I each took hold of the long edge of the blanket, our four hands at equal intervals along its length.

"Go ahead" said Morgan. He and Styles had reached over and were holding the skeleton steady. "Slow and easy."

Brooks and I pulled the blanket through smoothly until about a meter was on our side of the body.

"That's good" said Morgan. "We'll take it from here."

They wrapped one side of the blanket over the skeleton and tucked it in then wrapped the remaining portion over the top. The blanket was much longer than the figure in the bed.

The assistant got the stretcher which had been propped up against a wall and put it on the floor near the bed. He unfolded and unzipped a heavy, black plastic bag over the stretcher.

"Now if we can impose upon you gentlemen again," said Morgan, "we four can lift this lady onto the bag on the stretcher. Each take a corner please – that's good – up and over the footboard – now down - gently – excellent."

The task was done that quickly.

Morgan and Styles lifted the stretcher easily and placed one end's handles on the edge of the bed and the other on the dresser, then the Coroner and his assistant went to work zipping the blanket-shrouded body inside the bag and securing the bag to the stretcher.

"Let's make sure it's good and tight Mr. Styles. I don't think she'll mind," said the Coroner. "We'll have to tip this thing a good deal to get it out of the attic – don't want to have the lady getting away from us."

Between the five of us we got the stretcher with its fragile load out of the attic and down to the main floor. Word had got around and there were several people in the lobby when we arrived there.

One of these, recorder and digital camera in hand, was a part time reporter for the *Review-Mirror*, the local newspaper.

How he'd heard about this business so fast I couldn't guess. He swooped in quickly for a shot or two and I half expected the police officers to stop him.

They did nothing which, given a moment to think, was of course the right thing to do. All he got were some shots of a bag on a stretcher.

Sergeant Grant, back toward the stairs, stepped up one step and said in a loud clear voice, "I'll be happy to give whatever answers I can to your questions."

He had everyone's attention.

As the crowd of eight or ten people turned and moved toward Grant, Brooks quietly opened the main door. The coroner's assistant and Brooks wheeled their load out and the coroner softly closed the door behind them.

I went over and stood leaning my back against the door and listened to Sergeant Grant very earnestly and honestly tell anyone who asked a question absolutely nothing. He made it clear that nothing was known for certain, that he would not speculate and that an investigation would be started.

Within a few minutes it was evident that there was nothing to be gained by talking to the Police Sergeant so the reporter turned his attention to the coroner, and found him gone. He asked me where the coroner had got to and I said he had left a few minutes ago.

I had no thought of preventing anyone leaving so I turned slowly and opened the door.

As the reporter ran past me we all heard the deep rumble of the twin outboard motors of the police boat as it headed away from Gilmore Island. The group in the lobby broke up, returning to whatever work these few minutes of excitement had interrupted.

Sergeant Grant asked if I had a hasp and padlock to put on the attic trapdoor. These I was able to provide, having bought a set for a shed on the island. Grant borrowed a cordless drill and a stepladder and went off to do the installation himself.

While he was gone I ran over a couple of things with Kim. She gave me the layout of her opening promotion – letters and emails to Ontario Travel Associations, CAA, travel agents and such, as well as all local and regional newspapers which might give us a mention in their travel sections. We were trying to get the place filled right from the start if possible and it seemed we were well on the way.

I left Kim to carry on and took some coffee to the lounge. When Grant returned he gave me the second key for the lock – a sign of trust I hadn't necessarily expected – he said it was in case of more trees breaking into the attic - and we sat and chatted over coffee, catching up, in general terms, on what we had both been up to over the past couple of years. Soon we heard the return of the marine unit and Grant left.

Later that evening I was flipping through my antique notebook (Kim is always bugging me to get a BlackBerry or something) and came across the scribble about the Corbett Gallery. It occurred to me that I hadn't been out to any kind of dress-up event in a long time – not since I'd come here to Westport anyway – and I couldn't remember whether or not I had anything appropriate to wear to this fancy reception. Hanging in the corner of my half empty walk-in closet I found a suit bag which held a dark charcoal suit, a Harris Tweed jacket and a couple of pairs of dress pants. Nothing fancy but all in decent shape and not even from the previous century. No way was I going to be able to compete with the CK and Armani I would probably find while rubbing shoulders with the rich and famous of the neighbourhood but I wasn't really interested in competing anyway. As long as I looked reasonably respectable I'd be fine. A quick browse through the shirts and ties and I was satisfied that I could be passable without blowing this year's clothing budget. I was good to go.

Chapter 7

Sometimes, in the few quiet moments as the opening approached I found myself thinking about the Inn. Now that it was essentially complete, with a skeleton in the closet, so to speak, I wanted to know more about this place I was going to call home.

When I first saw the place it did not have a big sign saying "Gilmore House" although the island on which it sits is officially called "Gilmore" Island. I came to call the building Gilmore House after hearing that phrase from my real estate agent and later from local residents, my new neighbours, though they are rather farther away than you usually would think of neighbours as being. These were for the most part elderly, long-time residents of the area, some of whom had had relatives who had known the Gilmores, the original owners. I also gained lots of good information from the tradesmen who worked through the fall until the lake froze up and from those few hardy souls who came across the ice by snow machine through the winter.

As I talked to local carpenters and painters who had braved the stormy weather to come to work each day, and cooked for those who stayed on the island for periods of time, I built on my knowledge of the history of the island and of the building itself. The information I'd acquired from the Osgoode sisters at their bakery that day in the fall served as a base upon which to build my picture of the lives and events that made up the history of Gilmore Island.

The Gilmores were a wealthy family who had moved out of the "big city", Kingston, Ontario, in favour of a quieter life.

They purchased this moderately large island in Upper Rideau Lake, not far offshore from the village of Westport. Such sales of land and islands by the government were not uncommon at the time though few would become the permanent home to such a family as the Gilmores.

They began to build their new home in the spring of 1906.

A construction manager was coerced to come up from Montreal and many specialty items such as Italian marble and leather and English-made furnishings were imported. Otherwise all of the primary construction materials, mostly stone and wood, were local, as was most of the labour.

The Gilmore House is really a very large place, though it doesn't look it from either the land side or the water.

At three full stories above ground and a full though low-ceilinged basement (the Gilmores were ahead of their time here) it should stick out like a sore thumb. Somehow it doesn't.

That's mostly because Gilmore Island is heavily treed and has irregular terrain and rock outcroppings. The house has an odd arrangement of porches and terraces and a paint scheme of greens and browns and similarly coloured roofing which all but make the structure disappear from view. Even the turret on the north-east corner is unnoticeable from most points on the grounds and from the lake.

By 1910 it was finished and the family had moved in.

With no other islands nearby and nearly a kilometre to the Westport town site their privacy was complete. Perhaps too complete.

Most of the family was wiped out in the worldwide influenza epidemic of 1918, and those who remained alive moved back to civilization, though the Gilmore family continued to own the property for a while.

By 1920 the place was almost entirely deserted.

A series of caretakers, paid by a trust administered by a legal firm in Kingston, lived on or near the island and maintained it in the vain hope that someday the family would return. As far as was known, none of the Gilmores ever returned to the island. It was finally sold.

Between 1925 and 2000 the island changed hands several times, with each new owner bringing changes to the building and the property.

An elevator was a 1940's addition.

In the sixties someone added a beach. Barge loads of sand were brought in and spread at a low lying area on the west side of the island where there was a natural breakwater.

During the 1970s interior renovations were begun but a relative of the owner died after falling from the cliff into the rocky water at the north end of the island. This caused yet another change of ownership.

In the early eighties the large covered porch which had originally been only on the front of the house was extended along one side and across the back. Sometime in the early years cables for electricity and, later, telephone were run from the mainland and in the nineties both of these were upgraded, and cable for television was added.

In 2000 a fellow named Smythe bought the place with the idea of turning it into a hotel.

Renovations to the plumbing, electrical and heating systems were extensive. Smythe lived close by, in a rented house in Westport, overseeing every step of the operation.

The work was actually done very well and the result was a thoroughly modern small hotel with a Victorian/rustic look and feel.

Unfortunately the expense had been too much for Smythe, who was also having financial difficulties elsewhere and he was forced to bail out before the doors ever opened.

Smythe managed to pay off all the debts relating to the reconstruction, leaving nothing owing on the project, but was unable to carry on any further. He said at the time that he would soon return to buy the place back.

Rumour had it that factors other than money were involved in Smythe's final decision to abandon the island, but there are always lots of rumours about a place like this and it's hard to know which have basis in fact and which don't. The island went to a developer in 2002 but despite a lot of talk and planning, nothing further was done. Smythe did not return.

It fell again into disrepair. Fortunately few real vandals were interested in taking the boat ride so no serious damage was done, but time and weather took a toll and it looked awful, which is why, I guess, it stayed available until recently, when I came along.

Now I was almost ready to open.

I was glad that I had made the decision to not open until late spring. The task of getting the place in order had been a daunting one and having had the whole winter and spring to work at it took the pressure off and allowed me to think about things besides cleaning and painting.

Suffice it to say that there were lots of long distance phone calls made, lots of long drives to regional vendors and walks around the village to arrange the ongoing flow of supplies for the Inn.

There was credit to arrange where possible (not always an easy thing to do for a new place and an untried operator).

There were delivery schedules to set up. This involved both regional suppliers and local delivery people. I didn't think any of the big food service suppliers would deliver by boat. I didn't ask.

The local contacts were the most important to me personally. They would let me help support the village economy and keep me in touch with Frontenac County's producers and distributors. There are numerous farmers markets all over Southern Ontario and I'd spent time in the fall travelling around to a lot of them, from St. Jacobs, where I still like to buy my maple syrup, to North Gower where my friend Stavros sells me the best olive oil I've ever used.

Some stay open year-round and would be a good supply of fresh meats, poultry and eggs, and fruits and vegetables in season. Some of the sellers also do some importing of produce through the winter months.

Sergeant Grant knew that I was more than a little curious about the skeleton I'd found and was very good at keeping me informed about the investigation, though there was little to tell. Investigating a 100 year-old crime is a slow and tedious process and there was very little progress being made. As yet, no report had been made by the medical examiner: none that I was aware of anyway. I suppose it was because we had worked together previously that Grant seemed comfortable sharing details a cop would not necessarily share with a civilian. We talked regularly when he came to the island, though after the first few days he didn't venture over very often.

One day, shortly before the opening, he prevented me making an error that would have messed up one of the last remaining details that was needed to complete the look of the inn.

I don't even remember what it was that we'd been talking about.

Grant looked at his watch and stretched.

"Time for me to call it a day. The last three have been really long. I think I'll head back to Smiths Falls and grab a beer and a burger and watch the tape I made of the game I missed on Sunday. Too bad you're busy. You could join me."

"What makes you think I'm busy?"

"RJ. I'm sure I remember you telling me the other day that you have that fancy reception at the Corbett Gallery tonight. It is tonight, isn't it?"

I stared blankly at him for a couple of seconds. Grant waved his hand in front of my face and I returned to reality.

"I can't believe I forgot that. I've been trying to meet Cameron Alexander for months and now I have the chance and I almost screwed it up. Thanks, Mike. I'd better get moving."

Grant stood. "Me too. The longer I wait to watch that game the more likely it is that someone will tell me the final score and spoil the whole thing."

We left the room and parted in the hallway.

"I won't be back until later in the day tomorrow," said Grant. "I've a few leads to follow up at the shop."

"I'm giving myself a day off tomorrow – I can't remember the last one I had – nor do I know when the next one will be – so I'll be running errands and whatnot in the morning but I should be here, up in my suite, in the afternoon. Someone will be at reception making calls and hopefully taking more reservations. Have whoever's there call up and we can meet there and kick things around if you like."

"Sounds good," said Grant as he turned toward the stairs.

I went to the elevator and through it to my suite.

I got out of my work clothes and hit the shower.

After a careful shave I went to the walk-in closet and found the clothes I'd selected earlier. I hoped it would not be too bland for this event but I didn't have a lot to work with. Grey trousers, a Harris Tweed jacket and a white shirt with a patterned tie with grey, white and red and with black shoes and belt were it.

I'd called down to the boat house to make sure there would be someone available to get me in both directions, but found there wouldn't be anyone on later. I called Bascome's to arrange a water taxi both ways instead. Better that way anyway. There was no telling how long the reception would go on and I wanted to get a little private meeting time with the elusive Cameron Alexander.

The water taxi was there on time at six and the ride was uneventful, arriving at Westport about ten minutes later. I told the driver I'd call when I was ready to return and walked through the still hot evening, my jacket hooked on a finger over my shoulder, to the garage where my vehicle was stored. I got out the Lexus and drove to the far end of down-town. The Corbett Gallery is actually three old stores all joined together inside, on two floors. The Gallery is on the lower level and offices and the owner's residence above. Not too unlike my own setup at the Inn.

As I approached the Gallery the parking problems became obvious so I made a quick turn onto a side street and parked and walked the rest of the way.

The Gallery front was wide open to the early evening air and the couple of dozen people I could see were milling around inside and on the wide sidewalk. I waved my invitation in front of a fellow who was doing security and went inside.

I wandered briefly, looking at some of the artwork, until I became aware of someone at my elbow.

"You must be Mr. Harrison, from the Gilmore House. My name is Pamela Armstrong." She smiled as we shook hands. "I'm the office manager here. Welcome. Finally."

"I'm happy to be here. This is quite a place."

Pamela gestured with her wine glass. "The boss is over there in the corner with another client. They've been talking for fifteen minutes already and I don't think they can go on much longer without punches being thrown." Her half smile seemed to suggest that she was at least partly serious.

I looked at the far side of the Gallery. A tall, white haired man, perhaps a few years older than myself, in a medium grey Armani suit with a crisp white shirt, grey and red silk tie and highly polished shoes spoke earnestly to a much shorter, dark haired woman. She was late thirties to early forties. She wore a dark red dress with a wide black belt and black shoes with low heels.

The light bars over the artworks occasionally illuminated his Rolex and diamond solitaire ring and her bracelet and necklace as the two sparred over some topic unknown to me. Their conversation reached an end and they shook hands, cordially if not as between friends, then both walked in my direction. One passed by, headed for the exit, and the other stopped in front of me.

"Hello, Mr. Harrison. Nice to finally meet you. I'm Cameron Alexander." Her lipstick and nails were a perfect match for the dress which flowed like paint over her curves.

I'm not sure how long it took me to respond.

"Same here," I managed to get out eventually. "We've missed each other a few times. I'm happy that's been rectified. I must say, you're not what I was expecting. The name Cameron threw me off, I think."

"And you thought he," pointing at the tall, white haired man who had been waylaid at the door, "was me, so to speak.

Now I think I understand your somewhat surprised expression when I introduced myself. The name often has that effect and my staff like to play the 'How long can we keep people in the dark' game. I've struggled with the questions and the confusion all my life. My father wanted a boy apparently and when he didn't get his wish he insisted on a male name."

"Well, for what it's worth," I said, "I'm happy he didn't get his wish."

She made no response to that other than a smile.

"Since you're here we should take advantage and spend a little private time together. I think I can sneak away for a short while." She made eye contact with her office manager across the room and with a series of gestures indicated that we were leaving. Pamela nodded once and turned back to the group she had been speaking to. "Come with me to the store room and I'll show you a few items I've set aside for you."

She took my arm and steered me toward a door in the back of the gallery. From somewhere she produced a single key and unlocked the door, then released my arm and entered the darkened room.

Once illuminated the room proved to be a storage and work area almost as large as the gallery itself. There were dozens of paintings leaning against the walls and a considerable assortment of art pieces on shelves and tables. Large plywood work surfaces showed work-in-progress frames and display stands.

"This way please, Mr. Harrison," she said leading the way across the room.

"Only if you call me RJ."

"Very well, please come this way, RJ. Your items are over here," she said without stopping. She looked briefly over her shoulder. "You may call me Cam."

We stopped at a shelf unit which held dozens of small and medium sized art pieces, mostly Victorian looking but somehow rougher, less finely finished than I would have generally expected of Victorian art pieces and artefacts.

"Most of what you're looking at was made here in Canada, in Montreal, Toronto, Kingston. It was made here, for sale here and although the quality of the manufacture is quite good the equipment that was used to make these items was not up to the standard of that used in England at the same time, hence the somewhat less refined finishing on some of it."

"Okay. I understand. For my purposes that makes it all the better."

"I'd hoped you would see it that way. Some people don't want these kinds of items because they think they're less Victorian. It depends how you look at it, I suppose."

I examined the pieces closely. Some were actual art pieces but most were manufactured items which had been used in homes, offices, factories. They were the physical reminders of the history of the time when the Gilmores had built their home here.

I became aware of Cam watching me as I looked over her collection – my collection.

"How do we present these things in the Inn without risking having them all – removed shall we say – within a few months?"

"We have lots of ways to secure the artefacts – shadow boxes and frames are the easiest for these small items. I tried to stay with mostly smaller things for the rooms. Some of the larger pieces might be good in the dining room or the lobby. I have a crew of installers who will look after all that."

"Good. I wouldn't know where to begin."

Cam pointed to a number of framed prints which were leaning against the wall unit.

"I've selected some prints for you to look at as well. There are probably twice as many as you need so you can go through them sometime and choose the ones you like best. They all reflect the themes of the Victorian Era, the outdoors and nature as it was seen then and of hospitality, Victorian-style."

"You've been busy. Thank you for getting this all together."

"It's no trouble really. As soon as you decide which pieces you like I'll organize a small crew to put everything in place. I've decided to give you a break on the price – since you're just starting out – in exchange for some free advertising. We can work out those things later. Now we should get back to the party."

Cam took my arm again and led me back to the main room where still more people had crowded in. A lot of the pieces of artwork now had sold tags on them. Cam was obviously pleased by this.

"I'm going to have to go and mingle for a while. If you can stand it until the end perhaps we could have a quiet drink together. I'd like to hear all about the opening of the Inn. See you soon."

I watched her drift away into the crowd, wondering how I could make that happen.

I spent a long while browsing, looking at all the pieces, sold and unsold, to see if there was anything I would like for my own suite at the Inn. One in particular caught my eye. It was quite expensive and I'd already spent a lot of my settlement on the Inn. I caught myself thinking that I'd have to wait to see if I could afford it later and the phrase "if you have to look at the price, you can't afford it" came to mind. Then I realized with a start that, for the first time in my life, I was on the "can afford it" side. I bought the painting. It would look great in my living room.

I was still looking at the artwork and watching Cameron Alexander work the room when my cell buzzed. One of the live-in construction guys was calling to tell me that some kitchen plumbing had come unglued and was spewing water all over. Always something.

I waved to get the attention of Cam's manager. I told her that I had to leave and to please let Cam know that the items she'd selected for the Inn were fine and to go ahead with the installation as soon as possible. I also asked her to relay my apologies for skipping out so abruptly and promised to get in touch soon.

As I drove back to the garage where I stored my vehicle I hoped it would not be too long before I'd be able to have that quiet drink.

Don't think he knew who I was when I helped tie up the boat at the dock tonight. Sure gets around. Don't know what he was doin' here

Chapter 8

To say that everything went smoothly throughout the last few weeks of preparation for the opening would be untrue, but there were relatively few serious glitches and those were dealt with reasonably easily. This was mostly attributable to the significant organizational skills of Gilmore's Business Manager.

Kim Sinclair had a handle on most everything that happened at the Gilmore and was a calm and efficient leader. She had a quiet and easy style until they tried something she didn't like. Those who thought she could be pushed around quickly found out that they were mistaken. Few tried it twice and those who did found themselves looking for work elsewhere.

Kim and I were handling the final interviews for those staff positions not already filled. Mostly these were not front line jobs at this point, but we tried for as much experience as possible in our crew, though this was not the primary focus.

We were looking for people who liked working with people. A housekeeper's position at an Inn, as far as I'm concerned, is not just about making beds and cleaning toilets. It's about enhancing the guest's experience, making them feel comfortable and safe and welcome. A grumpy housekeeper who growls at the guests does not add to those good feelings, nor does a surly server or a miserable desk clerk who complains about having to be at work instead of golfing as the guest checks in.

Support people also have to get along with one another while they're on the job.

All in all the job of selecting the right people is a tough one and not by any means foolproof. We did our best and time would tell how successful we were.

I was looking forward to the end of one particular day because it meant, I hoped, the end of hiring. There were only three more positions to fill. Kim was handling one and I had the other two.

My second last interview was for a server position for evenings and weekends and the candidate was quite young and had little experience. What she had though was enthusiasm and a friendly and outgoing personality. She was a senior at the local high school and wanted to get away to college the following fall.

She wanted to work and seemed to sense my reluctance to hire her. She changed my impression by saying that although she came across as something of a party girl she was and would continue to be a reliable employee.

She was either very sincere or a very good actress and since I couldn't tell which I decided to give her the benefit of the doubt.

One more to go.

The last interview was for a part-time maintenance position in the Inn and the boathouse. Now that most of the construction workers were gone there was a need for someone to be available to handle small maintenance issues, change light bulbs, hang pictures and other jobs of that nature. The candidate was Bob Langdon, whose application introduced him as the husband of one of the kitchen staff we'd already hired. It said he had a construction background and there was little he hadn't done at some time or other – carpentry, roofing, landscaping, plumbing.

I was just about to call him in to start the interview when my cell rang and I was informed that there was yet another minor structural problem at the boathouse which would need additional funds to rectify. I'd told the carpentry foreman that I wanted to know about any cost over-runs before and not after the fact. I called Kim who had just finished her last interview, explained the situation and asked her to take Langdon.

He had been waiting in the lounge and as I left the dining room where I'd been interviewing, he had just gone into Kim's office. I saw only his back as he closed the door part way – a big man with a beard and short dark hair. I'd have to meet him and the others Kim had hired some time later.

All the staff was now on board, deliveries were arriving almost hourly. Old Bascome was proving a valuable ally, keeping up with the flow of goods and making sure all of my supplies and all my new employees got to the island safely. Staff training continued at a brisk pace and the folks from the Corbett Gallery were constantly around, installing art pieces and pictures throughout the inn.

The utter chaos of the last week or two is largely indescribable so I won't bother to try. There were lots of bumps and lots of frayed nerves but in the end we made it to our opening day, tired and anxious but ready for the test. At least I hoped we were.

I was mad she was found now I'm less worried. fools think she's that Victoria Gilmore who Disappeared from the island a hundred years ago. All the trouble I went to getting those clothes and the other stuff was worth the effort. I may come out of this okay after all. Fools !!!

still need to stay close so I can keep an eye on things.

Chapter 9

I really hadn't given any thought to how many people we were expecting to arrive on the opening day and perhaps that's for the best. I'd only have lost sleep worrying about whether we would be able to handle the crowd. We decided long ago to do a soft opening. For us that meant we opened officially on a Wednesday, a day which would not work as a check-in day for everyone. Some would arrive that day but others would not arrive until later in the week.

Guests did indeed arrive all through the day and were placed in their reserved rooms. The influx continued until Saturday morning when the last reserved room was filled. Kim's opening promotional efforts had obviously worked. Full house.

I worked in the kitchen fairly consistently. The first lunch was fairly calm but we had far greater numbers for dinner. The stress was palpable in the kitchen that evening but we were prepared and came through with only some minor aggravations. The first day ended late and with a certain sense of satisfaction we all retired to our respective homes and much needed rest.

Day two went well too but with more of a feeling of control and purpose, less of the feeling of panic present on day one, and the prep work and the services progressed well.

Late in the day a couple of days later, I took some paperwork along to the office for Kim to process, then headed to the lounge to see how the head bartender had made out dealing with his first days of dealing with real customers. Not long after I arrived there, Kim came into the lounge area and headed for the bar.

I was there with Thomas - that's with a European pronunciation please – emphasis on the last syllable – the head bartender. Any time I want wine or liquor for cooking I sign for it from the bar. This was one of Kim's ideas for inventory control. It keeps all the alcohol coming through the same door so to speak, and it makes life easier. I don't have to worry about counting and ordering wines and liquor and Thomas is in control.

I was just ready to leave with a bottle of Pale Sherry and a bottle of Kentucky Whiskey as Kim arrived.

"Hi, RJ. Hitting the bottle again I see."

Thomas gave Kim a sharp look but said nothing. Thomas is very serious about most everything as far as I know, not just bartending and getting his name pronounced properly, and does not think it appropriate that most of my employees treat me with what he feels is too much familiarity. He may mellow, slowly, but I think it will be a long process.

"Yes, Kim. I seem to have gone through a lot of this stuff already. The diners seemed to like what I did with it yesterday though, so I guess it will be worth the walk every few days. What brings you in here? We don't often see you in the bar during working hours."

"I'm looking for a guest actually. His name is Jeremy Greenwood. Joan described him and I was just about to look when I saw you. He had been to the reception area looking for me while I was out trying to clear up that marine fuel problem; seemed a bit upset according to Joan at the desk; wanted to talk to me as soon as possible."

"He is there at the table in the corner." said Thomas. "He has been here for about twenty minutes, having one drink only so far."

"Thank you, Thomas. I've no idea what this is about but I guess I'll find out in a minute. I'll see you later about the fuel business, RJ. I think I got it sorted out."

"I never doubted it for a minute," I said.

Kim flashed me a quick little smile and left the bar, heading toward the corner of the lounge.

I turned on my barstool to see who it was that she was meeting. The lounge was fairly quiet just then and her progress was direct and my line of vision unobstructed.

As Kim approached the corner table its occupant rose and the young man extended his hand to Kim. They greeted one another in a friendly manner and Kim sat down opposite him, her back to the bar, and they began their conversation.

I turned back to the bar and was reaching to pick up my two bottles when Thomas gently laid a hand on my forearm. I looked up at him and he nodded over my shoulder toward the corner table. I left the bottles where they were and turned to see Kim, twisted around in her chair, waving me to come over.

"Hold onto these for me please, Thomas. I'll pick them up later."

I left my stool and headed for Kim and Mr. Greenwood. As I made my way across the room it occurred to me that although I had certainly never met this man before his name was somehow familiar.

As I reached the table Greenwood stood again and we shook hands.

"Mr. Greenwood," said Kim, "this is RJ Harrison. He is the owner of The Gilmore House Inn and I think we need to include him as you tell your story. He's much closer to the situation than I."

"That's fine with me," said Greenwood. "I just want to find out what's going on with this business of the body in the attic."

"Why don't you tell us what it is that's bothering you and maybe we can help clarify the whole thing for you," I said as I pulled up another chair and sat down.

"I think it's you who need to have things clarified, not me. I've been reading the local paper this morning, that piece they did about your purchase of the island and the events leading up to the opening. I read about your impending opening a couple of months ago in a travel magazine. I decided then and there that I would have to see the place now that it's been fixed up. I have a personal interest, you might say. I like what you've done with the place but now that I've read the local paper I find that there are some inaccuracies in your account of the skeleton."

I hesitated a moment then asked, "And how would you know anything of the event?"

Greenwood leaned forward and rested both forearms on the edge of the table. "The article says you found the skeleton of Victoria Gilmore. Let's just say for starters that my mother, who is now in her seventies, will get quite a laugh when I go home to Toronto and tell her that *her* mother died in 1916, more than 20 years before my mother was born. Oh, wait a minute. That doesn't work, does it?"

Mr. Jeremy Greenwood sat back in his chair and looked at each of us in turn. To say his expression was smug might be a slight exaggeration but he was certainly pausing for effect and was enjoying the moment.

I looked at Kim, then back to Greenwood. Kim, seldom at a loss for words, seemed to be trying to say something but was unable to make any sound come out. I recovered slightly quicker and managed to start to ask questions.

"Your grandmother was Victoria Gilmore? Then Victoria Greenwood?" I managed to mumble almost to myself. "That's why I thought I should know your name; Greenwood. Kim, do you realize that we've had this whole thing wrong all along? Everyone has. Albert Greenwood and Victoria Gilmore really did leave together all those years ago," I glanced briefly at Greenwood who provided a confirming nod, "and – oh - do you know what else this means?"

I looked at the other two and since neither of them had anything to say at that instant I plunged on.

"I'll need to call Grant right away. I can't even begin to guess how much flack there's going to be about this." Greenwood and Kim both looked at me as though I was raving.

"If the skeleton I found in the attic is not Victoria Gilmore then who is it? You may have solved one mystery for us, Mr. Greenwood, but now we have a bigger one."

Been spinnin his wheels the past while. Now he's found out the skeleton in the attic isn't who he thought it was. Lousy luck. Who'd'a thought a relative of the long lost Victoria Gilmore would show up for the opening. Now that meddler Harrison will be sniffing around again. gonna to have to deal with him soon.

Chapter 10

For the rest of the afternoon I was rather preoccupied with thoughts of skeletons in the attic. The revelations of Jeremy Greenwood shook me.

Now there would certainly be a thorough police investigation with all the disruption that can involve. I wondered how no-one had figured out that the skeleton was not who we originally thought it was. I knew there had been no official report – Grant had told me that – but did no-one actually follow up? Do an autopsy? Anything? The official side just kind of slipped quietly away and was forgotten. If that was the case there would be hell to pay. I wondered if they'd lost the body. No. Couldn't be.

These things ran through my mind as my call to Grant was being shunted to voicemail: "The skeleton from the attic isn't Victoria Gilmore. A Mr. Greenwood – grandson of said person – says his grandmother was very-much alive until quite recently and that his next stop will be the police station in Smiths Falls to fill you in. Be prepared to be dumped on about police incompetence and such. Call me when you can."

As I mixed my newly acquired whiskey with maple syrup, pineapple juice, soy sauce and puréed garlic for the salmon marinade, I made a mental note to start looking into the previous occupants of Gilmore House a little more fully. I measured in brown sugar and olive oil, and a few twists of fresh black pepper and a pinch of sea salt, then poured some of the mixture into a shallow pan. Probably the skeleton belonged to someone with a connection to the island. Pretty unlikely that anyone would come all the way from Kingston or somewhere like that just to find a place to hide a body. This island qualifies as fairly remote, even to the locals.

I placed the salmon fillets in the pan and poured on the rest of the marinade, covered the pan with plastic wrap then put it in the walk-in fridge. While in there I checked over the supply of fresh local vegetables. Some of them would be included in tonight's featured entrées. I made a few notes for tomorrow's ordering.

Late spring in Ontario means asparagus and I'd found a fairly close grower who was willing to bring me as much asparagus as I needed every couple of days. Since that last late blast of bad weather it had been unseasonably warm and the asparagus had come on earlier than usual. These crisp green stalks would go perfectly with my International Salmon and multigrain/mushroom rice.

The sugar snap peas, also early because they'd been grown under plastic – a technique some farmers were using in order to get a jump on the season - would go with the other feature, a crispy, parmesan crusted chicken dish, served with oven roasted potatoes with fresh herbs from our own herb garden which was just beginning to come along.

We had a regular menu which we served every evening, hopefully something for everyone, meats, pasta, vegetarian, and then two features as well. It helped keep things interesting for the guests and for me and the other cooks as well. Cooking the same things all the time can get a little dreary, but adding two totally different items each dinner time keeps the creative juices flowing.

Speaking of juices, tomorrow we would need to make another batch of chicken stock, a staple in any commercial kitchen.

I paused on my way to the freezer to see how the salad prep was progressing. As with a number of my crew, Jeany was new to the food service work. This was her first time back to work after several years at home raising a family. Somewhere along the way, quite recently in fact, her husband had gone out of the picture and she had been forced to find an income. It had been rough for the first couple of weeks she was with us but once her family got used to the fact that she was not going to be home with them all the time they had begun to adapt. Jeany was now not only more friendly and less tired but was more efficient and more interested in learning about the kitchen work, from me and from Bud, my all around life saver in the kitchen.

"How are things going for you these days, Jeany?" I asked. She stopped her work and looked at me, a very concerned expression on her face.

"The home front is generally not bad; a few ups and downs but nothing too serious. Unfortunately I'm having trouble with Bob again. He still seems to think that I'm going to change my mind and we'll get back together."

"Even after a divorce and a restraining order?"

"Yes. I really don't want to call the police on him, you know, with the kids around and all, but he frightens me even more now than he did when we were married. I know what he's capable of. I still have the scars to prove it. I don't know what he'll do next." She turned away toward the wall and was quiet, possibly feeling that she'd said more than she'd intended.

"I know that this is not in any way, any of my business, but I want to help you however I can. Please let me know if there's anything at all that I can do." She nodded but did not turn to face me.

I went on to the freezer and then to the main prep table to where Bud was working.

Bud knows a lot about the food business from many years experience. He can do prep and cook and has a great work ethic, but he has no desire to lead. If he has an idea of how to do something better he says so – it took a while to convince him that I would not object if that happened – otherwise he does everything I ask him to do, and more.

I plunked down a couple of bags of assorted chicken parts and bones onto the table with more force than was necessary and Bud looked up from his work.

"I spoke briefly to Jeany as I was going to the freezer," I said quietly. "Apparently she's still having trouble with her ex. What do you know about this Bob guy?"

"We should get these bones into the walk-in refrigerator to thaw slowly for the stockpot tomorrow," said Bud with a sideways nod of the head to indicate that I should do as he suggested. With each of us carrying a bag of bones we went into the large refrigerator.

Bud turned to me as we entered. "Bob Langdon. He's quite a piece of work from what I hear. I don't think I've ever actually met him. I hear from some of the other staff here that he's been back in town for a while now and is being a real pain to Jeany."

"Wait a minute. Langdon. I'm sure a guy by that name applied for a job here, but Kim decided not to hire him for some reason,"

"Sounds like another good decision on her part," said Bud.

"Yes. Bud, I'm not asking you to *do* anything but please keep your eyes and ears open to anything nasty that happens between them and let me know."

"What are you going to do?"

"I don't know. Probably nothing. What could I do anyway? Maybe the situation will resolve itself. But if it doesn't smooth out by itself then something may need to be done to *make* it happen. I'm cold. Let's get out of here. Don't say anything to Jeany about this." Bud nodded his agreement.

We closed up the fridge and went on with our work. Jeany was still bent over the salad prep sink.

With bones on my mind again I went to my desk and fired up my computer, printed the ingredients for the stock for Bud for tomorrow, then opened a file I'd created to keep track of things that occurred to me about the skeleton. I noted the idea of looking into the past residents of the house and thought there might be some information to be had from the museum, and possibly from the *Review-Mirror*, the local newspaper.

I was brought back to reality when the convection oven snapped shut. Bud had put some potatoes in to bake and was headed to the walk-in to begin the last minute evening meal prep. I met him at the fridge door and took armloads of meats, produce and dessert ingredients as he passed them to me. Soon the large centre table's shiny stainless steel surface was covered with bowls and plates and boxes. We set to work organizing the various items. While Bud chopped vegetables for a vegetarian quesadilla I started coating chicken breasts which had been marinating in home-made herb vinaigrette salad dressing. The coating was a mixture of bread crumbs, parmesan cheese, granulated garlic and onion and parsley. Soon there were twenty or so coated chicken breasts on a rack ready for the oven. With the salad prep done, Jeany came over to the main prep table to lend a hand prepping a small mountain of fresh sugar snap peas.

And so it went.

By 9:00 I had just finished cooking the last of the evening's dinners for a couple who had rented a boat and hadn't realized how long it sometimes takes to navigate the locks. Bud had started the clean-up a while before and now Joey, the evening dishwasher, was almost caught up with the dining room dishes and the kitchen's cooking pieces.

I operate on a crew mentality here; everyone helps out with the clean up and everyone gets out that much earlier. That was part of the package when everyone was hired so there weren't any surprises. We also have a tip-out system. All the support people get a share of tips made by servers and bartenders; hence everyone has a stake in making sure each guest has the best possible experience. Seems to work.

As I finished cooking the last International Salmon I collected up my utensils and took them to Joey and then went back to scrub down the grill, but Bud had beaten me to it.

"Well," I said, "if you lot are good to finish the clean up I'll get some orders ready for tomorrow."

"Yeah, go on. We're okay," said Bud. "You'll probably be here long after we're gone anyway so you might as well get a head start."

"Thanks," I said. It wasn't as though I was going anywhere really. I headed to a relatively quiet corner of the kitchen where my desk, with phone and computer, is situated.

Once there I transferred the lists I'd made earlier in the day to real order forms in our computerized inventory program. Having been open only a short time there wasn't yet any history on which to build but we used the system anyway, noting areas where we were using nothing but educated guesses as the basis for ordering, and creating the history that would make this part of the job easier in the future.

So far we'd been lucky – no major shortages and not a lot of loss due to too much perishable stock. But it was early days.

By the time I'd finished all I could do, the rest of the kitchen crew had done with the clean up. We all headed for the dining room door and I, last out, killed the kitchen lights. In the lounge we met up with the last of the bar and wait staff who had just finished their work as well.

We all headed for the big main doors and having said our goodnights the departing group headed out along the lighted pathway which would take them to the docks and the boat to the mainland and home, using Bascome's last shuttle run of the day.

I watched them down the path then closed the huge door and went into the office to see the night desk clerk. It was Gwen this week. We spoke briefly about work and sports and the weather then I headed to the elevator which I rode up to the third level. I exited by the rear door of the car and entered my own private suite.

I went into the bathroom and dumped my cooking clothes in the hamper and changed into something more comfortable then headed down to my kitchen. I poured myself a glass of Valpolicella Classico and loaded up a small plate with some fruit and cheeses and crackers. Passing through the living room I turned on the music system and put on *Atlantic Suite,* an album by Phil Nimmons and his band. I'd listened to it a lot since coming here. The water I looked out onto was not the Atlantic but the general impression is the same. Nimmons 'n Nine Plus Six followed me as I went out through the sliding glass doors onto my balcony. I closed the sliding screen door and settled myself into a large comfortable lounge chair and sipped the wine.

The sun was down and the half moon was up. A sprinkling of clear bright stars were interspersed by a few silvery wisps of cloud.

I took a long while to unwind, watching the clouds and the moon – listening to the loons on the lake and the owls in the trees nearby. I finished my wine and my snack and rose to go in to bed.

As I began to rise I saw a shadow move below me, between the trees at the edge of the back lawn. It was leaving, walking slowly toward the beach, apparently unaware that it had been seen. When it passed out of the trees and onto the moonlit beach I could see that it was a tall and muscular man.

He turned at the water's edge and went up along the shoreline to the north, quickly passing from sight behind another grove of pines.

I stood frozen on the balcony, watching and listening for the man's return. A minute or so later I heard the sound of a small boat motor starting up and then fading away in the distance.

I took my plate and glass into the kitchen and put them into the dishwasher, then switched off the light and went up to the bedroom.

I didn't turn on any lights there but rather, slipped quietly from the dark bedroom out onto the upper balcony and stood watching and listening again. Finally, satisfied that no-one was around, I went back inside and went to bed.

Something about the shadowy figure was familiar, but I couldn't nail it down. Whoever it was should not have been there at that hour.

I replayed the scene on the moonlit beach a number of times before falling into a restless sleep.

I'm sure he saw me tonight but it was too dark for him to recognize me. stupid risk to take but didn't think I'd be spotted. No matter. boat was close enough that even if he'd tried to chase me I woulda had no problem getting away. need to be more careful.

Chapter 11

I remembered as my alarm was going off the next morning that I was supposed to be taking the day off. It was rather early in the game to be taking time off but things had gone so well in the first few days that Bud and I had decided to chance it. A brief rest would do us both good as we'd both been working crazy hours up to and through the opening. We flipped a coin and I went first.

Once I'm awake, I'm awake, so after a few minutes of staring at the ceiling I got up and headed for the shower, and then got dressed in jeans and a Henley T-shirt. Today I didn't even make the bed, but rather, just threw the sheet and duvet up over the pillow. One of the few perks of ownership I allow myself is that once a week the cleaning crew from the Inn comes to clean my suite. One of them would be here later in the morning after all the guest rooms were taken care of.

I went down to my kitchen and put on some coffee and set the egg poacher on the stove. Looking out the window I realized what a great day it was; sun shining, light breeze and already about eighteen degrees Celsius by the thermometer outside the kitchen window.

While the coffee was brewing and the water heating I went back upstairs and opened all the windows, including those in the turret, then went back down to the main level and did the same.

As I plunged the French press coffee maker I recalled last night's trespasser and wondered again why anyone would be around at that time of night. Maybe I was feeling suspicious after finding out that Victoria wasn't Victoria, or maybe I was just feeling possessive of my new Inn – either way, it bothered me. I poured my first cup of coffee, adding cream and sugar and then set to making breakfast. A few minutes later I was into my second coffee and was enjoying my poached eggs on toast. While I ate I finished off the list of stops I would need to make in town and made a shopping list for the grocery store.

After cleaning up the breakfast dishes I put on walking shoes and grabbed a light jacket. I went down the back stairs and out onto my private deck, locking the door behind me. I could hear the sounds of the kitchen as I passed close by that door, but I didn't stop in. The breakfast cook would be in control for now. Kim would see that the orders I had organized yesterday were placed today. Kim would also keep a close watch on the operation and call me if anything went awry. Bud would be in later to see things through the lunch and dinner rush. They all knew I was not going to be around today and they would handle whatever came along. I decided I would stop in later to see how they were doing.

Remembering again the shadowy figure of the previous night I went first toward the trees that lined the back grassed area, then followed what I thought was the route the man had taken to the water's edge and then off to the right, out of sight of the house.

There was not much in the way of a trail to follow but every now and then something seemed to stand out – a baseball-sized rock turned over showing a darker underside and leaving a hole, now partly filled with water – a length of driftwood perched between two stones, snapped in half by a now-absent weight.

A little further on and just as I was about to give up the search in favour of my planned activities for the day I saw a grouping of small rocks, about loaf of bread size and a little smaller, which had obviously been moved. I went for a closer look and gently lifted the rocks to look under and around them. Under the largest I found a frayed fragment of a rope, left behind as someone pulled out a rope without moving the rock.

Then the jackpot. In a line directly from the rope fibres to the water, barely visible on the wet stones were traces of dark green paint, evidence, at least to me, that someone had pulled a boat, probably a wood boat or it wouldn't likely have been painted, up onto the shore and had anchored it in place there with a few rocks.

I reached into the shallow water and dislodged one of the stones with the paint on it, taking care not to damage the fragile smear.

Satisfied that there was nothing else to find there I retraced my route back along the shoreline to the beach and then to my own back door. I unlocked the door and placed the stone and the rope fragment on the floor of the hallway behind the door where it would not be tripped over, relocked the door and went on my way.

This time I went immediately to the right and over a sparsely treed saddle of rock directly to the boathouse. No-one was around at that moment so I just went to the small office area and left a note saying that I was taking one of the boats.

My first choice of boats for this trip, which I make every week or so, was a 16-foot, 1937 Chris Craft, restored and shiny as new. I checked to see that it had not been rented for the day then pulled the cover off and climbed in, fired up the engine and left the throttle in neutral. I got out, freed the bow line, got back in. I stepped over the centre partition and untied the stern line and gave a gentle push away from the dock. I took my seat behind the huge old steering wheel and gradually eased the throttle ahead. The deep throaty rumble of the inboard engine rose as the sleek craft gained speed and arrowed across the water.

It was early in the day and in the season so there were few boats out. The sun was bright but not yet very strong and I was glad of my jacket as wind rushed over the low windshield.

Much as I enjoyed the boat and the calm water I had plenty to do so I headed straight for the public dock in the centre of the harbour at Westport and, reducing speed as I approached some other boats tied up at the dock, I looked for a place to tie up for a few hours.

There were few other boats and I quickly found a spot near the walkway, on the water side of the harbour. One benefit of having boats such as mine is that lots of people are interested in them and as such are willing, even eager to help tie up and talk.

I always indulge these friendly folks because it's the right thing to do and because I appreciate the help.

Also I do the same thing when I see a craft I want to know more about and never like it when I get blown off by some guy who thinks he's too busy or too important to talk to the people who just helped him tie up.

I spent a few minutes showing a guy the inboard motor and had the feeling he was unimpressed by my lack of knowledge about the thing, even though he certainly was impressed with the boat itself. We walked to the footbridge over the harbour and he went his way, to his boat further down the marina, and I crossed over and headed for town.

The walk over is at the foot of Spring Street. As I made the short climb uphill from the water I saw The Cove Country Inn and remembered the great dinner I'd had there a few weeks prior. I turned left at Main and went along through the business area to a residential area where I keep my vehicle.

Mrs. Samuelson, the property owner, is an elderly widow who lives in a big old house on the shore. There is a huge double garage containing my Lexus and little else except some toys her grandchildren use when they come to visit.

Mrs. Samuelson gave up driving several years ago when the car she had owned for nearly forty years finally packed up and she saw the prices of new cars. She embarrassed the heck out of her son-in-law, who had taken her car shopping, with language he had no idea she knew, let alone would use in public, and said she would never pay that kind of money for a car. She didn't, and hasn't. That leaves me with a good safe storage place and it costs me only a small amount of rent and occasionally a large amount of time talking with Mrs. Samuelson, who is endlessly interested in the Inn and anything else I would like to talk about.

It occurred to me as I walked under the young, bright green leaves that she might be a good source of information about the history of the area and of the Gilmore family.

I always stop at the house first, before driving away, to check on Mrs. Samuelson. She is often not home. She walks, whenever the weather permits, because she likes to walk and she has places to go - she's a member of boards and committees and groups and associations all over town.

Today there was no response when I knocked so I headed for the garage across the broad driveway from the house. I had fought with the old, beat up garage door when I first started to use the building so, late in the fall, I had a new door with an opener installed. When I pushed the button on my remote control the door jumped upward creating a vortex of dried up flower petals from the maple trees around the yard.

As I drove out of the driveway I glanced back to see the dark green door, which I had had painted to match the colour of the original, descend to the ground. I turned right onto Main, windows down and breeze blowing in, and heard the sound of a small boat passing by in the harbour. The engine noise was similar to what I had heard the previous evening. I braked hard and pulled to the curb. I shut off the motor and listened but the boat had passed behind a house and was gone.

I sat for a couple of minutes wondering if I was being foolish to think that this could be anything other than a coincidence and then, not having reached a satisfactory conclusion, I moved on. There must be dozens of boats with exactly that same motor around here, I thought.

The parking lot at Kudrinko's Country Grocery was not even half full at that hour. I parked at one side, where I knew there would be shade for a while, and headed through a walkway between the grocery store and its neighbour, to the next street. I would return to buy my groceries later.

Directly behind Kudrinko's and facing onto Church Street is an L shaped building housing several businesses, among them the local LCBO and The Cottage Coffee House. My second stop, after Mrs. Samuelson's, is always The Cottage Coffee House. Not only do they serve what I am told is very good ice cream, but they are the local supplier of excellent quality, Fair Trade and Rainforest Alliance Certified coffee. They can tell you, if you want to know, in what country, on what farm and by whom your coffee was grown.

The coffee here is roasted and ground (if you want it ground) on site, and served in the shop with some very excellent pastries, breakfasts and sandwiches. Cottage Country Coffee is a franchise, dealing in Fair Trade Coffees. I use only Cottage Country Coffee at the Inn, not only because it is very good but also to support the concept of Fair Trade Coffee.

This is one place that's always busy and the regulars were already outside, under the huge cream coloured canvas umbrellas, sipping their favourites and relating the morning's news.

I stopped briefly to talk with Wil Bascome and one of his friends and then went into the shop.

You have to know that this is the best-smelling place in town, with the possible exception of the Osgoode bakery, and partly for the same reason. Here the fragrance of freshly baked pastries is blended with the aroma of brewing coffee. I ordered my usual coffee and a danish from the young woman at the serving counter and while it was being prepared went to the back area to talk to the owner about a bulk coffee order.

I gave him two orders. One was my own personal order for one kilo of whole beans, my own blend which we had agreed upon several months ago after many attempts to get it just right. The other was for the Inn, fifteen kilos of ground coffees of several different strengths and flavours. These would be ready to be brought to the island on Monday morning, along with many other deliveries. My own coffee I would pick up in a couple of hours.

I sat on one of the tall stools at the front window of the shop and watched the people passing while I ate my pastry and drank my coffee. Wil Bascome and his friend were headed along Church Street, probably back to the Bascome Marina; one of the Osgoode sisters, I have no idea which one, passed by on the far side of the road and Harold Morrison, uncle of Andy, of Morrison Boatworks came from the walkway to Kudrinko's, glanced briefly at the coffee shop, and then crossed Church street and went into the Pro Hardware opposite. Harold worked for his nephew and was sometimes around the Gilmore boathouse doing maintenance on the old boats. Maybe he was in search of something for a repair on one of them. I was reminded at that moment that even though he was around the Inn from time to time, I had never actually met him face to face.

When I'd finished my coffee I went next door to the LCBO to check on the arrival of a case lot of wine I had ordered. I paid for that and for a six pack of beer I would use for cooking and asked them to hold onto both until later.

After a stop at the drugstore I went back through the alleyway to Kudrinko's where I picked up a few groceries. I loaded the bags into the vehicle then drove around the block where I picked up my wine and coffee orders.

I got another coffee to go and then headed out of town, by way of Concession Street and on toward the community of Rideau Ferry on 42.

I inserted a CD of West Coast Jazz by Dave Brubeck and relaxed and enjoyed the drive.

I stopped at farms where I bought my eggs and some asparagus and then headed across the intersection at Highway 15, and on to Fairfield. After picking up some cheeses and cooking sauces I was on my way back toward home when I was struck by an odd feeling. I twisted my head around quickly as an older pickup passed me on the other side of the highway, headed toward Fairfield. I had the impression that I had seen it before that day – not just once but more than that. I watched in the rear view mirror but the truck kept on until it was out of sight.

I was so absorbed in my thoughts about the pickup that I almost missed the turnoff to the storage area I had been using for some of my odds and ends. I went in and opened my unit, a much smaller one than I'd had when I first came here, and took out my golf clubs. I thought that now that things were up and running at the Inn and now that my leg was feeling significantly better I might sometime get a chance to play again.

I loaded the clubs in the back of the Lexus and headed back into town and went to the public dock. They have trolleys there for the use of the people loading and unloading boats and they come in very handy. I hauled all the accumulated stuff of my day's shopping to the boat in one load. I left the clubs in the car.

That done, I took the Lexus back to the garage and checked again to see if Mrs. Samuelson was home. Again there was no answer so I walked back to the marina and headed back to Gilmore Island, the afternoon sun warm on my face and the breeze even more pleasant than it had been a few hours ago.

Guy wastes a lot of time driving around the countryside. Nothin' better to do than that and make my life difficult. Golf now. Shit.

Chapter 12

The next morning I was awakened by the ringing of the phone beside my bed. It was Gwen, just ready to go off her overnight shift on the desk, calling to inform me that the police were here, again, and that they would like to see me as soon as possible. I asked Gwen to get them seated in the lounge with some coffee and to say I'd be there soon.

I showered and dressed quickly and was headed out the door in record time, noticing as I left my suite that it was only 6:45. It was going to be a long day.

As I crossed the lounge I noted that Sergeant Mike Grant was accompanied by Marine Constable Allard. Gwen had thoughtfully provided an extra cup at the table where they were seated so I slid into a chair and poured myself a cup, offering refills to the others at the same time.

"Well, good morning Sergeant Grant, Constable Allard," I said, making myself comfortable in the low chair. "You're certainly on the job early this morning."

Mike Grant smiled slightly and said, "Sorry about that Mr. Harrison. We would have waited for a more reasonable hour but some of the brass are a little anxious about this case all of a sudden. They seemed to think that if we stormed the place at dawn it might startle a confession out of someone, so here we are, doing what we were told to do."

"Yes, I can see you're really driven to a frenzy of activity and endeavour."

"Something like that," said Grant. He glanced over at Allard who had so far been silent. "We are here to do a job and we're going to do it as well as we're able but I see no reason to be jerks about it. Our new C.O. is a little heavy handed sometimes and is feeling a bit embarrassed that we didn't see the true picture about the skeleton in the first place. Now he thinks quick decisive action will clear things up and gloss over the fact that we were less than 100 percent initially."

"Surely no-one can blame you for the fact that the body was more recent than we first thought. Even the Coroner was fooled when he was here," I said.

"No, but there's lots of heat and the sooner we can figure this thing out the better for all concerned," said Grant.

Allard spoke for the first time. "And we have decided that we can follow orders and hopefully solve the case and not be too disruptive to your business in the process."

"Thanks for that," I said. As I reached to the table for my coffee cup I wondered how much of this politeness and pleasantry was for real and how much might be intended to lull me into a false sense of security. It occurred to me for the first time that I myself might be considered a suspect in this case. I'd been here a long time before any guests or staff or construction workers. Yes, if I were them, I'd be checking me out very carefully. Still somehow I didn't quite believe they thought I was the guilty one in this.

"I notice too that you're not in uniform today," I said.

"We thought it would be better if we were less conspicuous while we're here," said Grant. "No doubt the word will get around soon enough but in the meantime there's no point in attracting unnecessary attention."

"Sounds good. How can I be of help?"

"We'll need you to provide us with a list of all the trades companies that worked on the renovation with you, and we want to get all you know about who might have had access to the place before you took ownership," said Allard. "We're thinking that possibly one of the previous owners may have some insight."

"Insight. Yes. As to a list of construction companies, I can have that for you in short order. The history will take a little longer and to be honest I'm still finding out things about the place, so I may not be the best one to ask. What I can do is give you a list of people who will know a lot more than I do about the island and the surrounding area, people who've been here all their lives."

"Good," said Grant. "I think what we'll do is this: I'll take the list of construction companies back to Smiths Falls and start calling and setting up interviews. Josée will come back here, after she drops me off at the Westport dock, and collect what history you can provide and your list of possible sources of more."

He looked briefly at Josée Allard who nodded once in acceptance of the plan.

"Okay," I said. "I'll go to the office and start pulling together the list. You can relax and finish your coffee if you like. I won't be long with this I hope."

As I rose to go Mike added, "Oh, I almost forgot to tell you. A forensic team is coming from Kingston to go over the attic room. I don't guess there will be much for them to find after all this time but they're pretty thorough. You just never know. By the way, do you still have the spare key for the lock I put on?"

"Yes, it's in a secure drawer in the office. I can have Kim get it out and give it to Constable Allard."

"That will be fine. Thanks."

I went out of the lounge and around to the office. As I had hoped, Kim was there and, after a brief explanation, I was able to have her get what I needed from the computer. A task which would have taken me much time and aggravation, Kim did almost without thinking and we sent Sergeant Grant on his way, lists in hand. Kim would get the attic key out later.

While Constable Allard was taxiing Grant to the Westport dock where they had left his vehicle, I went back to the office to scrounge a few sheets of lined paper then went into the dining room to get some breakfast.

This is something I seldom do, first because I usually eat in my own suite and second because when I do it everyone somehow feels that it's some kind of test.

I had the feeling that it was going to be a busy day and that I might not get the chance to eat again before I started to work in the kitchen for the evening meal so I decided on a serious breakfast. I ordered steak and eggs with sautéed mushrooms, hash browns, toast and coffee.

While I waited for my food I began to work on the information I was providing for Constable Allard, one page for previous owners, one page for people who were likely to be able to give the police more local insight than I was able to, and some more pages to sketch out what I knew of the history of Gilmore Island.

When my breakfast arrived - steak medium rare, eggs over easy, toast light - all as ordered, I packed up all the papers but one. The list of contacts I continued to work on as I ate.

I think the food was fine. I have to say I'm not really sure because I was concentrating more on writing than on eating. Anyway, when asked, I told Michelle, the server, that everything was fine. I'm not sure I was convincing. Michelle, lean and hard at 40-something and a restaurant worker all her life, accepted my response without comment but with a look that said she could have given me a piece of old football and I wouldn't have noticed today. Maybe she was right.

I signed for the meal and left the dining room by way of the French doors onto the deck. As I did so I heard raised voices coming from the kitchen. I went back inside and entered the kitchen from the dining room. A couple of servers and a guest gave me a look as I went through the swinging door. Jeany was at the prep sink as usual for this time of day. Bud was at the main prep table but he wasn't working. Instead he stood less than casually with one hand firmly gripping a 45 cm cast iron fry pan, watching the interplay at the prep sink.

"You can't keep ignoring me. You're my wife and I'm coming home whether you like it or not." He was somewhere under two metres tall and paunchy with thinning, dirty hair and a full beard. His clothing was wrinkled and one worn runner was untied. He grabbed Jeany's shoulder and spun her around to face him. At that instant Bud's fry pan was raised and Bud was on his way around the prep table. I was on the move too, raising my hand to slow Bud's approach.

"Hey, enough of that," I said loudly. "What the hell do you think you're doing?"

The man's hand dropped to his side and his fists clenched. "Mind your own business. This is between me and my wife."

"Your *ex-wife* you mean and I *am* minding *my* business. You are harassing my employee, in my kitchen, in my Inn, on my Island. You have no business being here. I'll go one step further and add this: You are not welcome here, and you are being warned, in front of witnesses, that if you ever return here for any reason whatever I will call the police and have you charged with trespassing."

I stopped for breath and waited for the next move, wishing the local constabulary weren't already on the boat.

"You can't do that." His face reddened and a sheen of perspiration appeared on his forehead.

I spoke more quietly this time. "Try me. I can do it and I will. Now it's time for you to leave, quietly, with no damage on the way out or I'll have to call the police now. Go out that door, out of the Inn and off the island." I pointed to the rear exit from the kitchen, the one leading to the back deck.

He turned and walked to the door, then before leaving had his parting shot. "You'll be sorry for this, both of you. You're an interfering do-gooder," he said pointing to me, then, "and *you* won't find a restraining order of much use against me," pointing to Jeany. He turned and left, slamming the door as he went.

"I'm sorry RJ. I ..." I interrupted her.

"Stop. There's nothing for you to be sorry for. This was not your fault. Now, I know you don't want to involve the police again but I really don't think you have any other option. You know he's dangerous and now he's angry too. More than he was before. Having the police involved now and having the restraining order enforced, especially if he winds up in jail for awhile, will be painful to your children, yes, but it will be a lot less painful than having them grow up without a mother. Think about it."

I picked up my papers from the counter and turned to go. Bud had returned his weapon of choice to its hanger over the main prep table and was mostly working on the batch of cookies he had been making. He nodded to me as I passed on my way back to the dining room. Looks of relief had replaced the anxiousness of a few minutes before. When I went out to the deck to work on my lists I saw no sign of the ex. I didn't know how he had come or gone but it didn't really matter as long as he *was* gone.

No-one was having breakfast outside so far this morning – the weather was still a little cool at this hour – so I pulled a chair off the stack near the railing, slid it up to a table and continued my work.

Not much later I heard the French doors open and looked up to see Constable Allard emerging from the dining room with Michelle close behind carrying a tray with a coffee service. Michelle set the tray on the outdoor dining table and turned to leave.

"You should have a jacket sitting out here. It's not July you know," she said as she reached the door. "Oh and nice job in there. I hope it works."

"Thanks for your concern, Michelle, and thanks for the coffee."

She came as close to smiling as she ever does as she closed the glass door.

Josée Allard pulled out a second chair and sat down as I poured the coffee. "Your staff, they are quite protective of you, are they not?"

Before I could respond she continued.

"So, I see papers there. Do you have something for me already?"

For the first time I noticed a slight hint of Quebecois accent around the edges of Josée's English. I thought it might be a good idea to revise my pronunciation of her name. And I wondered what she would look like if she was not quite so serious.

"Yes, I've been working on some lists for you." I turned two of the papers toward her and continued. "This first one is a complete list of previous owners. I got to know it pretty well during last winter as I dug around old contracts, leases, land transfers – stuff like that. I'm fairly sure they're all there but some of the dates may need to be verified if that matters." I changed pages. "This is a list of people I can think of who will probably know more about this area than I do. Wil Bascome is the owner of Bascome's Marina. He's about 75 years old or so – been here all his life – knows the water and the islands cold and is very up on what goes on around town."

"Semi-retired and not enough to do, so spends at least part of his time minding other peoples' business?" suggested Constable Allard.

"Not far from the truth," I said. "This next one is Mrs. Samuelson. She lives in town and is let's say 85 roughly. She would probably have been born not too long after the time of the Victoria Gilmore disappearance, not that that has any particular significance I guess, since we now have a skeleton which is not Victoria Gilmore. Anyway Mrs. Samuelson is another one who seems to know most of what happens around here. The next few are people I know less well but who have been around a long time, so they may be of use to you."

"Anyone under retirement age on the list?"

There was a little bit of a smile as she finished the question. Much better.

"You'll want to talk to Andy Morrison who owns the Morrison Boatworks and the Osgoode sisters who run the Osgoode Bakery."

"Anyone else?"

"Not that I'm aware of actually," I replied. "Oh wait. I've just thought of someone else. He's not as old as the first few on the list but he's worked a lot of places – kind of a handy man. He works here part-time occasionally in the boathouse but I don't know if he's ever had any association with the island before this. His name is Harold Morrison."

She wrote the name on the list. "This is a really good start. We would waste a lot of time finding proper places to start asking questions without something like this. Thanks."

"You're welcome. I hope it helps. I'm still working on my rendition of the history of the island. I only know what these same people have told me," I said, pointing to the lists of names.

"No matter. Whatever you give me will serve as a base of information. Others will fill in the blanks, we hope, and eventually we will have what we are looking for – the identity of your skeleton and an answer to the questions of how and why she ended up in your attic."

I took a sip of coffee and said, "I acknowledge ownership of the attic but I'm beginning to wish people would stop calling it *my* skeleton."

This last elicited a real smile from Constable Allard who leaned forward over the table and said, "I will try to remember that, but no promises."

I was in process of pouring more coffee when her phone buzzed and she answered. She listened briefly without speaking then said, "Understood. I will see you there in twenty minutes."

She closed her phone and stood up. "I have to go for a while. I am to meet the forensic team at the town dock and bring them out."

I stood up as well, picked up the coffee tray and we headed for the dining room door. I realized there were some guests being seated for a late breakfast so I steered us away from that entrance over to the kitchen door. We went in and through the kitchen, where I deposited the tray near the dishwasher, and out through the dining room and lounge toward the main entrance.

"We need to stop at the office so you can get the key for the attic."

"Right."

Constable Allard went into the office to see Kim, returning quickly and walking toward the door, putting the tiny key in an inside pocket.

"I will be back in less than an hour I expect," she said as she opened the door.

"Come in this way and have someone find me. I'll take you up to the attic trapdoor."

"Thanks. See you."

She went out and closed the huge oak door. I stood there a moment then headed for the kitchen. I was late for work in my own Inn.

watched him yesterday as he went on his little rounds of the town, getting supplies and seeing his friends. Probably shouldnta followed him out of town but I had to know where he was going. All that for asparagus and eggs. Pitiful. storage area might be a good place to lay a trap. Maybe the garage where he keeps his truck too. have to think about that. Doesn't seem very interested in the skeleton anymore good.

Cops were out at the Inn again today. Maybe this aint going away after all.

Chapter 13

Some time later when the lunch rush was over, one of the dining room servers breezed into the kitchen to inform me that the police were looking for me - again. I said I'd be out in a few minutes.

I was in the middle of making a custard base for a dessert and needed to see it through or see it ruined. The orange-flavoured custard was almost cooled enough over its ice bath to fold in the whipped cream. Once that was done I would pour the mixture into a flat dish and put it in the freezer. Later it would be served sliced with fresh fruit and more whipped cream.

Five minutes later I was on my way out the door and through the dining room. Bud stopped me.

"I didn't want to say anything earlier but I hear Bob's been seen following Jeany around town the last few days. She hasn't said anything more about him since he was here earlier but I know she's worried, not just for herself but the kids as well. Someone said she had commented that every time she turns around while she's coming to or going from work he's there in that old red pickup."

"Okay Bud. Thanks. I'll see what I can do."

I met Constable Allard and the forensic team at the front desk and, after brief introductions we all headed up the stairs to the third floor.

When we arrived at the attic entrance it became very obvious that the forensic people were not interested in tolerating our continued presence so Constable Allard and I started back down toward the main floor as the others climbed the ladder.

It suddenly occurred to me that I might get some time alone with Josée if I invited her for lunch in my suite. I wasn't yet all that hungry but I decided to not pass up the opportunity. Nothing to lose by asking, right?

"Are you hungry by any chance, Constable Allard?" I asked as we reached the head of the stairs.

Allard stopped and looked at me. "Yes, I am," she said. "It's been a long time since breakfast for me."

"Me too. Let's go into my suite and I'll get us some lunch and we can discuss the case."

"I suppose that would be all right. Lead the way."

I got a strange look from Allard when I led her into the elevator and closed the doors. We rode down one floor and I then reached up to the secret switch and opened the rear door.

"Nice trick that is," she said as we departed. "I will have to remember that if ever I need to get into your suite again."

I re-closed the door. "The next floor up has the bedrooms and bathrooms," I said waving my arm vaguely in that direction. "You're welcome to go look around if you like."

"Another time perhaps."

We went to my kitchen. "Living room and dining room are through there," I said, indicating the open doorway. "Pull up a stool and sit there at the counter if you like." I opened the fridge door and peered inside. "What would you like to eat? I have some lunch meats, or how about some salmon salad?"

"A salmon salad sandwich sounds good, and before you say anything else I have to warn you. If you continue calling me Constable Allard when we're alone I may have to arrest you or something. My name is Josée, as you well know."

During her speech I had ceased my search for ingredients for the sandwiches. I looked at Josée a moment then smiled. "Yes. I do know. And I'm RJ. Do you like red pepper?"

"Yes, thank you. Is there a washroom nearby where I could wash up?"

"Just around that corner," I said, pointing to the hallway.

Josée rose without further comment and left the kitchen. I watched her go, then, for a moment, watched the place where she had been. I then returned to my search for what I needed from the fridge.

By the time Josée returned I had pretty much finished grating carrot, chopping celery, red pepper and green onion for the sandwich filling. She watched as I added a little salt and pepper, a teaspoon of relish, a very small dab of horseradish, a bit of ranch dressing and some mayo. After I mixed these together with the salmon I retrieved a loaf of fresh, whole wheat bread.

"I have some cucumber to slice on these if you'd like. Do you want yours plain or toasted?"

"With cucumber please and toasted," she answered.

I cut four slices of bread and put them into the toaster. "So, is there anything more I can do by way of helping with the investigation?"

Josée hesitated a moment then said, "I do not think my superiors would be very impressed with an amateur being involved with the case." The toast popped and I began building the sandwiches. "Besides, I am not sure what more you could do. You have provided a lot of information already and you should probably just let us do our thing now."

"What would you like to drink with this?" I asked, handing Josée a plate.

"Water would be great, thanks," she said.

I filled two glasses, one with water, another with milk, and brought them to the counter. "Would you like to eat outside on the deck?" I asked. "The weather seems to be warming up and there's a decent view of the lake."

"Sounds good to me," said Josée.

We picked up our plates and glasses and went out through the sliding glass door onto the deck, and sat at my small Bistro table. I had switched on a CD of Oscar Peterson as I went past the entertainment unit. Great jazz piano drifted quietly out onto the deck.

As we stepped onto the deck , Josée gestured back toward the living room. "That is a lovely piece of pottery on the sofa table in there. Is it from around here?" she asked.

"It's by a potter named Leta Cormier, from around North Gower I think. I have a couple of pieces of her work here. You might find some at the Corbett Gallery in town, I'm not sure. She's quite well known and has pieces all over. "

Sunshine was just beginning to reach around the west side of the building.

We ate in silence for a couple of minutes, each engaged by our own thoughts, watching the trees and the water.

"I do not believe I have ever had a salmon salad sandwich with so many things in it. Usually it is with only a little onion and celery. Very good."

"Thanks. I just experimented until I found a combination I liked."

Josée perked up briefly as a very large and distinctive power boat flashed past, much too quickly in the no-wake-zone close to the beach where some of my guests were sunning. It was still too cool for most people to be in the water. She said nothing but I had the feeling she had registered the incident for future reference.

"I won't be around as much after today," said Josée. "Now that the case has been taken over by the detectives I'll be back on water duty."

What the hell. Nothing to lose right? It'll be either yes or no and there's nothing I can do to affect that that I haven't already done.

I turned my gaze from the lake and looked at Josée "That's too bad really. I was getting to like seeing you around. I'll miss that."

Josée looked at me very seriously as if weighing the truth of what I'd said. "Perhaps we will see one another anyway."

"Perhaps that would be more likely if we planned it .... Okay, here's the thing. I'd like to go out with you sometime, sometime soon I mean ... a date ... I'm kind of rusty at this and you're not making it any easier."

Her smile, which had grown as I babbled, disappeared and she was again very serious. "I am sorry. I did not mean to make fun of your discomfort. I think I would like to go out with you."

I must have looked relieved because she smiled again.

I was just about to speak when her phone beeped. She answered, listened briefly then ended the call. "I have to go. The forensic guys are done for now but they want to keep the attic off limits for the present. We will let you know what happens next."

"Okay. That's not a problem. I can't think of any good reason why anyone would need to be up there anyway. You can lock it up again and hold onto the key."

We rose from the table and headed into the living room.

"Thanks for the lunch. It was very good. I'm looking forward to doing this again soon."

Yes!

We dropped off dishes in the kitchen. "You're welcome. You're invited anytime you're here and I'm not working."

We went through the elevator and out into the second floor public hallway. "I will go up and collect the guys," said Josée, "then I will be going back to the mainland."

"Okay. I'm headed for the main kitchen. I'm on this afternoon and evening. Bud will be wondering what's happened to me.

"I'll see you soon," I said, and extended my hand.

Josée took my hand, then moved in very close and gave me a quick little kiss on the cheek. She released my hand immediately, turned abruptly and disappeared up the stairs.

Again I watched her go, then I went down the stairs to the main level and to work in the kitchen.

As I cooked that afternoon and evening I thought about my lunch with Josée, and about what had brought us together - the skeleton of a woman; a woman who needed someone to find out who she was and how she came to be in my attic. I didn't really doubt that the police would put in a decent effort; Mike Grant certainly seemed serious enough and now others were involved too. But despite Josée's admonition about amateurs muddying the waters, I would continue to poke around and see if I could help resolve some of the questions surrounding the mystery woman. After all, I hadn't always been an amateur.

I also thought a moment about Jeany and her ex. I wondered if I could or should get involved in that situation. I'd been trying to put my previous life behind me – that life of sometimes dealing with dangerous people, some of whom preyed on others. I'd dealt with more than a few. I hadn't always been in the relatively tame world of insurance investigation. I didn't really want any part of that life but I wondered whether or not I could draw a line where I could live with it.

heard them come out of the elevator while I was around the corner. Need to be more careful sneaking around here almost caught me today. To many question if I get seen in the house.

seems to be getting pretty cozy with the lady cop. Maybe something I can use there.

Chapter 14

Not much happened over the next few days that related to the investigation. Not specifically at least. I called Josée and made a date for dinner in Smiths Falls.

Life at the Gilmore House Inn moved slowly on and the rest of the world was for the most part of small concern to us. For the most part. One thing was always there in the back of my mind. A problem waiting for a solution.

On my next day off I did some chores around the place then headed off to Westport to continue my own course of inquiry and to deal with my annoying little problem.

I tied up the boat as usual at the town dock and walked over to get the Lexus.

I knocked on Mrs. Samuelson's door and, to my surprise, she was home. She invited me in and we sat in her kitchen and chatted for a few minutes. I asked her if the police had been to visit.

"Yes. A very nice young man, officer I mean, named Grant I think, came to see me day before yesterday. Asked a lot of questions about people I might remember who'd gone away under unusual circumstances – sudden like or anything. I told him I'd been around a long time and a lot of folks have come and gone in those years. He said maybe in the last thirty years or so. I think he was being funny, thought I'd be stumped by that little time. Seemed kind of surprised when I rattled off -

about fifteen I think. Probably I missed some but not too many."

She stopped for a sip of tea and I got a word in.

"Do you think you could give me the same list? I'm checking out a few ideas of my own. Mostly I'd just like to have this business settled and have the Inn back to normal." Not that it's been exactly normal yet was what I thought but did not say.

"Remember that time, soon after you found your skeleton, when you came to tea and we sat and talked about the Gilmores and the island and all? Well I thought then that you'd probably not just sit back and let the police look into the matter. No. You seemed then like you'd be in it up to your neck."

"If you had that idea then, you had it before I did. I really didn't have any plan to do any investigation myself."

"So you say. You'd told me you were some kind of investigator in your, what did you call it, your previous life. Maybe it's harder to give up than you thought."

I looked closely at her and mulled over that idea. She was leading up to something. "So you think I was planning this all along?"

"Maybe not planning exactly but ... I thought after I spoke to that nice Sergeant Grant that you might be interested too so I jotted down the names for you. I think I may have added a few to your list that aren't on his." She reached into a shallow drawer in the side of the table and removed a mauve envelope. "Here you are." She looked closely at me and went on. "I don't know if you've thought about this but there has to be some possibility that whoever did this terrible thing may still be around here. You just be careful, RJ."

I stood to leave and said, "I will Mrs. Samuelson. I learned to be very careful of crazies in my – previous life."

"Good. See that you remember that. Oh by the way, were you here on Tuesday night – late?"

"No. Why?"

"There were some noises out by the garage and when I turned on the outside light I thought I saw a man's shadow heading past the trees there. Probably just a randy cat making the noise – maybe the shadow was just an old woman's imagination."

"I'll have a look when I take the Lexus out."

"Thanks, RJ. You come back and see me again soon, okay?"

"I will. 'Bye for now."

I went down the porch steps and over the gravel driveway to the garage. I had a close look at the door and the area around the building before I used my opener. I checked for signs of tampering but nothing seemed amiss. As I reached for the Lexus door handle I realized I still had the mauve envelope in my hand. As I slipped it into my inside pocket I caught a hint of fragrance. The envelope, like Mrs. Samuelson and everything in her house, smelled of lavender.

As I drove away I rethought my conversation of a few minutes earlier.

If I had given Mrs. Samuelson the idea that I was going to get involved in the case, who else might I have given the same idea too? The person who put that woman in the Gilmore attic maybe? If Mrs. Samuelson was right and the killer was still around, I might have let him know I was looking for him. Not a comforting thought.

Before going to do my grocery shopping I went in search of the Roadside Motel. A few well placed phone calls had got me the present location of Bob Langdon. Word was that when he wasn't following his ex around, he was doing mostly nothing and doing it mostly at the Roadside. I parked the Lexus at the end of the row of rooms and walked halfway back toward the office to number six. As was the case with all the other rooms here the screens hung half out of the windows and drapes were drawn across grimy windows. I knocked on the door and a flurry of peeling paint drifted to the cracked sidewalk. I knocked again.

"I'm coming. Quit banging," said a voice from within.

The door popped open and there in his underwear stood big bad Bob. Almost before some flicker of recognition slid into his face I heaved on the partially open door and knocked him backwards. Had the room not been so small and the bed so close to the door he might have recovered his balance. As it was he stumbled back, hit the bed and didn't stop rolling until he hit the floor, face down, on the far side. By then I was around there too, sitting on him and holding both arms behind his back.

"What the ... ," I slapped him across the back of the head.

"Shut it, Bob." He stopped talking.

"This will go a lot easier for you if you just shut up and listen. I don't want to have to break your arm to get your attention but I will if I have to. You understand?"

Silence.

"I'll take that as a yes. You don't know much about me but you're about to find out. You probably think I'm just some Innkeeper with a wonky knee. But if you think you can intimidate me the way you do your ex-wife, think again. In a former life I dealt with scumbags all the time, guys who make you look like a Boy Scout. You know how I *got* this bum knee? I was shot. The guy who did the shooting didn't survive to tell about it. I still keep in contact with some guys from back then, guys who would be only too happy to return a favour for me. Not the kind of guys you want to tangle with. You reading me, Bob?"

Again silence but this time a nod and a sniff.

"All right, Bob. Here's how it's going to work. You're going to pack your bag and pay your bill and leave town, today. I will be watching. There will be no visits to town, no working in the area, no passing through. Nothing. If you cross me, I'll make a phone call. One way or another neither Jeany nor I will ever be seeing you again. Go far away from here and get on with your life. Okay, Bob?"

"Okay." Sniff.

"Good. I'm going now. Remember what you agreed to and remember I'll be watching."

I got off him and stood up. He didn't move. I left the room and went to the Lexus, where I waited for about fifteen minutes. My hands were shaking. I don't like that kind of confrontation at all. Also I'd not spouted that much b/s in a long while. I was lucky to have made it work, if I had.

Before long, Bob came out of the room carrying a backpack with a Toronto Argos logo and a green garbage bag with a pant leg hanging out through a hole in the bottom. He hurried along the walkway to the office, emerging some minutes later then went to a red pickup and drove away. So far so good. Hopefully that was the last any of us would see of Bob Langdon. And if Langdon was my late-night trespasser that wouldn't happen again with him gone.

After my hands stopped shaking I drove to Kudrinko's. I planned out the rest of my day. First I would see to some supplies and get them into the Lexus where I had added a cooler that ran off the otherwise-unused cigarette lighter, to take care of the perishables. After lunch at The Cove I would have a look at the museum. It had been closed for the season when I had tried to see it when I first arrived but once we hit the May long-weekend, it had opened, and this was the first chance I'd had to check it out. I didn't know if I'd find anything useful there or not but it was worth a try. Later I would go to the Town Hall and see where they kept their archives.

As it happened I got no further than the museum for quite some time. There was a lot to see and to read and I began at the beginning.

The town began in 1828 as a lumber destination and other things grew from that.

Even though they were only here for twenty years, there were frequent mentions of the Gilmore family, who arrived after the town was over 50 years old.

There were stories and pictures of the steamships and the steam locomotives that came and went with freight and passengers from Kingston, and of the people who came with them.

There was a reasonable assortment of artefacts from the town's history; saw blades from the lumber mills; boat bells from steamships; farming tools and clothing of all sorts.

I had heard that there had been a fire about thirty or so years ago which had destroyed some of the clothing and artefacts from the early 1900's. Fortunately not too much had been lost.

The history lesson had been interesting and I had learned a lot about the town. I also learned from fairly close observation that the dress I'd found the skeleton wearing was a very old style, something over 100 years. I made a mental note to see if I could get someone to find out if the dress was in fact from the period or if it was a reproduction, and if so, from when.

My next stop was the Town Hall, a small, grey stone building on George Street.

In the basement were the town archives but since I didn't have anything specific to search for the resident expert suggested I check out the newspaper office instead. He remembered a large spread with lots of historical information which had been published during the town's 150th Anniversary Celebration, about 35 years ago.

I took the suggestion and went straight there. With the help of their staff I soon located the papers from 1978 and quickly found the right weeks. The papers were a wealth of information. I waded through all sorts of articles, some about the early years of the town, some about the current celebration.

My eyes were starting to feel weary and I was about to quit for the day when I hit pay dirt.

A whole section, a colour insert from a special weekend edition, was dedicated to a huge ball, a period costume party, to which it seemed most of the residents of Westport had gone. Along with mayors and councillors past and present, and a smattering of out of town politicians and celebrities were pictures of the everyday folks of Westport at the time.

It was one of these that caught my eye, not for the people, a couple I did not recognize, but for something else in the photo. I had seen their clothes before.

I was fairly sure that the man's suit had been hanging in the wardrobe in the Gilmore attic, and I was positive the woman's dress was the one recently found being worn by the skeleton.

Maddeningly, there were no names attached, as there were not names with many of the other photos in the spread – too many people and only one photographer, probably.

I got the archivist to make me a copy of the picture and left the building, heading for my next stop.

I would have to keep digging but this was definitely a good start.

Now I know he's trying to find me. the museum, the town archives, the newspaper office. left with a pile of paper.

Not good. heard he was an investigator of some kind before he came here. Its startin to show. Not just random now. Research. Looking for a trail to follow. trying to find out about her.

better make sure I Don't leave a trail for him. think it's time for a more Direct approach.

Chapter 15

In the evening, after I'd seen to a few jobs around the suite, I went out onto the deck with my dinner, my laptop and a stack of papers from the newspaper office.

The people at the *Review-Mirror* had been very helpful with finding further information about the big costume ball at the 150th Anniversary Celebration. Since it was such a big deal at the time, the articles had been entered into the paper's computer (at a later date of course) and so I was able to fill a USB stick with all the pertinent stuff.

A CD of Peter Appleyard on the vibraphone played in the background as I worked my way through veal parmesan with roasted potatoes and roasted fresh asparagus. I also worked through the pages of information on my laptop.

Search as I might, I couldn't find anything to identify the two people in the photograph I'd spotted earlier. By the time I finished eating, the light from the sunset had almost gone and with it my desire to continue going over the files.

I closed up the laptop and pushed it to the far side of the small table. I sat my plate on top of the machine and poured the last couple of ounces of wine from the half litre decanter into my glass.

Turning my chair toward the last dim glow of the recently departed sun I stretched out with my feet up on the deck rail, sipped my wine and tried to figure out what my next step should be. A few wispy clouds drifted near the horizon showing tinges of faded pink and mauve from the recent sunset.

The snap of a twig told me that someone was in the shadows among the trees, perhaps the same someone I'd seen leaving a few days earlier. Bob?

I set my wineglass down on the table and stood up in hope of getting a better view of the grounds below. I saw nothing.

I put both hands on the rail and leaned out as far as I could. I didn't want to start shouting and disturbing the guests but I felt the need to make a point. I spoke as clearly as I could and only as loud as I thought necessary to reach the trees.

"I know you're out there. This is the second time I've heard you and this time if you don't show yourself I'm coming down after you." It was an empty threat. I knew it but he didn't, whoever he was.

I stood and waited, not expecting anything to happen.

"Okay. Have it your way," I said.

I hurried to the doorway and slid open the sliding screen, stepped inside and closed the screen loudly. I moved a few feet from the door into the darkness of the room where I hoped to be out of sight of whoever was out there, then turned and waited.

I figured the person might suspect a trick but I also guessed that he or she could not risk waiting to find out. I got down low and crawled back to the glass door where I arrived just in time to see a shadow move among the other shadows, away from behind a large tree. I slid the screen open quietly and staying low I crept out onto the deck and peered between the upright supports of the rail.

As before the figure moved through the trees toward the water, hurried but not running and making relatively little noise. The same figure; the same size and a slightly odd gait which I had not registered before.

Soon I heard the now familiar sound of a small boat motor as my visitor made his retreat.

I got up and stood watching and listening for a few minutes, then picked up my computer and dinner things and went inside.

As I cleaned up from my dinner preparations I resolved to find, hidden away among my seldom used possessions in a cupboard somewhere, a million-candlepower flashlight. It would be living on the deck for the next while, in anticipation of a return visit from the shadow on the beach.

I slept badly that night, waking frequently, all the minor sounds of the Inn magnified by my imagination.

I awoke earlier than I needed to, my mind replaying my encounters with Bob Langdon. He fit the physical parameters of my night-time prowler, and I wondered if maybe he was planning some retaliation for my interference in his life. If it was even him.

With the early morning came a brief, light rain, then brilliant sunshine. Several guests were enjoying a late breakfast on the dining room deck when I finally dragged myself downstairs.

I'd had breakfast in my suite so I headed straight out to the beach to have a look around again. Since I was not due to work in the kitchen until the afternoon I decided to make a more extensive search of the beach than I had the last time my visitor had appeared.

I had on my jeans and hiking boots from L.L.Bean, along with a sturdy T-shirt and a small pack with a bottle of water and some other supplies over my left shoulder.

I went out through the trees to the stony beach and, turning right, headed up the shore toward the northern tip of the island, called Loon Point. The going was slow over the loose stones, but not particularly hard. I walked at an easy pace, watching the ground for signs of recent activity. I passed the spot where I'd found the paint and the rope and continued on. I stopped abruptly, trying without success to remember if I'd seen the rock and rope fragment where I'd left them. I couldn't remember.

For the rest of the beach I saw nothing obvious.

As I neared Loon Point the loose stones of the beach gave way to solid rock, great jagged slabs rising sharply, thickly covered with spruce and aspen, all pale green at the branch-ends with new growth and swishing softly in the light breeze.

I picked my way carefully along the narrow path which rose ever upward as I moved toward the highest and most northerly point of the island, a narrow rocky outcrop, jutting out over the water at a height of about 15 meters.

I'd been this way many times before and each time was impressed with the scene, the vista of rock and water and trees in every direction as far as the eye can see.

As I made the final approach to the ledge I pushed through some new growth of sumac. As the small branch moved in front of me another, much larger moved toward me from behind and to the left. Almost as soon as I registered the movement it caught me with terrific force in the middle of the back and sent me stumbling headlong toward the cliff edge. I tossed aside the shoulder pack and forced myself to fall to the rapidly shortening stone surface. Landing on my knees I used what little leverage was available to roll at least partly sideways rather than straight to the edge. Now on my back I slid along the stone to the edge farthest from my entry point and as I started to go over, caught hold of a spruce sapling, luckily well rooted in a deep, soil-filled crevice. I caught and held and stayed at the top of the ledge, my legs dangling over the edge.

I pulled myself all the way back to solid rock and stayed there for a few minutes, resting and regaining my composure and massaging some bumps and bruises. My heart still raced and my breaths were more like gasps. That had been a very close call.

My crashing about had briefly silenced the birds and small animals in the area and now they resumed their interrupted routines. I rose stiffly and hunted up my pack, unzipped it with shaking hands, found the water bottle and drank some water, then went back to the place where my little adventure had begun.

The trap had been set with infinite care.

One supple branch, about five meters long and four or five cm thick had been very carefully bent back and up from its original position at the opening to the lookout. I could see where it had been bent in a tight arc and tied to a larger branch with rope, and another length of rope had been attached to the branch I had pushed out of my way as I stepped out onto the outcrop from the trees. I had walked right under it.

If, when the branch released, it had not propelled me slightly sideways but directly toward the edge as it had no doubt been intended to do, I would not have survived. Fifteen meters to the water is not a long fall but there are lots of jagged rocks around the shoreline which would have made for an unpleasant landing.

One of the other things in my pack was a small digital camera. Inside the bag it had survived being thrown into the trees. I took a lot of pictures of the scene and resolved to bring either Sergeant Grant or Josée out to see the place as soon as possible. I had not told them of my previous encounters with the figure on the beach but now the situation had changed.

My phantom had expected that I would try to follow his trail and had set out to kill me when I did.

The note I'd found when I first arrived at the island had said that I'd regret my decision to buy the Inn. Maybe the writer had begun to work at making that so.

I still had my suspicions regarding Bob Langdon but I couldn't figure out how or why he could be connected with the note. Or if he had the outdoor skills to pull off this sort of thing.

I knew I'd have to be a lot more careful from then on.

Chapter 16

When I got back to the Inn I went straight to my suite without being seen and got cleaned up for work. This proved to be more of a chore than I'd expected. As I looked in the mirror after my shower I determined the reason for the stinging sensation I'd felt when the warm water and soap had flowed over my arms and head.

The scrapes on my arms were more noticeable than I'd thought they were and there was a longish scratch on my left temple and a smaller one on my left ear. Nothing serious but enough to get people asking questions.

I touched up the scrapes with antiseptic and got dressed in my cooking clothes: black socks and jeans and a loose mid green polo-style shirt. We all wear the same in the kitchen; cooks, prep people and clean up crew.

With only a few minutes to spare I headed for the phone and called the OPP detachment at Smiths Falls. Mike Grant was there and after a short delay we were connected.

I told my story as concisely as possible, without embellishment or emotion and Mike listened quietly.

"Well, you seem to have got someone's attention, haven't you." It was a statement, not a question. "I'll be out there tomorrow morning early. There aren't a lot of hours of light left today but I want to see the location before anyone has a chance to mess with it. I'm also going to arrange to have a boat swing by at intervals through the evening, just to let whoever it was know we're watching."

"Thanks. That sounds good. I'll be working in the kitchen for the rest of the evening so just have calls put through there if you need to reach me tonight."

I went down to the kitchen by the back way through my private stairs and started to work at the prep table without anyone noticing I'd come in, or so I thought.

The specials for the evening meal were Chicken Cordon Bleu and Pickerel with cilantro-lime butter. Nothing to match fresh caught Pickerel.

I could see that Bud had a small mountain of cilantro chopped and was working on zesting some limes. I started on the cheeses for the Cordon Bleu. Ordinarily there is Swiss cheese in the dish but I like to use Emmenthal and add a little really good cheddar, finely grated, along with it and the smoked ham. On my way out of the walk-in fridge with the ham I saw Bud watching me.

He walked over to my table and stood looking at me a moment, then said, "You look like you got hit by a bus, boss." He grinned a little sheepishly at his joke then was serious again as he waited for me to respond.

No point in denying that there was a problem. "I was out hiking this morning and had a close encounter with a tree branch."

"Whole damn tree from the looks of you. You sure you should be working?"

"No, I'm not sure. I'll know better in a while. What I do know is that if I sit in my room I'll just get stiff and feel worse than I do now." I inhaled deeply and the pain must have showed on my face. "I'll do what I can. If it gets to be too much I'll pack it up. You will probably have to carry the load tonight."

Bud gave me a quick smile as he turned to go back to his limes. "So what else is new?"

I decided I could make the compound butter. Some of the cilantro and some of the lime zest were mixed into softened butter. The mixture was then formed into a log shape, rolled in plastic wrap and refrigerated. Later the firm log would be cut into slices and one slice would be placed on top of each hot pickerel fillet as it was served.

The long painful day turned into a long painful evening. By eight o'clock I had done all I could. My back and arms and knees hurt fiercely. My ribs hurt with every breath. The dinner rush was over and I didn't feel too bad about leaving the rest of the evening to the crew.

I went to the dining room and had dinner there. I didn't feel up to cooking for myself. I had the Chicken Cordon Bleu with some roasted potatoes and steamed vegetables, and a couple of glasses of Pinot Grigio from The County. Skipping dessert and having had only half my cup of coffee I left the dining room and headed around to the main entrance. As I walked to the elevator I thought I might as well stop at the office to see how Gwen was doing tonight.

Gwen took one look at me and shook her head. "My dad used to come home looking like that now and then after a night out with the boys. But you've been working. Did you say something to annoy Bud?"

"As if Bud would do anything like this even if I did annoy him, which I do regularly by the way. No, just a little accident out on the trails."

I moved on toward the elevator. "Sure, if you say so. Have a good night. If you can," she said. "Oh, by the way, that newest cookie recipe is a hit with the guests we send off with bag lunches. The one Bud calls the All Canadian Fruit Cookie. Best one yet." The gate closed and the cage began to rise.

"Thanks, I'll tell Bud."

I got out of the elevator into the dark second floor hallway and turned toward the kitchen to get a glass of water to take upstairs with me. I didn't make it to the kitchen.

As I exited the elevator alcove a dark clad figure burst down out of the stairwell and smashed me against the wall opposite, then grabbed hold of my shirt and threw me down that same stairwell to the landing halfway down to the next floor, then hurried down after me.

Bruised and dazed I remained where I was, my back on the landing and my head at an odd angle against the wall, half expecting a further attack. It didn't happen right away. The figure, now not more than a dark blur, stood over me briefly. Perhaps he thought I was dead, my neck broken. He gave me a good hard kick in the ribs, just for good measure and then ran up the stairs toward the lower level of my suite.

I'm not sure quite how long I stayed on the landing before I was able to force my battered body to move. I was determined to go up after him but, as I raised myself to a standing position I could feel blood running down my face and the pain in my ribs was bad so I decided to go back downstairs and get an assessment of the damage. And, I didn't think it would be a good idea to encounter my attacker again just yet. He might still be around somewhere, possibly waiting for me upstairs.

I staggered in through the back entrance of the kitchen just as Bud and Frankie, the afternoon and evening dishwasher/prep helper, were finishing up. Bud heard me enter, took one look and jogged the few steps to where I was, took my arm and led me to the chair at my office area.

"What the hell have you been up to now?" he said, reaching for the first aid kit. "Frankie. Go get Michelle, please."

"Someone was waiting for me upstairs when I went up after dinner, bashed me against the wall then threw me halfway down the stairs."

"Same someone hit you with the tree earlier?" asked Bud.

"More than likely, I expect."

"I'm going up there and see if anyone's still around." said Bud.

"He was up there a few minutes ago but he's probably long gone. Leave it for now," I said. True, but also I didn't want Bud taking on someone who was willing to kill me.

At that moment Frankie arrived with Michelle, our senior first-aider, in tow.

Bud had placed a compress from the first aid kit over the cut on my forehead while asking his questions, but Michelle now took over.

"Take that off for a minute please, Bud. Let me see how bad it is."

"Doesn't seem to be any concussion," said Bud. "Eyes look all right and he seems to be pretty coherent; as much as usual anyway."

"I expect he'll live," put in Michelle. "A butterfly bandage will close up the cut. Shouldn't need stitches. Get some crushed ice from the bar please, Francis, and a couple of clean bar towels. And don't let Thomas give you a hard time about it."

Frankie hesitated briefly, then realized it was he who was being called Francis, and dashed off to the bar.

"You know, Michelle, you only confuse the kid when you call him Francis," said Bud.

"If his mother had wanted him called Frankie she would have *named* him that."

"If anyone cares I think I will go back up and go to bed now. I've had about enough of this day." I got up slowly from the chair and was immediately, if gently, pushed back into it.

"You're not going back up there 'til we see if anyone's still there," said Bud. At that moment Frankie returned, with Thomas following close behind. Frankie gave the towels and ice to Michelle and she put them to use.

As if by pre-arrangement the three men each took a heavy cast iron pan from the overhead rack and went out the door to the stairs leading to my suite.

As they disappeared I heard Frankie, last in line, say to the others, "Try not to hit anyone with these okay. I'll have to wash them again."

There were no sounds of battle from above. A few minutes later the three returned to the kitchen, pans in hand and told me of their foray.

"All clear up there," said Thomas.

"We checked over the whole place, both floors," added Bud.

Frankie piped up. "Now that I think about it I thought I heard someone coming down the stairs just before you came back down. Maybe it was your attacker? Probably went out the back door to your deck."

"Well, that maybe accounts for how your friend left, even if it doesn't for how he got in," said Bud.

"I'll call the police in the morning and have them check the place out thoroughly. Oh, maybe I don't have to. Sergeant Grant is coming out to investigate my first incident. Now he'll have two things to look into. I'm going to bed."

"I think we should report this to the police now and let them decide about coming out tonight or tomorrow," said Bud. "I'll make the call, and I'll tell them you've gone to get some rest and can't be disturbed."

The bleeding had been stopped and Michelle had put on the bandage.

"Good idea, Bud. Make sure you leave the message for Sergeant Grant specifically, since he's already got stuff happening here."

This time when I got up no-one tried to stop me. Michelle walked to the door with me. "Don't worry. I'm all right now. I'm going to take a small handful of something to dull the pain and fall into bed. What shift am I on tomorrow, Bud?"

"As from this moment you're not on for the next two days. Never mind arguing. We'll be fine. Frankie's been wanting to work the main dinner rush so this will be a good chance to try him out. He's even been practicing at home, making hot dogs and KD. Right Frankie? Frankie?"

"Oh yeah. Right, Bud. Sure."

I wasn't sure, in my current state, which, if either, was kidding but it didn't matter. I shook my head, once only because it hurt, then headed up the stairs.

Somehow my trap failed. He's very lucky. He wouldn't be the first to be killed falling onto the rocks of Loon Point from that lookout. I should know. He's pretty beat up . Maybe thisl convince him to quit.

Decided not to wait. knew he was hurt so I figured I'd get to him again quickly while he was weak.
got in and waited in the stairwell where he'd come up from the kitchen. hit him hard and sent him crashing down the stairs. He didn't move for a long while. Looked like his neck was broke. heard voices from the kitchen so I left. hope he's dead.

Chapter 17

Various and sundry aches and pains had me awake several times in the night and by the time I decided to get up I didn't feel very rested. I went down to my kitchen and made a pot of coffee then went back up and had a really long soak in my whirlpool tub filled with water as hot as I could stand it, sipped my coffee and thought through all that had happened to me in the last twenty-four hours. I was less stiff as I dressed and returned again to my kitchen.

The morning thus far was rather grey and foggy – another *Atlantic Suite* morning. Nimmons' clarinet somehow helped sooth away some of my aches and pains.

I began chopping peppers and onions for a western omelette. I had assumed up to now that the attacks were solely in response to my presence here. From the note writer. Now I began to wonder if my encounters with the mystery man might be related to the questions I'd been asking about the skeleton. The idea of my finding out who she was and who had put her in the Gilmore attic was potentially very important to someone. Perhaps the two things were even related somehow – the note and the skeleton. As I ran my knife through a couple of mushrooms and some leftover ham I wondered what would be next. Now this guy had me angry and I was not going to retire quietly and leave the thing unsolved.

I whipped a couple of eggs with a little salt and pepper and the finely chopped vegetables and ham and poured it into a heated pan, then put the pan into a preheated oven.

While the omelette was setting I found some cheddar and got out a plate and cutlery. If the guy was nervous enough now to do violence there was no telling what he might be capable of when I became a real threat to him. And I *would* become a threat to him.

When the omelette was almost ready I dropped a couple of slices of bread into the toaster and poured a fresh cup of coffee.

After grating on some cheddar I folded over the omelette and buttered my toast, then headed, mug and plate in hand, to the dining room table where I could see the scenery as I ate breakfast.

Where to begin?

I thought about what I knew and decided that my only real lead was the picture of the 150th Anniversary Celebration in which a woman I did not know was wearing the same dress the skeleton had been wearing when I found her in my attic. The man in the picture was wearing a suit which could be the one we found hanging in the wardrobe near her bed. Until I heard the Medical Examiner's report I was guessing about the woman's age. The newspaper photo gave a possible time frame. If I was right that the dress was indeed the same and not merely a similar one then the events leading to the woman's death must have occurred after the 150th party. But how long after? Even if it was the same dress, was it the same woman?

Since my employees had told me I didn't have to work for a couple of days, I figured this was a good time to go to the mainland and ask some more questions. Nothing too strenuous. I could take my time and be thorough, without the pressure of having to be back at a specific hour to work. I knew Kim and Bud could handle most anything they might encounter and they both knew how to reach me if they really had to.

It was nearly 10 o'clock by the time I had cleaned up, slowly, from breakfast and was on my way down the back stairs.

As I emerged from the doorway I looked out past the trees to the water and saw a police boat glide past the beach and on around the island. Apparently Mike had kept his word about running extra patrols. I wondered, as I walked toward the boathouse, if he had come out to look over the spot at Loon Point where I'd been clobbered by the tree branch. Probably had. I'd have to remember to get him the pictures I'd taken of the scene, just in case anything had changed. I'd download and email them when I got home later. Listen to me. Mr. Technology.

The overcast had lifted by the time I reached the boathouse and I found one of our young part-time guys without anything pressing to do so I asked him to take me to the mainland. I'd decided not to take out a boat alone given all my aches and pains and what was going on, whatever that really was. All I needed was to have this loon launch an attack while I was out on the water and least able to defend myself.

The sun was warm, the breeze light, and I tried to enjoy the ride but each time the light craft bounced over a wake I felt jolted and in pain. Maybe I had a cracked rib or something. Should probably get checked out.

Soon we were at Westport and I told the driver that I'd call the Inn when I wanted to go back.

I made the trek to Mrs. Samuelson's place in record slow time and stopped at the house to see her but there was no answer. Just as well. I didn't relish the idea of having to explain my current condition. I took out the Lexus and headed east up Main Street to Rideau, then left on Concession and out of town. Might as well go for eggs and cheese while I was out. I'd decided to try a chocolate-raspberry cheese that I'd tasted previously at Fairfield. Maybe it was something I could work into a new dessert.

The drive was uneventful and by the time I got back to town I was ready for a coffee. I parked in the lot near The Cottage Coffee House and, taking my newspaper-clipping photo along, went inside. The shop was crowded, some people sitting at the tall tables in the window and some just standing around talking and drinking coffee.

The owner was behind the serving counter and I gave him my order then laid the photo on the counter as he poured my coffee.

"I'm doing a little research on the area and I'm trying to locate these people. Any idea who they are?"

He sat my drink down on the counter and looked closely at the picture. "There's something slightly familiar about the guy - maybe - but I don't know for sure. I don't think I've ever seen the woman. I haven't been here all that long really."

"Lots longer than I've been around," I said. "The picture was taken at the 150th party. Maybe the costumes are throwing you off."

"Maybe, but that was still long before my time. Still there's something about the man, but I can't get hold of it."

"That's fine. Thanks for the effort. If you happen to think of anything let me know, would you please?"

"Sure will. Maybe you should try old man Bascome. He's been here all his life. Maybe he'd know them."

I handed over my payment for the coffee. "I'll do that. As a matter of fact I may do that right now. Thanks."

As I went outside I felt again the warmth of the sun on my face. I looked up at the sky and as I did so someone passed by hurriedly and bumped me into one of the outdoor umbrella tables. I righted myself without spilling too much of my coffee and looked around. Whoever it was had gone around a corner.

"Some people got no manners," said someone nearby. I had to agree.

I wondered if it was possible that Bernie knew only the man in the photo and not the woman because the man was still around when Bernie had come to town but the woman was not. It was very possible that he was still around.

It wasn't far to the Bascome Marina, and I met a few people along the way. It was slow going what with tourists wandering along the sidewalks and some folks I knew asking what had happened to me and what was going on with my skeleton. I related parts of the story many times and assured those who were concerned that I was going to be fine and that the police were working on it and that the mystery would eventually be solved.

By the time I reached Bascome's it was almost noon and I was thinking about where to go for lunch once I'd finished here.

Bascome was an interesting character and I was looking forward to talking to him. I always enjoyed our chats. And there was a good chance that he would have some ideas about the people in the picture.

As I mounted the wide wooden stairs to the entry I thought something was odd. The huge double doors were closed. Bascome almost never closed during daylight hours in the tourist season. If he wasn't there one of his staff was.

I turned the handle and pulled gently on the door. It opened easily and light from the street flooded into the dim interior. The inside light should have been on at that time of day.

"Hello. Is there anyone here?" My call was met by silence.

I moved slowly across the sales room floor, around free-standing counters and tables of boat parts and accessories, toward the door to the office which was behind the counter. The office door was open and I strained to see into the darkness there.

So thorough was my concentration as I passed the open end of the parts counter that I failed to see the figure crouched there until it was almost too late.

As the figure lunged upwards at me I was able to lash out with my left arm. He was too close for a punch to land but I managed to catch him in the side of the head with my elbow. His momentum carried him into me but his resolve was shaken by the blow and his element of surprise was gone. He regained his balance and pushed me hard with both arms and I bounced off the door frame, then he backed off slightly and set up to throw a punch.

Rather than wait for the shot to land I ducked under it and hit him as hard as I could, just below the ribs, with both fists in rapid succession and with all my weight behind them. He didn't go down but at least I had his attention.

He stepped back and bumped into the counter, sending some stock crashing to the floor. Then he charged at me again. He was bigger and heavier than I and this time he heaved me against the door frame with such force that I was momentarily stunned. He seemed not to realize this and hesitated, perhaps deciding if he had made too much noise crashing around the store - if he should finish me off or retreat while retreat was still possible.

He apparently decided on the latter.

All this time he had had his back to the light coming in through the open door. Now as he turned to leave I thought I saw something familiar in the silhouette. It may just have been the halo of light around him or it may have been the head shot I'd just taken but I was sure this was a person familiar to me. I also thought I detected a slight limp as the man went out through the open doorway. And maybe a beard?

I sat there on the floor for a couple of minutes to assess the damage and let my head clear, then slowly and painfully got to my feet and went in search of Wil Bascome.

He was not hard to find. I flipped on the light switch as soon as I entered the office and immediately saw the prostrate body on the floor.

Bascome was on his back, legs apart and arms flung out straight. There was a large gash on his forehead. *Still bleeding. Good. Means he's probably still alive,* I thought as I approached. I quickly rooted around in cupboards and found an old sweater, a first aid kit and a folded blanket. All my sundry bumps and scrapes were suddenly back and hurting and it took me what seemed ages to get down to the floor.

I checked respiration and heart rate, both of which were satisfactory and put a compress on the head wound. I took out my cell and dialled 911 and gave the emergency operator all the information and assured her that I would remain with the victim until help arrived. I rolled the sweater in a long tube shape and encircled Bascome's head, tucking the ends gently under his shoulders so that his head would not move too easily if he regained consciousness. After rechecking that the bleeding was controlled I covered him with the blanket and then parked myself in his office chair where I could keep an eye on him and wait more-or-less comfortably for help to arrive.

Police and ambulance had to come from Smiths Falls and Perth respectively as we had neither in Westport. It took only about ten minutes for the police to arrive. A cruiser was on patrol not far away and knew the most direct route to the town. The constable verified my findings about Bascome's condition then started asking questions and taking notes. As we heard the first sound of the ambulance siren I remembered to tell the patrol officer that Sergeant Mike Grant was working a case which might well overlap this one. The constable used his radio to call Smiths Falls. Sergeant Grant, it seemed, was already on his way.

The ambulance arrived and Bascome was removed from the marina office and driven away to the Perth hospital. The constable hung around and paced the front boardwalk until Sergeant Grant arrived a few minutes after the ambulance left. The two men had a brief chat at the roadside then the patrolman left to continue his assigned duties. Grant mounted the stairs slowly, watching me closely where I stood in the doorway.

"I'm going to have to get an office here I think," he said. "So, are you injured?"

I thought a second then replied. "Not much more than I was before, I guess. A bump on the back of my head to go with the one on the front from yesterday's little altercation. For what it's worth I think I gave a couple of bruises this time instead of just taking them."

"Well, that's positive. I think. Are you ready to leave?"

"I'm going to wait a few minutes 'til someone from the staff gets here to run the place for the rest of the day or to just be here while the crime scene people do their thing. The guy from the store next door knows someone who knows someone so he made some calls and arranged for coverage. Are the crime scene guys coming, by the way? Will they want to close the place temporarily? "

"They'll be here any minute. They were processing a possible arson in Merrickville earlier so they'll probably come straight from there, or as straight as it's possible to come anywhere around here. We got lucky with the timing. Ordinarily they would have had to come out from Ottawa or Kingston. And yes. They may want to close the store. We'll see what happens."

We were still standing on the porch when the police van arrived and the two Crime Scene Investigators climbed out. As they mounted the steps one of them gave me a mock frown and commented, "You seem to be turning up at a lot of crime scenes recently. People are going to start to talk about you if you're not careful."

"People are already talking about me far more than I'd like. Just don't be adding fuel to the fire."

As he passed me in the doorway his frown turned to a smile. "Don't worry. We know how to keep quiet." He gave a jerk of his thumb toward Sergeant Grant. "Him I'd be worried about though."

"Yeah, Yeah. Thanks for nothing," said Grant. "How 'bout you get on with the job so we don't have to hang around all afternoon. We're late for lunch already."

The two men passed on through the door without further comment. Grant followed them in to show them where to find the specific location of the trouble, though they would process a lot more than that one room.

While he was gone I parked myself in one of Bascome's big old wood porch chairs, tipped it back onto two legs, carefully, so as not to hurt myself yet again, and closed my eyes to rest a few minutes. I must have dozed off. When I suddenly came awake Mike Grant was talking to a young fellow I recognized as one of Bascome's staff. I shifted my weight and the chair banged down onto its four legs on the wooden porch. The Crime Scene van was gone and the shadows indicated that it was past noon.

Grant saw and heard that I was awake and came over.

"The guys wanted to wake you up to say goodbye but I told them you needed your beauty sleep. It's getting on toward one thirty and I need some lunch. Are you interested in tagging along?"

"Yes. Where were you going to go?"

"I usually go to The Cove Pub when I'm passing through here. Food's good and at this time of day it'll be quiet enough that we can talk without attracting too much attention or being overheard."

"Sounds good. You buying?"

"You wish. I have enough trouble getting the powers that be to pay for my meals on the road, never mind anyone else's."

"Fine then. I just thought I'd check."

I guess Grant thought I might be feeling as beat up as I looked or something because, 'though it was only about three blocks to the Cove, we piled into his unmarked police car and drove to lunch.

Chapter 18

The Cove is a large white building on Bedford Street at the corner of Main. It houses a restaurant, a lounge and several very nice rooms with all the amenities to be found in big city hotels.

We had planned to sit in the lounge and have lunch but there was work going on there so we had to sit in the dining room. Not that that was any hardship. It is a lovely room with a high ceiling, pale yellow walls and hardwood floors that gleamed in the early afternoon sun that flowed in through floor to ceiling windows and French doors.

We sat at a corner table as far out of the way of general traffic as possible. After we ordered, Grant launched into his inquiry about what was going on. The opening surprised me.

"Officially I am required to tell you that you need to back off and not be carrying on your own personal investigation. You should be leaving it to the proper authorities, that is to say, me."

I thought about that a moment. "Officially?"

"Yes. However, in my spare time back at the shop, when I haven't been out here trying to keep you out of trouble, I've been doing a little checking up on you and finding some interesting things. Seems you were a pretty highly regarded investigator before you - retired. 'Intuitive and tenacious' I believe were the words used by your former employer. Your former boss has left, in case you hadn't heard, but *his* boss was very helpful."

"Nice to be remembered well," I said, "but, as you will also have found out, I was not quite intuitive enough and as I found out, being tenacious can get you shot."

Grant was silent a moment, looking intently at the iced tea in his glass. He picked up the glass, swirled the ice around a few times then took a sip. "I can only imagine what that was like. Most cops can go through a whole career in this country without ever even drawing their weapon on the job, let alone firing it. Hardly any ever get shot. You were private. Not armed and doing what should have been a routine job.

"I had one lousy experience with a shooting but I was on the other end from what you were. It must have been just after we met in Rainy River – a couple of years before I came to this area."

"What happened?" I asked.

"Bank robber in Kenora. I was on highway patrol at the time. The bank robber went into the bank a bit after noon with a bag in one hand and a shotgun in the other. No effort to conceal. No caution. He told the teller he'd been watching for weeks, the bank and me. Told her he knew for sure that I'd be a long way off at this time of day."

"But you weren't."

"No. There had been a vehicle crash about ten kilometres outside of town. I was almost on top of it as I left Kenora and it took a couple of hours to get it sorted out and cleaned up. It was a little after noon when I wrapped it up so I decided to head back into town and grab a bite of lunch before continuing my patrol. The café I was going to was right next door to the bank. I'd just pulled up and got out of the car when this maniac came charging out of the bank, bag in his left hand, full this time, and shotgun in the other. He saw me right away of course and as he raised the gun I ducked and the first barrel took out most of the right side windows of the cruiser and some of the right rear quarter panel and light lenses. Then he ran. The noise of the shotgun blast and breaking glass pretty much cleared the street of people. I moved around the front of the car and onto the sidewalk, drawing my gun as I went and hollered for him to stop.

"He took a quick glance over his left shoulder and decided to gamble. He started to turn, using the heavy bag as a counter-weight, and swung the shotgun in a wide arc so he could have another go at me, but I didn't let him. I fired three. The first caught him in the left shoulder as it came around, accelerating the momentum the bag had given him, and throwing off whatever aim he might have had. It's almost frightening how clear it all comes back. The second shotgun blast went off into the air, raining down pellets on cars a block away. No-one was hurt. My second shot hit him square in the chest as he pivoted from the first hit, and the third hit him in the forehead as he went over backward from the second impact. Dead before he hit the concrete."

"Sounds to me as though you did what you had to do."

"Isn't fun though. Not doing it or living with it. Or the paperwork that goes with it either."

"I was lucky to walk away from my encounter," I said. "Well, I didn't exactly walk away. Some of Waterloo Region's finest got into a firefight with the character after he shot me and he didn't walk away either, figuratively or literally. It was only luck that a patrol car was passing close by at exactly the right time, just when the radio call had gone out, and diverted to the address specified in several 911 calls. They kept him from finishing me then and there.

"As it was I spent a couple of weeks in hospital and a year in rehab and I still limp if I exert too much. On the plus side I can always tell when it's going to rain."

Grant laughed.

"You said 'officially'. What does that mean, exactly?"

The waitress arrived with our lunches and we were quiet for a couple of minutes. Grant had a Club Sandwich and home made fries. Mine was Rainbow Trout with rice and fresh mixed vegetables. It was excellent.

"What I was saying before we got sidetracked with our respective encounters with guns and your departure from the insurance investigation business was that I'd heard that you were tenacious and intuitive. I guess I'd be a fool to think you're going to just sit quietly in the corner and wait while we work the case. I would also be a fool to not avail myself of help from the person closest to the case, who also happens to be an experienced investigator. Unofficially."

I was very surprised to hear that.

"So. You really *have* been checking up on me."

"Yes."

I let that sink in. Somehow I wasn't very surprised to hear it. I wondered how deeply Grant had dug.

"So you're saying that we, that is, you and I, can collaborate on this case. As long as no-one else hears about it."

"Yes. This is just between you and me. If the brass find out we're working together they'll have me issuing parking tickets in Moosonee."

"Yeah. I'll bet they would. Well. Okay. Thanks for the chance to help. I'll try not to be too obvious about it."

Grant hesitated briefly then said, "I found a short gap in your work history that's unaccounted for; after college – before Med. Rock. Europe? Care to fill in the blanks?"

"No. I wouldn't."

Grant watched me closely but didn't pursue the idea. I had the feeling he'd filed it away for later.

The waitress came by again at that moment and asked if there was a problem with the food. We assured her that there was not and began eating our now cooling meals.

A few minutes later I wondered out loud, "Would you consider letting Josée in on our arrangement? She's already starting to give me grief about amateurs involving themselves in police affairs."

Grant pulled a decorated toothpick from a quarter of his sandwich. Before taking a bite he said, "I'll think about it."

Over coffee Grant got things moving again. "So, do you have any idea who it might be? You've had a couple of close encounters now."

I took a moment to think then said, "I have the feeling now that it must be someone I've been in contact with or that I've seen around the town or on the island. I wouldn't have said that with any certainty yesterday – well I'm really still not certain - but after this morning I'm reasonably sure I've seen the guy before, been close to him. The size, the build and other things I can't quite put my finger on yet, all give me the impression that I should know who he is."

"Any accent? Any sounds or smells – food or fuel or anything like that? Smells can be really important."

"He's never said anything to me. Just a few grunts and groans when we were struggling are the only sounds I've heard. But now that you mention it there was a smell – oil or gas or something - not very strong, but there none the less. And body odour. I hadn't thought of it before."

"That's good. Keep replaying the encounters in your head. Try to remember as many details as possible. Something you haven't thought of yet may lead us to him."

I finished my coffee and waved to the waitress who came with the bills.

"I'm getting stiff sitting here. After all my falling down and such over the past couple of days I feel like one giant bruise. Let's walk a bit while we talk."

We each left money on the table and headed out the door to the street.

The sun was warm and bright, ripples on the water sparkled and the light breeze carried the scent of freshly cut grass. We walked the short distance up Bedford and went left on Church. We passed Murphy's Barber and Sport Shop and a few other stores. The sidewalk was crowded with people and the street was busy with cars.

"This has turned out to be a less than wonderful idea. Nice to be out in the sunshine but not much good for carrying on a conversation," I said as we dodged around kids in strollers and dogs on leashes.

Grant dodged around a woman with a walker and said, "Yeah. We need to find a quieter place to talk. I still have questions that I need answered before I go back to the shop."

We kept on another half block or so then made a left at Spring and another at Main, heading back toward Bedford and the Cove where Grant had left his car.

We were just passing Kudrinko's market, with only half a block or so to go, when we heard squealing tires, car horns and a lot of frenzied shouting. We both started to run in the direction of the noise, Grant much faster than I, and by the time I rounded the corner he was kneeling over a person lying in the roadway. As I approached I could hear the chatter around the scene: "He's lucky to be alive." - "That guy tried to hit him on purpose." - "I couldn't believe how fast that old red pickup was moving." - "If this fella hadn't looked over his shoulder when he did he'd'a been a goner."

Grant had found a first aider to tend to the victim who was not badly injured but very shaken up. As the only police officer present Grant called in the incident then started taking witness statements before too many people drifted away. A cruiser arrived a few minutes later, the same one that had left Bascome's Marina only an hour or so before, followed closely by an ambulance. The victim was checked out by the paramedics and had a couple of cuts and bruises tended to, and was released after giving his account to Sergeant Grant.

I was sitting on the broad stairs of the Cove when Grant finished and strode over.

"This is turning into quite the exciting little town. Probably not the kind of excitement the locals would welcome though."

I stood up slowly and came down the stairs to the sidewalk. "You can bet on that. I hope they don't figure out that I'm at the centre of this little storm. I could get run out of town on a rail. I take it the guy is all right. No serious damage?"

"He'll be fine. Maybe a bit stiff for a couple of days. Right now I'm more concerned about you. Did you happen to notice the general look of the victim?"

"How could I not? He was wearing practically the same clothes I am, same colours anyway, and his hair is the same colour, though maybe a bit longer than mine. From the back he would have looked almost exactly like me."

Grant put a large hand on my shoulder and slowly turned me around, at the same time pointing with the other hand toward his car, still parked at the curb in front of the Cove.

"Seems like maybe we have a new lead," he said as we walked to the car. "Our boy probably drives an older model, red pickup, probably with some modifications to judge by the comments about its performance. And he knew to look for you at the Cove."

"Yup. He seems to be keeping a pretty close eye on me, but not constant or he would have known we had left already. Now that I think about it, I've seen a red pickup quite regularly recently. I wonder if this guy was around the café this morning. Maybe he heard me mention that I was going to see Bascome. That's the only place he could have got that bit of information. *I* didn't even know I was going there until I was leaving the coffee shop. Unless it was just a big coincidence."

We climbed into the car and were engulfed in a sudden silence.

"I don't believe that and I don't think you do either," said Grant. "He was there alright. But so were a lot of other people, I bet."

"Yes. The place was full and so were the outside tables."

"So there's a good chance that one of those people is the one we're after." Grant hesitated a moment, considering his next move. "Whoever it is he's getting too close. Do you have any rooms available at the Inn right now? I'm thinking of trying to put someone out there to keep an eye on things."

"Thinking of moving in to keep me company are you?"

"Well, yes. That's sort of what I have in mind. You've had a couple of close calls and I don't want anything more serious happening. You won't be any good to anyone if you wind up like our mystery woman."

"I agree that I don't want to get killed over this but I'm not so sure that I need a baby sitter."

"You don't know who I have in mind for the assignment. You might get to like the idea."

"Maybe. In the meantime we need to do a little quick and positive damage control."

"Meaning what?" asked Grant.

"If this guy is as close to me as he seems to be he may be aware of the list of names I gave to Constable Allard. Or maybe he'll figure some of them out himself. If he's been at the Inn he may have even seen the list. Now he's had a go at Bascome he may try some of the others. I may have ..."

Grant interrupted. "Don't be beating yourself up unnecessarily. I have a copy of the list in my case in the back seat. We'll start now and see all we can find and tell them to be careful." Grant paused briefly. "That should be interesting. We don't know who to tell them to be careful of."

I reached up over my shoulder and pulled down the seatbelt. As I did so I had an idea.

"You know, I might just have an idea for a suspect."

"Go on," said Grant.

"The ex-husband of an employee fits the physical description and has a red pickup. I had a run-in with him at the inn not long ago."

"What sort of run-in?"

"He was in the kitchen, where he had no business being, and was giving his ex a hard time. I intervened. He left and he wasn't happy."

"Okay. Better than what we had a few minutes ago. It's pretty thin as a motive for running someone down in the street but you just never know what will set some people off or how far they'll go. I'll put the call out and we'll see if we can pick him up to answer a few questions."

It occurred to me briefly to tell Grant about my second encounter with Bob Langdon, but I thought better of it. Maybe later.

"We'd better get going on catching-up with the people on the list. Could you drop me off at the house where I keep my vehicle? I'll start there with Mrs. Samuelson and then go on to some of the others."

Grant looked at me a moment as if trying to decide whether or not I was serious. "You want to go out alone and see these people and risk having another encounter with our buddy?"

"I'll be much more careful from now on. Besides he has a long head start on us if he's going after those on my list. The quicker we get to all those people the more likely we are to prevent any of them ending up like Bascome."

"Fine. We both have cells so let's keep in touch. I want to know every place you go, when you arrive and when you leave. If something happens at least I'll have a starting point to look for your body."

"Thanks for that cheerful thought. I'll try not to get into too much trouble while we're apart."

Grant started up the car and we drove the few blocks to Mrs. Samuelson's place. Much to my relief she was there, out weeding the garden beside the front door, when we arrived.

I unbuckled my seatbelt and opened the door.

"Be careful. And remember to call me."

"Yes mother," I said as I closed the door.

Guys got 9 lives !!! wasn't even him on the street too many people saw the truck today get him tomorrow.

Chapter 19

Mrs. Samuelson stood up from her freshly weeded flower garden as I crunched across the gravel driveway.

"RJ, you don't look very much better than the last time I saw you."

"No. Well, I've been having a few little setbacks shall we say."

"Yes. Right. You'd best be careful. You let yourself get too beat up and you'll be ages getting over it."

"Yes, well I hope to be putting this behind me very soon."

"That's good, dear."

"I'm on my way out to see Mr. Barnes out on 23 – he may have some information to contribute to our investigation - but I have a couple of questions I'd like to ask you first if you don't mind."

"Certainly, RJ. Anything to help."

I took the overflowing basket of weeds from one hand and the trowel and shears from the other and helped Mrs. Samuelson step over the raised border of the garden onto the driveway.

"Shall we sit out here on the bench or would you rather go into the kitchen?" she asked.

"Outside is fine. Let's go over to the bench," I said. "This will only take a few minutes, I hope."

An ancient garden bench sat in the dappled shade of an even more ancient little leafed linden tree, its miniature, new, pale green leaves flapping madly in the afternoon breeze, awaiting the emergence of small white flowers. As we crossed the yard we passed through several distinct curtains of fragrance; thin, mild smoke from an early campfire blew on the breeze from across the water; the strong sweet smell of hemlock near the house, it's multi-flowered white heads waving gently; rhubarb pie cooling inside the open window in the fresh air.

Mrs. Samuelson lowered herself to the bench with a sigh. I sat beside her and the old structure groaned under our combined weight. Mrs. Samuelson seemed not to notice.

"So, what's on your mind, RJ?"

I decided to begin with the picture in the hope that she would recognize one or the other of the people.

"I got this picture from the newspaper archives. I wonder if these two people look familiar at all."

I handed her the photo and she held it in her lap, adjusted her glasses and looked at it intently.

"Yes, dear. I do believe I've seen these two before but, well, I'm not real sure where or when. To judge by the outfits, this picture looks like it was taken during the 150th. That's a long time ago and much as I don't like to admit it, my memory isn't what it was. Perhaps it's just that I've seen this picture before."

I waited for more.

"Now I look some more I think maybe I do know the girl. I've no idea what her name is but I think she was a person who came here to work for the Arts Council – you know we have a big art festival here every August – yes, of course you do. Well, RJ, I think she worked for them one year. Didn't stay here long though. Heard she got a better job somewhere and moved on rather suddenly. If it's even her." She paused to collect her thoughts. "There's something familiar about him too but I can't say more than that."

"That's very good. You've given me a place to start looking for her. Do you know anyone around now who would be familiar with the Arts Council from back then?"

Mrs. Samuelson adjusted her position on the hard bench then looked up into the tree.

"You know, it's just possible that Wil Bascome may know, or maybe George Lester. You know George, don't you? He's the owner of the property adjacent to the arena where the Art Festival is held each year. He's almost as old as me and a little fuzzy about yesterday the way a lot of us are at our age, but he can tell you anything you want to know about what happened fifty years ago. Some things you don't want to know too. Let me look at the picture again, please."

A sudden squealing of tires and a roaring exhaust drowned-out our conversation. When it passed I continued but the train of thought regarding the photograph was derailed. When I looked back at her, Mrs. Samuelson had tipped her head back and was looking over the tops of her glasses, watching the rippling linden leaves.

Now for the other reason for my visit.

"You mentioned Wil Bascome a moment ago. Unfortunately he was injured earlier today and is in the hospital in Perth," I said. Mrs. Samuelson's attention returned to me. "It was a deliberate attack and we think it may have had to do with this thing we're investigating."

Mrs. Samuelson resumed looking at the linden leaves.

"Part of the reason I came here today was to warn you to be careful of strangers and, if you're out walking anywhere, watch out for an older red pickup. It probably isn't the man in the picture but someone is nervous about the questions being asked and is taking steps to see that we don't find out too much."

Mrs. Samuelson rose slowly from the bench and picked up her tools and the basket of weeds.

"Well, you've warned me and I'll keep a sharp lookout. Now you'd best be off to see George Lester. Most likely this time on a weekday you'll find him at the pub, but not here in town. He drives all the way to Merrickville to the Goose and Gridiron. Says the beer is better there, or some such nonsense. He and his cronies sit around all afternoon most days solving the problems of the world. If the person you're after was associated with the Art Festival he'll quite possibly know that."

I stood up as she began walking toward the house.

"You'd best get a move on. George Lester isn't as tough as Wil is and his old body won't take kindly to being knocked around."

"Okay," I said. "I'll get going. You be careful and if you see anything suspicious call the police." I headed for the garage where my vehicle was stored. "See you later," I called.

Mrs. Samuelson pulled open her door and turned to me.

"I'll do as you say. But I'll also go dust off my old shotgun just in case."

As I stared dumfounded at her, she smiled.

"Stop in after you find George and I'll give you a piece of that pie you were smelling earlier." With that she turned and went into the house. I heard the deadbolt slide home and the chain go on. I felt a little better. I just hoped she was kidding about the shotgun.

I got the Lexus out of the garage and headed for Merrickville. For the next half hour or so I mulled over where I was with the case.

I parked up the block from the pub and, dodging the ever-present tourist traffic in Merrickville, walked along the sidewalk and went into the Goose and Gridiron. Even in full daylight the bar was not very bright. There were few patrons at the bar and none of them looked old enough to be George Lester.

There were several women working the bar and the adjacent dining room and I took a seat at the bar and asked one of them to help me out.

"Do you happen to know George Lester?" I asked. "I hear he comes in here most days and it's important that I find him as soon as possible."

The bartender looked at me a moment, as if assessing my character. "He was here earlier but he had to leave. He said he had a doctor's appointment I think." She pulled a draft and delivered it to a fellow further down the bar. "Isn't that what he said, Charlie?"

Charlie accepted his beer from the bartender and looked along the bar at me. "That he did."

"You know you're the second person looking for George today," said the bartender.

That bit of news rocked me. "What did he look like, this other fellow – I'm assuming it was a man?"

"Yeah. A man alright. Not nearly as polite as you. Big guy with a beard, strange gravelly voice. He was wearing old clothes, clean you know, but old – old style - like he'd had them for thirty years."

"How old was he? Best guess."

"About fifty to fifty-five maybe. Probably not much more but it was kind of hard to tell for sure, what with the beard and all."

"I don't suppose George said where his appointment was, did he?"

Charlie piped-up from his stool at the end of the bar. "No. But I know from some past talks we've had that he goes to Dr. Marshall, and he's in Westport."

"Doesn't that figure? Thanks for your help." I took a step to leave, then sat back down on my bar stool. "Have we met before, Charlie?"

"Don't believe so."

I nodded in response, then pulled out one of my Gilmore House Inn business cards and gave it to the woman behind the bar. "If you happen to see George Lester again today please give him this and tell him it is extremely important that he call me right away."

I got down from the stool and walked toward the door.

"Hey, hold on," she called after me.

I turned around to face the bar again but continued walking, backward, to the door. "Yes, what is it?"

"He had a bit of a limp," she said, "and he smelled of oil or something."

I nodded my thanks then turned quickly and went out the door. I was dialling my cell as I descended the steps and by the time I reached the Lexus I was being connected to Sergeant Grant's message service.

"I'm working the list. I gave up on old man Barnes for today and went to Merrickville to try to find George Lester, a senior from Westport whom Mrs. Samuelson said might be able to help us. I missed him here and he may be back in Westport already, possibly at the office of a Dr. Marshall. You need to try to locate Lester. He is definitely in danger. Our boy was here looking for him before I arrived. Talk to you later."

I threw the phone on the passenger seat and started the car. A moment later I was leaving Merrickville for the drive back to Westport.

I think that must have been the only time I've been to Merrickville without visiting Mrs. McGarrigle's.

Chapter 20

As I drove back to Westport I realized that my discussion with Mrs. Samuelson had been sidetracked and I hadn't seriously questioned her about whether or not she knew the man in the picture. She had not said she did, but neither had she said she didn't. Some investigator.

Sergeant Grant called as I drove, to say that he had tracked George Lester to the doctor's office and had missed him there, but had his address and was going to the house now. I altered course slightly as I entered town and headed for the address Grant had given me.

I parked the Lexus less than well at the curb, behind Grant's unmarked, and hurried up the walk. As I reached the front steps Grant came out and closed the door.

"He's fine. I showed him the picture you gave me and he did recognize both the people as being from around here at some point but he couldn't name either of them. He did however, give me a possibility of someone who will probably know."

I waited for the rest.

"Do you know the Osgoode Bakery in town?"

"Yes. I get all the breads and other baked goods from them for the Inn. Why?" I asked.

"Well apparently one of the Osgoode sisters once worked doing secretarial work for the Arts Council and Lester says she was friends with our mystery woman. He doesn't remember her name but seems quite sure she is the one Mrs. Samuelson was referring to."

"I know both the Osgoodes and they would only have been about five years old at the time of the 150th."

"Well, maybe there's another one. An older sister? Or maybe it was their mother or an Aunt. The old fellow seems a bit fuzzy on the details of most things. Could be it's all so much nonsense."

"Could be, but I think we'd better follow it up anyway," I said as we walked back to the road.

"Could you take this one? I have to go back to Perth. Wil Bascome has regained consciousness and I want to talk to him as soon as possible. I probably won't be back until tomorrow but I'll call you if I find out anything interesting from Bascome."

"Okay. Sounds good. I'll let you know if I find out anything here."

Without further talk we got into our respective vehicles and drove off, Grant to Perth and I to the Osgoode Bakery.

It never fails to amaze me how good a bakery smells. As the door swung shut behind me, closing in the warm, moist atmosphere, I stood, rooted almost, lost in the heady aromas of yeast, cooking fruit, gently browning pastry, heated sugar and alcohol and in the background the pervasive fragrance of freshly brewed coffee. Give me a comfortable chair and a good book and I could gladly have stayed there. All day. Maybe longer.

I was roused from my reverie by the sound of a coffee mug being set firmly on the old wooden counter. As I refocused my eyes and my brain I saw one of the Osgoode sisters - I've long since given up trying to tell one from the other - standing there looking at me.

"Good afternoon, RJ," she said. "Enjoying yourself?"

"Immensely, yes."

"Well, wipe that silly expression off your face and come in the rest of the way and have a coffee."

I walked to the counter and picked up the mug, inhaled the aroma once more and took a sip.

"Excellent as usual. How are you today, Sandi?" Her slight smile didn't tell me if I was right or wrong. I took a seat on a tall stool at the counter.

"Very well thank you, RJ. I hear you've been having a rough week what with being attacked by trees, falling down stairs, wrestling robbers – how is Wil Bascome by the way? Have you heard anything?"

"He's recovering. Sergeant Grant is in Perth right now interviewing him to see if he can provide any information about who attacked him."

"Glad to hear it. Good thing you turned up there when you did or he may have been even worse off than he is. So what can I do for you today?"

I debated as usual for about one second, then decided. "I believe I'll have a Butterhorn today, thanks. I'll have it here and while I'm snacking I have a couple of questions for you."

Sandi, if that's who it was, extracted a delicious-looking pastry from the showcase and put it on a plate in front of me. "I thought there might be more than a craving for a pastry in your coming here today." She put a couple of napkins beside the plate and refilled my coffee. "So, what's on your mind?"

I took a bite of Butterhorn and savoured the richness of texture and flavour combination. Then, returning to reality again, I began to refocus on the problem at hand. I added a little more cream and sugar to my coffee and stirred thoughtfully.

"As you know I've been looking into finding out who the woman was whose skeleton was found in my attic. You were kind enough to give me some valuable background about the town and the local history. I'm wondering if you would mind helping me a little more, please?"

"Yes. Of course. I'm happy to help if I can," she said.

"Thanks. I've recently heard that George Lester thinks someone named Osgoode used to work for the Arts Council around the time of the 150th celebrations. I wonder if you know who that might have been?"

"That was my oldest sister, Constance. She worked for a secretarial company and was placed with the Arts Council a few times when they were busy."

"That's great. I didn't know there were three of you Osgoode sisters."

"There are seven actually, but only five are still living in the area. And then there's our brother Ken, of course. He has the family farm out on 26. He stayed on there when all the girls moved away. I think he wanted to put a little distance between himself and the rest of us once he grew up. I can't imagine why. He must have had a great time growing up with seven older sisters in a town this small, as a Catholic minority and in a 1200 square foot house with only one bathroom."

"Possible he was looking for a little – what would you call it?"

She looked at me closely. "No need to be over polite. Peace, quiet, sanity, space – all words that come to mind. He's remarkably well adjusted for all his ordeals at home. A real nice fella. You should meet him sometime." She motioned me to approach the office door and pointed across the small room to a framed photograph on the wall. "That's him there in that picture. We girls all got mom's build and colouring. Ken takes after Dad." I looked at the photo and saw eight small red haired women and two tall, dark, bearded men.

"Perhaps I will." Momentarily I was distracted by the large young man with the beard. I dragged my attention back, away from the picture, to the business at hand. "For now though we're getting off the topic. I need to talk to your sister Constance about identifying some people in a photo I have. Do you think she would talk to me about it?"

"I'm sure she would. Con retired a couple of years ago but she still takes in typing jobs and such at her little home office. It keeps her occupied and in touch with things. I could call her if you like. Probably better than just showing up to ask questions about dead people when you've never met before."

While she had been talking I'd finished my pastry and coffee. I wiped my fingers on my napkin and stood up. "Could you call now, please? I'd really like to make some more progress with this today, if I can."

"Sure. You amuse yourself for a minute. I'll be right back. Call me if anyone comes in, please."

She went through to the office and closed the door. I heard the phone buttons beeping and the muffled sound of her voice. When she came out I would have to have a closer look at the family portrait on the office wall. I thought possibly I'd have to give Ken Osgoode a little more thought. Sandi came out in a few minutes with a smile for her success.

"You can go right over. Con says she's been looking forward to meeting you and this would be a good time. She hasn't any pressing work to finish up this afternoon. I'll write down the address for you." While she did that I looked over her shoulder and studied the picture.

She gave me the address and we said our good byes. I paid for my coffee and pastry and went outside. As fresh and cool and fragrant as the late afternoon air was, I missed the aromas of the bakery instantly. Good thing I don't work in one. I'd soon not be able to move.

I parked on the street and by the time I'd gone half way up the walk the front door opened. There in the doorway was a somewhat older version of the person I'd just left.

"Hi there," she said. "You must be RJ. I've been hearing about you for quite some time. Come on in."

I followed her down a short hallway and into what was obviously her home office. Constance motioned me to a chair and sat down in an identical one beside me.

"So, Liz tells me you have a photo you want me to look at."

"Liz called you? I thought it was..."

"Are they still playing that game?" she interrupted.

"Apparently they like to keep me guessing about who's who. I have the impression that it's an ongoing game; played with any new people in town."

I took the photo out of my jacket pocket and handed it over to her. She hesitated only briefly. "Yes I know who this is," she said, tapping a finger on the image of the woman in the picture. "The man must have lived – may still live, around here too but I don't know his name. I worked in Kingston for a number of years beginning just before this was taken and I haven't seen him that I remember, since I returned. Her name is Veronica Graham."

Chapter 21

"Are you sure?" I asked.

"I can assure you it is true. There's nothing wrong with my memory. Or my eyesight. Frankly I never thought to see her or hear of her again. And seeing these two together brings back some – uncomfortable feelings."

I gave her a moment to reflect. "Perhaps you could elaborate on that thought, if you don't mind, please?"

Suddenly she seemed much older than her sixty or so years. Her face became drawn and lined and had lost its colour. A tissue had somehow mysteriously appeared and was held firm between clasped hands in her lap. She looked at the ceiling and spoke softly.

"I felt at the time that I should have said or done something, but I didn't. I had no real facts or information – only feelings and those would have been of little interest to the authorities.

"As I said, I went to Kingston just a few days before the 150th, to work at what was to be a short job. I ended up being hired on full time so I was there for nearly ten years rather than a few weeks. For years it bothered me that I wasn't there to help Roni in her time of trouble."

She paused to collect her thoughts so I asked, "What sort of trouble was she having?"

Constance Osgoode continued staring at the ceiling. "Man trouble – of the worst kind. We had become friends – not terribly close but more than just work acquaintances. After I moved away we corresponded by letter fairly regularly. I was alone in Kingston and she was alone here and it gave us both a sense of kinship I guess, to say nothing of just having something to do and something to look forward to. At first the letters were just innocuous stuff; the weather, people we knew, local gossip; that sort of thing. I think she sort of looked at me as a big sister – someone she could talk to.

Then after a month or so – we wrote pretty much every week – she started to tell me about some problems she was having with a local man. She never mentioned his name.

"He seemed to be obsessed with her. He believed they should be together; that they were soul mates. He followed her around constantly and called several times a day on the phone. At first she treated the whole thing calmly and politely, trying to make him understand that she was not interested. That didn't work. She tried being sharp and unfriendly, and later on even loud and rude but still he persisted. I could sense the fear through the bland and everyday wording of her letters."

She stopped speaking and wiped a tear from her eye.

I spoke softly. "Did she ever say how or where they had met?"

Now her tone changed from wistful to angry. She poked several times at the photo in her lap. "Here, damn it. Right here at that stupid 150th party. I guess the photographers were rounding up people at random to have their pictures taken – putting together groups and couples, taking the shot and then moving on. Probably someone was supposed to be following along to write down the names of the people in each picture, but some got missed. Some, like this one, appeared in the newspaper without any caption at all."

She paused again but I had the feeling more was coming so I kept quiet this time. In a moment she continued.

"In one of her early letters she mentioned that she had been paired with some guy she didn't know, to have a picture taken and that he had hung around her a lot for the rest of the evening. She had not thought anything of it at the time. Later, when the calls and visits started but were not yet a serious issue, she mentioned that the guy from the party was calling and visiting her more often than she was comfortable with.

"He would show up at her work at times when no-one else was around and hang around in the street near her home. As I said, she never told me his name or what he looked like. I was never able to visualise him. I hadn't seen this picture 'til today. Now I feel quite certain that this is him. This is the person who drove Roni away from Westport."

She fell silent again. I waited a moment then asked another question. "What do you mean he drove her away?"

For a time I wondered if she wasn't going to answer. She looked intently at the photo then closed her eyes. Soon the resolve returned and she spoke again.

"He made her life hell. It got bad enough that she finally called the police. Their response, since he had never actually done anything, was to wonder what she had done to 'lead him on' as they phrased it. They said he was probably harmless – just infatuated with her – if she ignored him he would eventually give up and quit bothering her. He didn't quit so she called again. This time they said they would talk to him. If they did – and I would have doubts about that – he wasn't deterred.

"Her last letter from Westport was desperate. She was at the end of her rope and had decided to leave town. She was afraid that if he found out she was going he might follow her, so she decided to pack up secretly and just disappear in the middle of the night. And she did."

Constance got up and went to the window, tipped back her head, closed her eyes and took a couple of deep breaths;

soaking up some of the late-afternoon sun; gaining strength to continue, then she returned to her seat.

"I heard from my sisters later that she had just vanished one night. Her car and all her personal belongings were gone. Don't know how she got it all in. She had one of those old, oh, not Corvette but something like that name. Corvair. That's what it was. Strange looking thing. Funny the things you remember. Anyway nothing remained in the rented house but the furnishings it had come with. No-one in Westport ever heard from her again."

"Your choice of words tells me that there may have been another communication of which the folks in Westport weren't aware."

"Yes. I got one more letter. It was a strange and distant letter saying in effect that she had found someone to be with and was starting over and would not be having anything to do with people from her old life. The letter was typed as all the others had been and was signed in a very shaky hand. It felt as though it had been written by someone else. The letter was postmarked in Montreal. That was the last I heard from her. She had no family and as far as I know, no-one ever came looking for her."

We both sat quiet a while. The rays of the early evening sun streamed in through the spotless glass of the office window, dancing off shining brass desk accessories and fracturing into a psychedelic rainbow through a cut crystal vase on the credenza. I'd have to remember to ask her who did her windows. The Inn could use someone who did that quality of work.

"You're looking a little pale. I hope I haven't upset you too much. Can I make you a cup of tea or something? I can usually find my way around a kitchen pretty well."

"Something to drink would be welcome," she said, "but I think I need more than tea. I had finished working for the day and had just opened a bottle of wine when you arrived. Maybe we could both do with a glass. It must have breathed enough by now." She stood and moved toward the door. "You sit. I'll get it. I need to move around and think a bit."

With that she left the office and I heard her opening cupboards and drawers. Soon she returned with a tray bearing a bottle of red wine, two glasses and a small board with cheese and olives and an assortment of crackers, which she set on the edge of her desk.

"Would you pour, please? My hands are a bit shaky all of a sudden." She sat back down in the chair she had been in before.

I stood and poured a generous portion in each glass and handed one to her and sat back down.

We were quiet again briefly, sipping our wine, each reviewing the story that had just been told.

"Now that I've identified the woman in your photo and told you all I know about her perhaps you would answer a question for me."

"Certainly I will if I can," I said. I had a feeling I knew what was coming.

"You've been trying for a while now to identify the person whose skeleton was in your attic. It's no secret – it's all over town. I can think of only one reason why you would be going around town showing people *this* picture, and I don't even want to ask, but I must. Do you really think that my friend Veronica is your skeleton?"

I was right. I had known what was coming. Not at all unreasonable that an intelligent person would make the correct connection and ask the correct question, yet I had not been prepared for it when I came here. There was no good answer. Certainly not one that would not add to the anxiety I had already caused. I hedged.

"You understand that I have no proof, only speculation; feelings if you like. I'm trying to piece this mess together any way that makes sense, following what little actual evidence there is and modifying my theories as I go. Following the trail and seeing where it leads. This picture is of two people who were around at the same time the 150th party happened. Today I determined from someone else that the woman was *possibly* a woman who went away soon after that event. Until today I didn't know anything about her or the man. Now I do. Now, with what I've heard from you, I'm reasonably sure that this is the woman I've been hearing about, who departed so abruptly."

I hesitated again, not wanting to lie but still not sure what the truth was.

"Now, having heard your story, it seems possible – even likely - that she didn't run away to Montreal as you were led to believe. Maybe she was killed and maybe this guy is the one who did the killing. So, to answer your question, yes, I do believe that your friend and the skeleton in my attic may be one and the same."

We both sat sipping our wine and staring at the walls, not knowing what to say next.

"If I'm going to make it back to the island before dark I'm going to have to get moving soon. For what it's worth, I'm not sure you could have affected the outcome of this tragedy, presuming that it is as we suspect, even if you'd called the police. Those were different times and the idea of stalkers as we think of them today was pretty much unknown. No-one would have expected then that the thing would play out the way we think it did. And it is by no means *certain* that it did. Remember that we're guessing about a lot of things here still. This guy in the picture may be entirely innocent of any crime and be living happily with a wife and kids in Edmonton. And your friend may be alive and well in Montreal."

"Or not," she said. "You'll try to find out more won't you?

And you *will* let me know what you find? Now that this can of worms is open I want a satisfactory solution found. I have a bad feeling that Roni is dead and that this," tapping the picture, "is the one who killed her. Catch the bastard. I will help any way I can."

"Thanks for the offer. I may need more information as the investigation progresses. I'll let you know if I do. In the mean time I'll be talking to Sergeant Mike Grant who's running the case – my involvement is strictly off the record, just in case anyone ever asks. He is going to keep an extra watch on a few people associated with the case and you're going to be added to the list. Just a precaution but you should be a little careful until this is wrapped up. Keep the doors locked and watch out for any strangers around the neighbourhood. Be on the lookout for an older red pickup hanging around."

We exchanged phone numbers and I was ready to be on my way.

"One more question occurs to me, if I may. Do you recall her middle name, Veronica's I mean?"

"It was Agnes. I remember because it's the same as mine. Why do you ask?"

"Just needing to file away a coincidence is all. Thanks."

On the way to the public dock I called the Inn so they could send the boat for me. I made a quick stop at the grocery store to grab something for dinner and then returned the car to Mrs. Samuelson's garage.

Her house was dark and quiet, no lights on anywhere, but it was early still. I walked around and checked the doors and peeked in the windows. Then I remembered the shotgun comment and thought better of looking in any more windows. Nothing seemed amiss so I scrawled a quick note and stuck it between the door jamb and the screen door at the back. I wanted to let her know I'd be back for pie tomorrow.

As the sun began to disappear behind the tree-covered hills I walked to the public dock. It was deserted at this hour so I had a few quiet minutes to reflect on my day's work. I'd found out a good deal but there was still a lot to be determined. I felt a little guilty about my over quick suspicion of Ken Osgoode. Constance Osgoode could not possibly have failed to recognize her own brother in the newspaper photo and though I was sure I wasn't imagining her sincerity about that, I'd pass the idea by Grant anyway. Have him checked out.

Soon the bright headlamp of the courtesy boat could be seen rounding the point and the smooth purr of the motor was audible in the early evening quiet.

The boat arrived with the same driver who had left me at the dock earlier in the day. He inquired about my day and I answered in some noncommittal way. Thereafter we continued in silence until we reached the island where I disembarked, said good night and headed for the house with the few groceries I had picked up. As I walked toward home I heard a soft sound on the evening breeze; a sound I had not heard over the deep rumble of the antique powerboat. It was the now familiar sound of a small and distinctive motor, out on the lake, and moving slowly away from the island. Had my buddy been following me home or had he been on the island? I strained my eyes in the direction I thought the sound was coming from, but in the dark couldn't see a thing. The way sounds travel over water, he might be anywhere – impossible to follow him tonight - if it was even him.

I continued inside and went in the door off my private deck. When I opened the door I looked deliberately behind the door for the rock and rope fragment I'd collected off the beach. They were gone. After that I went directly up to my suite, checked all around and found nothing of concern. I put away my groceries and then called Mike Grant's office in Smiths Falls to let him know what I had found out and, as an after thought, mentioned the missing rock and the possibility that our quarry had been close-by not long ago.

Suddenly I heard the cage door of the elevator open.

wasn't careful enough today. acted without planning. almost caught me at Bascome's and I coulda been identified on the street outside the Cove.

Gonna hafta move against these two old women who're helpin him. can't take a chance they remember me. They have to go. Him too. Him first !!!!

Chapter 22

The next morning I was scheduled to be back in the kitchen. Bud needed a day off and had waited longer than he should have because I was injured. I'd had only the one day off but I felt better and was ready to go. With the rest and the feeling of progress in the investigation I felt rejuvenated. I'd called Bud and told him to take the day off.

I left Josée sleeping peacefully and showered and dressed as quietly as possible. It had indeed been a surprise of the better variety when she stepped out of the elevator the night before and told me she had been assigned to keep me safe. And that she intended to be very vigilant.

I arrived in the kitchen at 6:00 a.m. and was starting to get things ready for breakfast when Jeany and Francis, alias Frankie, came in. Frankie was learning some prep cooking as an aside to his dishwashing duties. I wasn't sure if Bud had actually let him cook while I'd been off. I'd have to ask about that. They both asked how I was then got busy with the work at hand.

Bud had done the menu planning for the day since I hadn't been around to do it, and I began to prep the breakfast special. As with the dinner we serve a basic breakfast menu every day and add a special, a different one each morning. Today was an upscale version of scrambled eggs with red pepper, green onion and back bacon, with garlic hash browns and toast.

As I chopped peppers and onions I thought about my next move in the investigation. Grant would be there soon with information he'd picked up from Wil Bascome, and hopefully that would point us in the right direction. Grant would also be showing the newspaper photo around a little more vigorously now that we were reasonably sure that the man in it was the one we needed to question. Even if it turned out that he wasn't involved with the case he could still have valuable information. But, my gut told me that he was involved.

The dining room staff had arrived and were taking out loads of cutlery, coffee cups and glasses to start setting up the tables for breakfast. Frankie dropped off the first load of washed and cut up potatoes at the main prep table. I transferred them to a giant steamer to do a pre cook, after which they would be held until needed. One of the nice things about working a small kitchen and serving a clientele who are not generally in a big hurry is that with a relatively small amount of prep most things can be cooked to order entirely. Everything hits the table as fresh as it can be.

"Did you two eat this morning already?" I asked without looking away from the pancetta I was cutting. Jeany answered first.

"Yes, thanks. I had breakfast at home today. How about you, Frankie?"

There was no answer. This could mean one of two things. Either he had not eaten and didn't want to say so or he had eaten and would be glad to eat again, being an average late-teenage boy.

"So, what will it be," I asked. I looked over my shoulder at him. "You want the regular stuff or do you want to try the special?"

Without much hesitation he answered. "I'd like to try the special, please. Long as there's enough."

"No reason there shouldn't be enough since we're just making it now. I'll let you know when it's ready." I looked over at Jeany. She was looking my way. She smiled, shook her head and raised an eyebrow, just one, then bent back to her soup preparation. I wasn't quite sure what all that had been intended to convey but I had other things to consider at the moment. The timer went off for the potatoes and I pulled them off the stovetop and lifted the lid. Steam billowed out, creating a cloud over the stove. I dumped the hot potatoes, which were only partially cooked, into a steam table insert and dropped the insert in its place. Before closing the steam table lid I took a large serving spoon and put a decent portion of the potatoes onto the now hot and olive oil-coated flat-top. A few slices of thick-cut, local back bacon were close by.

While the potatoes started to brown I set a pan on the gas stove top and cracked a couple of eggs into a small bowl. There was one person I needed to catch up with again. By now Mrs. Samuelson might very well have remembered the person in the picture. She'd been around during the time of the 150th and as far as I was aware, had not left since for any length of time, perhaps not ever.

I smashed a clove of garlic and took off the skin, then smashed it again. I minced the remainder as finely as possible, mixed in a little coarse salt and ran the flat of the knife over it to smooth it to paste, ready to add to the potatoes. I took the bacon off the flat-top and diced it up then put it back on and turned the potatoes. I'd need to get to see Mrs. Samuelson later today, as soon as I finished working in the kitchen. I tossed a small portion of finely chopped red onion onto the hot surface. With any luck Grant would be able to go with me and we'd make some more headway.

The cubed bacon was browning nicely so I tossed in portions of red pepper and green onion then started them cooking. I added the garlic to the potatoes, continuing to turn them over now and then with the steel spatula.

"Okay, Frankie," I said. "You can put in whatever kind of toast you want. This is almost ready."

I beat the eggs with a little milk and put it in the pan with the bacon and veggies and after a moment stirred the mixture. Slowly, scrambled eggs formed around the other ingredients in the pan. I mixed the now caramelizing red onion into the potatoes. A minute later I heard the toaster releasing its golden contents and readied a plate for the rest. "Here you go, Frankie," I said as I plated the meal. "Go sit and eat in peace for a few minutes. No working and eating at the same time." He added his toast to the plate and headed for the door to the dining room.

"Thanks, RJ. This looks great. I'll be back in a few minutes."

As soon as Frankie had left, Jeany spoke from her station at the salad sink.

"Seems Bob has left the Roadside. I heard from a friend who works housekeeping here, who knows someone who cleans at the Roadside Motel, that he paid up and beat it a day or two ago. Don't s'pose you had anything to do with that?"

"Me? What could I have done?"

I turned back to the prep table and my preparations for the rest of the day. I couldn't help feeling a little gratified that my visit to Bob had had the desired effect. Hopefully it would stick. I wondered whether or not Grant's people had turned up anything on Bob since I'd fingered him as a possible suspect. I guessed Bob would be even less happy with me if he found out I'd sent the cops after him. Not that I cared what Bob thought.

I made up some seasoned bread crumbs for the evening's Chicken Parmesan and cleaned and trimmed asparagus for the other evening special, Salmon en Croute with Asparagus and Hollandaise.

About fifteen minutes had passed since Frankie had gone to eat when Jeany and I heard what sounded like a rifle shot followed instantly by breaking glass and a lot of shouting. As I ran toward the dining room, I called for Jeany to notify the police.

Chaos reigned. Dining room staff were crawling away from the main window through which a bullet or some such projectile had entered the room. There was a small hole surrounded by a spider web of tiny cracks, and there was a coating of fine glass particles all across the room. The sound of breaking glass we'd heard had come from juice glasses hitting the floor as staff had upset tables scrambling for cover. It looked as though Frankie was the only one who would be sampling the breakfast special in this dining room today. Frankie.

I looked round at the room and the few people still in it but there was no sign of him. "Anyone seen Frankie?" I called out to no-one in particular.

Someone in the doorway to the lounge answered back. "He was outside on the deck having breakfast. I haven't seen him since the shot."

I crouched as low as I could and went to the glass doors. Peering around the doorframe I tried to see if he was out there, but the angle was bad and I couldn't see enough to tell. I turned the handle on one side of the French doors and slowly pushed it open and crawled outside. The deck was in shadow from the house and some of the tables and chairs were still stacked along the wall. A few leaf fragments swirled around in the breeze and insects buzzed overhead. I looked both ways and seeing nothing, crawled further out past an overturned table.

Sticking out from under a covered stack of deck chairs was a pair of legs.

"Frankie? Frankie, are you all right?" Stupid question. Even if he wasn't hit he would not be all right.

"I'm, I think I'm okay, RJ," said a muffled voice. "I think someone was shooting at me. Why would someone do that?"

"Don't know, Frankie. You stay down. I'm coming over to you." I stayed as low as possible and made my way across the deck to where Frankie was lying half under the chairs. I slid under with him and did a quick check to see that he hadn't been shot. There was no blood anywhere.

"We'll just stay here for another few minutes. Whoever it was is probably long gone but we'd better not take chances. How are you feeling?"

"Pretty shaky to be honest. I never been shot at before. Not much fun."

"Damn right it isn't. Scared the hell out of me when it happened, I can tell you. It passes though. Did you see or hear anything while you were out here?"

"Both, I think. I think I saw who shot at me."

"What? Tell me."

"I was almost finished eating when I heard a small boat passing by the beach area. Sounded like it was a fair ways out. I turned around a bit and looked out through the, what is it? Um… lattice stuff there around the deck. Just as well I didn't stand up I guess. It was some guy in an old green motor boat. He cut the engine and picked up something long from the bottom of the boat.

"I turned back around and went back to my breakfast. I thought it was probably a fishing rod he had. Now I'm not so sure about that."

My mind flashed back to my walk on the shore the morning after my first encounter with the stranger in the dark – the dark green paint on the rocks where a boat had been secured to the water's edge.

At that moment Sergeant Grant and Josée burst through the french doors and dropped low, their guns drawn.

"RJ? You all right? How's Frankie?"

"We're both fine. Frankie says there was a small green boat with a single occupant out there on the water off the beach. Anyone there now?"

As I watched, Grant slowly peeked out over the deck rail and scanned the waterfront. "Seems to be all clear for the moment. Let's get inside."

"Your timing was pretty good. Didn't even have to call this one in," I said.

"I was on my way already."

We all moved, still crouching unnecessarily, to the dining room door and went inside. Immediately Sergeant Grant was on his cell calling in the incident and Josée was running for the door.

"I'll get a boat and see if I can catch up with whoever it was," she said as she ran.

"You two head for the lounge," I said to Grant and Frankie. "I have to be sure someone is taking care of the folk who were in the dining room, in case of splintered glass injuries – hopefully nothing more than that, then I'll bring some coffee and meet you there."

I stopped in the kitchen and talked to Jeany then went around the back way to the reception area. Kim was just arriving for her day's work. "Kim. Good to see you. Sorry to do this to you before you even have your jacket off but we have a problem. Someone fired a bullet through one of the dining room windows. There's glass everywhere. There is also no chance that it will be cleaned up in time to serve breakfast here. Jeany is making sure everyone who was in the dining room is all right.

"I need you to call any and all local restaurants and see if they will honour a voucher from Gilmore House for breakfast for our guests. Make a list of those who say yes and then print up something simple on the computer with that list on it so people know where they can go. The restaurants can attach the food bills to your printout and send it here for payment. Does that sound all right?"

Kim took a second to process the idea then nodded. "That should work. I'll let the boathouse know they'll be busier than usual this morning. I guess if any of the guests just want to take coffee and pastries to their rooms that would be good too."

"Good idea. Include the rest of the regular breakfast menu as well. No room service but if anyone wants to take a bowl of cereal or some toast or whatever to their room they can. Give everyone the option. Maybe we'll be cleaned up in time for lunch. Speaking of which, any of the staff who want to stay and help with the clean up after the police are done can do so with my thanks, and full pay for the time. Oh. Maybe best not to mention to the restaurants why we're doing this – just say a maintenance problem or something? No doubt some of the guests will have heard the shot. Rumours will start soon enough."

When I arrived back at the lounge with the coffee there were only two people in the room. Josée was back from her quick tour around the island. She and Grant had talked briefly about starting a search on the mainland but decided that by the time they rounded-up enough people the shooter would be long gone. There were too many tiny bays and inlets where he might have hidden the boat. Grant took the tray from me and I sat down.

"I took Frankie's statement and sent him back to work. He was getting pretty fidgety and said he wanted to do something so he wouldn't be thinking about what happened. You can check on him later and see how he's doing. Send him home if you need to."

"Fine. I'll do that." I poured three coffees. "Now, can we three agree that Frankie was most likely not the intended target of the shooter? All of the cooking crew wear the same clothes. I think the shooter thought he was shooting at me."

Grant leaned forward in his chair, coffee cup poised halfway to the table. "And I think we got lucky that the water has a bit of chop this morning. He was not *that* far away from the beach. He should have been able to tell that it wasn't you but maybe he rushed. He took the shot because you and Frankie are similar in height and colouring and you were both wearing the same colour shirt. Can't have been easy to aim standing up in a rocking boat."

Josée Allard agreed. "I can see no reason why anyone would want to shoot Francis. You on the other hand seem to have annoyed someone. Why do these repeated attempts on your life not have you hiding under the bed?"

"For one thing there's not enough room under the bed. For another I'm getting kind of annoyed myself. I've been shot at before so it's not exactly a novelty. I didn't like it then and I don't like it now, but I don't plan on hiding. I want this guy, and soon, before he hurts anyone else."

Grant was thoughtful a moment then stood up. "You were shot once and lived to tell about it. Don't push your luck. Josée will be sticking with you from now 'til we wrap this up. She's in on our little arrangement now and won't tell."

Grant looked at me, then at Josée, then back at me.

"If the inn has an empty room maybe Josée could move in there for the duration. If not," here he paused briefly, "I'm sure you two can work something out."

I noticed that Josée's skin had pinked a bit. Grant did not look at her as he stood to go.

"You can continue to check leads if you still want to after this. But take Josée with you and please try not to get killed. I would hate to have to explain to the powers that be why you were in the line of fire, so to speak, and the paperwork would keep me in the office for weeks." He shrugged into his jacket and as he turned to leave added, "This guy is escalating. There's no telling what he'll do next. Be careful. Both of you." He looked over his shoulder toward the main entry. Men in suits were arriving. "The crime scene guys are here. I have to go. Oh, by the way, RJ, I got your message and have people digging up all they can find on Veronica Graham. Nice to finally have a name to work with. The right name."

"You can tell the crime scene guys that the bullet is in the side wall of the dining room just past the swinging door – almost in the corner. I noticed the hole and a little pile of plaster dust as I came through the last time."

"Thanks, RJ."

As Grant walked away I rose and picked up the coffee tray. "So, you're going to be sticking with me are you?"

Josée raised an eyebrow but did not comment.

I carried on. "I'm going to check on Frankie and leave some additional instructions for the clean up with Kim. I know there's some kind of emergency glass repair company in Perth. Maybe we can get them here quickly so we can open for dinner at least, maybe even lunch. After I talk to Kim, you and I are going to head for the mainland for a repeat visit to someone who might be able to shed some light on this thing. You up for that?"

"Sure thing. I am your shadow, day and night until we solve this case. You up for that?"

"I guess we'll see, won't we?"

"By the way," she added, "I almost told Sergeant Grant I'd just arrived when he got here. No need to complicate things, I thought. Now I think he suspects I was here overnight."

"I don't think I'd worry about that. Grant won't have a problem with it."

"I hope you're right. Shall we go?"

"Yes. We need to get this cleared up soon or I won't have any staff or any guests willing to stick around here."

Chapter 23

There was a stiff breeze blowing when Josée and I went out to the dock and the water was choppy. I'm no more than a smooth water boater at any time so I was happy to have Josée to run the motor launch. She controlled the boat expertly, facing into the wind and waves as much as possible for most of the trip then running hard and fast with the waves as we dashed for the safety of the small harbour. I was glad to be on dry land again. Josée seemed hardly to have noticed the roughness at all.

Our destination this trip was Mrs. Samuelson's place, not to get out my vehicle, but to see if Mrs. Samuelson could help us in our hunt. I hoped to catch her before she went out anywhere, otherwise we'd be all day trying to find her. We walked as quickly as I was able, along the tree lined street to the familiar driveway.

As we passed the halfway point of the wide gravel driveway an engine revved and a red blur appeared from beside the garage. An older red pickup with darkened windows blasted across the driveway directly toward us, engine roaring and fountains of stones flying from all four tires. Almost before we registered the threat the truck was upon us. We both dove to the side, I to the right into the carefully tended flower bed, Josée to the left.

As fast as the danger had arrived it ended.

I hoisted myself up slowly, pulling assorted greenery from my clothing and hair. As I bent to brush the dirt from my black work jeans I saw Josée, lying sprawled face down in the gravel at the far side of the driveway.

I called her name as I hobbled across the driveway but she didn't move. I hauled out my cell and dialled 911, gave the address and situation to the operator as I moved and finally arrived at Josée's inert body.

Her head was turned facing away from the house, feet toward the roadway. I knew not to move her unless it was absolutely necessary. I brushed back the hair from her neck and felt for a pulse, and watched for breathing. Both were there, at least for the moment. So was a spider web of shallow gouges from the gravel of the driveway.

I jumped as I heard a crunch of gravel behind me and rose and turned as quickly as I was able, ready to fight if I had to. Mrs. Samuelson stopped mid stride as I stood up. "Is she all right?"

"Definitely not all right but alive so far. Ambulance is on the way," I said as I crouched back down to Josée. "A blanket would be a good idea, if you would please."

I heard her turn and retrace her steps noisily across the stones, go back into the house, the old wood-framed screen door banging loosely as it closed. The wind rustled the leaves above and somewhere on the water a loon called. Far in the distance a siren drifted in and out on the wind as Mrs. Samuelson made her return trip. She walked around Josée and helped me spread the blanket. A scent of lavender soap drifted up and was gone on the wind.

We were still for a few minutes, Mrs. Samuelson hovering above Josée and me, shifting her weight from one foot to the other, sighing audibly from time to time, annoyed by her inability to make things better.

At once we realized that the sirens, not one but several, were much nearer. It occurred to me that there had been probably more sirens heard here in Westport in the past week than there had been in the last several years combined.

Four vehicles screamed onto the quiet street, lights flashing, and came suddenly to rest. In the deafening silence that followed, police and paramedics emerged from their vehicles and began to work.

The paramedics came with armloads of gear and a gurney loaded with more. "What happened here?" asked the first to arrive. He crouched down to take my place beside Josée and I rose and stepped back a little. The other began unloading gear onto the ground. Mike Grant stood, white faced and grim, and close enough to hear the answer without being in the way.

"She was hit by a pick-up truck. I don't know how hard," I said. "I know she dived at least partly out of its path but obviously she got clipped. The cut on her forehead was bleeding. I stopped that but that's all I did other than check pulse and breathing. I didn't want to move her once I knew she was breathing properly. She hasn't moved at all since it happened."

"Okay. You can let us handle it from here." With infinite care and confident efficiency they went to work and soon had Josée checked out, braced, wrapped and loaded, first onto a back board then onto the lowered gurney.

Mike and I watched as the two paramedics carried the gurney to the ambulance so as not to bounce Josée over the rough gravel surface. One of them jumped in the back with Josée while the other went to the driver's door. "We'll go to Perth first and let them check her out. They may want to move her to Ottawa or Kingston later," said the one in the back compartment. He didn't wait for a response but pulled the door closed. The ambulance moved slowly out of the driveway and as soon as it hit the road the lights and siren were once again in use.

As the siren sound diminished Grant pointed and nodded over my shoulder, indicating that I should look at something. I turned my head and saw that Mrs. Samuelson was still standing in the driveway, but now nearer the front of the house, as though she had drifted that way in the wake of the departing ambulance. "She looks pretty shaken up," he said. "So do you for that matter. You should take her into the house. I need to talk to the uniforms and get them looking for that pickup, then I'll meet you inside."

I did as requested. Taking her arm I led Mrs. Samuelson along the drive and up onto the front porch. After a last look over her shoulder she pulled open the screen door. I held it as she went in and I followed her, along the hall, past living room and dining room, to the kitchen at the back of the house. As we entered she gave her head a little shake as though displacing the memory of the past half hour.

"I'll put on a pot of coffee," she said. "You said in your note yesterday that you'd be back today for some rhubarb pie. Wasn't expecting all this excitement though. Trouble does seem to follow you around these days, RJ."

I nodded thoughtfully. "Trouble seems to have been here waiting for me today. Whoever that was couldn't have known I was coming here. I didn't know myself until a little while ago." I left off speculating about who the truck driver might have been looking for here if not me, but Mrs. Samuelson interpreted my hesitation.

"You think he might have been looking for me," she stated rather than asked. "Don't guess I'd have fared as well as you did if he'd caught me in the middle of the driveway like that, no sir, I wouldn't." She went, shaking her head, to the stove to retrieve the coffee pot then to the sink to fill it with water. There was a knock at the front door.

"I can get that if you like," I said.

"Yes please," she replied without turning.

I went along the hall to the front door and met Mike Grant there.

Since I'd told Mike about my conversation with Constance Osgoode he had had people working to dig up whatever could be found about Veronica Graham's sudden departure.

"Nothing new yet on Veronica Graham. How's Mrs. Samuelson doing?"

I motioned him to follow me into the living room where we stood and talked briefly. "She seems better now. Seems to have figured out that she may have been the target this time and isn't pleased about that."

"I'm calling some extra help. Yesterday the brass were unimpressed with the idea of spending more money on what was a rather nebulous theory – their word, not mine. Now a cop has been injured and suddenly the budget got a lot bigger. There will be a car on all the primary sources from now 'til we roll this up."

"Good. I was hoping you'd say something like that. Let's go back and tell her that. I'm sure she'll be more comfortable knowing that someone will be looking out for her."

As we walked to the kitchen Grant told me he'd had little success in his interview with Wil Bascome. Bascome wasn't able to identify his attacker.

We went to the kitchen and found Mrs. Samuelson sitting at the table with a copy of *Canadian Living*, closed, in front of her. She looked up as we came in. "The coffee's almost ready. I think we'll just have it here if you don't mind. Could one of you tell me who the young lady was – is?"

Grant spoke first. "She is an OPP officer connected with the marine group locally. Her name is Josée Allard. She's been helping to investigate the body in the attic business."

"Well I hope she'll be all right. Coffee's ready."

"I'm ready too." I said.

Mike Grant spoke quietly. "I'm sorry to have had this happen here. We're trying to catch up with whoever is tracking RJ. We think there's some possibility that the person we're looking for might be trying to silence anyone who could help us in that. From now on there will be a police officer close by day and night until the person is caught."

She had been looking down at the closed magazine. Now she looked up. "That's very good of you, Sergeant, looking after an old lady. I appreciate it. I really do. I hope your officer will come in and have tea with me once in awhile. And I hope he won't mind following me around town a bit. I have things to do you know and I won't let some criminal have me hiding in my house." She waited for a response.

"I'm sure we will be able to accommodate your busy schedule," he said without sarcasm. "Just don't run him around too much. He is here to protect you after all."

"Of course. Are you ready for pie and coffee now?"

We were.

Went to get the old woman but no luck. The other two showed up. Got the cop but maybe not him too much Dust in the air to tell. Haveta come back for the old woman

Chapter 24

Mike Grant was on his cell phone trying to get an update from the Perth hospital and I was washing up the plates and cups from our snack. Mrs. Samuelson turned from the cupboard where she had just put away a plate she'd dried and asked, "RJ, why were you and Officer Josée coming here today? With all the goings-on I never did hear the reason for your visit."

I almost dropped the next cup. With all the *goings-on* I seemed to have left my brain out in the driveway. "You're right. We were coming here to have you take another look at a picture from the 150th."

"Of course. The famous picture. I was wondering when you'd get back to me. You've showed it to most everyone else in town since you were here last. I was beginning to think you weren't going to bring it back here at all." The tone of petulance was a put on I knew. It was only yesterday that I showed her the picture, but I apologized anyway.

"Sorry not to get back to you sooner." I reached for my jacket which I had hung over the back of one of the old wooden kitchen chairs.

A loud snap diverted our attention to Sergeant Grant. "No news so far," he said pocketing his phone. "What were you two doing?"

"I was just about to show Mrs. Samuelson the picture again, see if she has any more recollection this time of who the man might be," I said as I took the paper from my pocket and unfolded it.

"I've been thinking about these two since the last time you were here, RJ. I think I may have an idea."

Mrs. Samuelson reached one hand for the paper and the other for her glasses which were tethered on a cord around her neck. She settled onto a chair and spread the faded photo on the table and gave it her full attention. For about ten seconds.

She looked up at me. "Don't you know who this man is?"

Grant, ever the diplomat, said quietly, "Well ma'am, that's kind of why we brought it to you. Because we didn't know who either of them was before and we still don't know who he is. Her name, by the way, is Veronica Graham."

She digested that a moment, then continued.

"Yes, well, I suppose you wouldn't know the girl. If this is who I think it is - Veronica? - she left town long ago – long before either of you were around here. But the man, RJ – really – this man works on your island sometimes. He should be familiar to you."

"Who? No. Surely I'd recognize someone I see regularly? I don't think even aged thirty-five years I could miss – ." I faltered there. Could I really have not seen this? I could almost see him - older, but the name and the face wouldn't come into focus.

Mrs. Samuelson came to my rescue. "Now maybe I'm being too hard on you. He has changed a lot and I've seen the changes happen gradual-like. Yes. A lot of changes now that I think about it. I should have recognized him the first time you showed me the picture – maybe would have if we hadn't been disturbed by that delinquent next door with his loud car." She drifted in thought briefly. "Lots of changes since this was taken."

"What changes might these have been, Mrs. Samuelson?" prompted Grant.

Mrs. Samuelson seemed lost in memories for a moment. "He was always a strange boy – quiet – reclusive – never wanted to take part in things. First-class mechanic though. His father and uncle saw to that. Always happier around an old boat than he was around people. Had a couple of run–ins with your lot, Sergeant. Lookin' in windows, bullying. Later it was drinking and fighting. That's how he got his leg broke – never did set quite right. Still has a bit of a limp though it doesn't seem to slow him down much. That happened later though – a while after this was taken." She was quiet again for a few minutes and just as I was about to say something she began again.

"He was a good lookin' fella in those days, wasn't he? That was before the fire. He had his quirks all along but the burns on his face and hands seemed to tip him over the edge. That's when he grew the beard and moved out of town somewhere. Maybe, Foley Mountain?"

We knew the answers to the next couple of questions but we wanted to see if anything new would be forthcoming.

I let her think a moment then asked, "How does this woman fit into all this? Did they have any kind of relationship at all? You said she left town? When was that?"

"There was a lot of talk at the time. That's the only reason I remember it at all. Soon after the 150th, soon after this was taken, he did a lot of bragging about his new love. Her. I never knew her name." She tapped the photo with a blunt finger nail. "He was adamant that they were an item. But nobody ever saw them go out together, and I heard from someone who knew her that it was all his imagination. She never had any interest in him, as I heard. People laughed at him behind his back. Everyone knew that it was all just empty talk but he kept it up for a few months. Then she left."

Grant and I looked at each other. *She left all right,* was the thought that occurred to me immediately.

"It was odd you know," continued Mrs. Samuelson. "He changed a lot after that. Everyone thought he'd be madder'n hell when she upped and disappeared like that. But he wasn't. He was jumpy and meaner than usual, if that's possible, for a while. But not upset. You'da thought loosing his *true love* like that would have had him raving. But no. Odd I call it." She sat slowly shaking her bowed head at the memory.

Sergeant Grant was unable to contain the question any longer. "Please, Mrs. Samuelson. You still haven't told us who you think this is."

She stirred from her reverie and looked from one of us to the other then back again as though wondering what we were doing in her kitchen, then, with a little head shake and a couple of blinks her eyes cleared and she sat up straighter. She looked at me as she answered Grant's question.

"This is Harold Morrison. He's the uncle of the current owner of Morrison's Boatworks where your old boats were stored all those years. He works as a mechanic for the boats at your Inn, doesn't he?"

I carefully took back the picture from her and looked at it again. A lot of changes, indeed. After a moment I let the picture fall to the table and went and looked out the window at the leaves being tossed around on the breeze. I must have been lost in thought longer than I realized.

"Now *you're* doing it. Staring into space," said Grant quietly. He had moved beside me at the window. "What's up?"

I took a moment to answer. "I don't know exactly. Something's poking at my memory. Harold Morrison? Boats? I don't know. One thing's for damn sure, we have to find Morrison. Even if he's not the murderer, and I'm betting he is, he may know something about the disappearance of Veronica Graham."

"I'm going outside to see if the Constable is here to do guard duty," said Grant. "While I'm out there I'll get Smiths

Falls to start a search for Harold Morrison. Provincial MTO will probably be quickest. If he's driving legally he'll be on record with them."

"Well you two can do what you like. I'm going to take a nap," said Mrs. Samuelson. "This has all been rather taxing. Lock the door on your way out, RJ. Goodbye, Sergeant Grant. Good hunting." With that she headed purposefully for the kitchen door.

"Mrs. Samuelson," I called after her. "Do you know if Harold Morrison was seriously injured in that fire he was in?" She didn't stop or turn.

"Oh yes. Quite bad I think. He has some burn scars on parts of his hands and face and smoke and chemical fumes made his voice sound strange – kind of gravelly."

She continued on down the hall and soon Mike and I could hear the creak of the old stairs as she climbed to the second floor.

"I'm going to stay here for a few minutes and make a few calls then I'm going back to the island. Not too likely that our boy will have another run at me there, with a lot of people around. Not where he can't use his truck as a weapon. I'll have to stay away from windows though, since he seems to like guns too."

Grant looked at me over his shoulder as he headed for the door. "Good idea. Don't do anything or go anywhere else. As soon as we have an address I'm headed there. I'll let you know what we find."

"And Mike. Keep me posted about Josée's condition, please,"

"Definitely."

With that he was gone out the door.

Chapter 25

I took out my cell and began to dial the Inn to let them know I would be a while longer. As I dialled I realized I'd have to run the boat myself to get home. I wondered how Josée was doing. I hoped the water wasn't as rough as it had been earlier or I'd be in trouble. Thoughts of water and boats brought back the feeling that there was something about boats that would prove important somehow, but it still eluded me.

The silence of the house was shattered by the slamming of a car door, the rev of a big V8 and the rain of gravel on the sidewalk and walls. I stood and looked just in time to see Grant's unmarked car bounce over the end of the gravel drive and onto the paved road. Grant hit the siren and switched on the flashing light just as he disappeared behind the trees lining the edge of Mrs. Samuelson's yard. Apparently he had hit pay dirt.

I resumed my interrupted call and reached Kim at Gilmore House. I asked her if she'd seen anything of Harold Morrison that day. She hadn't but said she would keep a lookout for him. I didn't want to alarm her so I said that I had a job for him but wanted to talk to him privately about it. I asked her to not say anything to him if he was around but to call me and let me know. Pretty lame but it was the best I could do on short notice. I said I would be there soon and signed off.

After that it took a few minutes to check all the lower level windows and make sure the front door was locked. I took my jacket from the back of a chair in the kitchen and let myself out through the back door, checking carefully to be sure the lock had engaged. I closed the old screen door slowly so it wouldn't bang then headed down the driveway toward the street. I waved to the Constable who was on guard duty and turned on to the street, heading for the public dock. He nodded in response.

Morrison. Mrs. Samuelson had reminded me that I had a connection to that family. It was at least possible that Andy Morrison might know where to find his uncle. I had told Grant that I'd go straight back to the Inn but this idea was too promising to ignore. It was only a couple of blocks out of the way anyway.

I cut through an alley and a parking lot, hurrying in the afternoon sun. I arrived at the Morrison Boatworks in about ten minutes and jogged up the stairs. The door was closed but unlocked as I would have expected it to be at this hour. No one was behind the counter. Probably Andy was in the back working on a boat. The sign wasn't up but I rang the big brass ship's bell on the counter anyway and waited. No-one came so I rang again. After a few minutes I decided to have a look in the back area.

Perhaps Andy was far enough back that he couldn't hear the bell.

I opened the door to the work shop and storage area and called out to Andy. Receiving no response I started to walk further into the shop. As I passed a large tarp-covered boat a small noise caught my attention. Too late I knew I was in trouble as an oar flashed out of the shadow and connected with the side of my head.

He's been very lucky. I almost got caught. shot at the bastard from the boat but I missed water was too rough for a clean shot tried to run him down with the truck again but only got the cop. Now his luck's run out didn't think he'd look for me here but it couldn't be better. I have him and he won't bother me any more. It's over. soon anyway.

As I regained consciousness I was in total darkness. I quickly realized that there was some kind of cover over my head.

My hands were free for some reason and I started to push myself into a sitting position. A wave of nausea hit me and I stopped moving. My head throbbed and I could feel the place I'd been hit. The nausea passed and I moved a little more.

I heard a chair squeak as someone changed position but no-one spoke.

Finally reaching a sitting posture I slowly removed the cover from over my head. The light was muted, still daytime but I was deep inside the very old boat shed. Wood plank floors; boats all over the place. I recognized this room as part of the boatworks. I'd been here a couple of times before. It was where Andy Morrison had brought me to inspect the old boats. There was still some long term storage there; some boats and a couple of old cars.

The chair squeaked again and I turned slowly toward the sound.

A figure sat in an ancient Muskoka chair, relaxed, lounging almost, face obscured by shadows.

In his right hand, resting on the wide arm of the chair, was a very old and very large gun. On the other arm was a spiral note pad and a pen.

"Hello Harold," I said slowly. "Finally we meet."

A short sharp intake of breath told me I had guessed right, but the man didn't move. I could feel his eyes on me in the shadows, deciding.

"I can't believe – I really can not believe that we have never actually met face to face before now. You've done some work on the boats at the Inn since it opened. I've seen you around a lot, always at some distance or at times when I couldn't get a chance to talk to you. I've meant to meet you properly several times but something has always got in the way. Now this. My guess now is that perhaps you've been avoiding me?"

Very slowly he moved to a more upright position, still sitting, arms still resting on the chair, no longer relaxed. He reached into the breast pocket of the plaid shirt he was wearing and took out his glasses; put them on. His face came into a shaft of sunlight shining through a skylight; drawn, haggard. Scar tissue showed on his cheeks and around his eyes. The black beard was ragged and greying in places.

"How did you know it was me?" asked Harold Morrison calmly. His voice was raspy.

"I didn't. Not for sure. Not until now."

"Bullshit!" less calmly. "You've been hounding me for weeks. Ever since she was found, everywhere I turned, there you were, dogging my footsteps, making my life hell."

"Your paranoia is showing, Harold."

"I'm not paranoid. You have been making my life miserable ever since you found her."

"It's you who's been making your life miserable, Harold, but not half so miserable as you made hers, I'll bet. Her name was Veronica by the way, in case you'd forgotten; Veronica Graham. Let's call her by her name. She's been anonymous for too long already. You saw to that, didn't you?"

"Shut up! You don't know what yer talking about."

"Oh, I think I have a pretty good idea what a sadistic whack job you are, Harold."

I was pushing my luck and I knew it but I figured I'd been stupid enough to let him get me in this position and I was probably going to get shot again as a result. I was betting that if I could make him angry enough he might just decide to beat on me a little first, instead of just shooting me and I could have a chance to fight back. At the very least I might make him mad enough to throw off his aim a bit. It was a long gamble.

The light level changed as clouds passed across the sun and a rising breeze blew scents of fuel and fish and cooking through the gaps in the old building.

"You have a vivid imagination, Harold. It's your guilty conscience that's been hounding you these past few weeks. You killed Veronica and mummified her body by sealing her up in the Gilmore House attic and you hoped she'd never be heard of again."

An odd scent passed by me at that moment, something out of place. It distracted me briefly. When I reoriented Harold was standing, pacing, waving the gun around and talking rapidly, in a much louder voice.

"No. No, that's not what happened. I didn't kill her - couldn't kill her - I loved her. Only her. Ever. Tried to get her to love me but she wouldn't even try - wanted to leave. Couldn't let her go away. I loved her. Made a place for her in the attic so she could stay with me while she learned to love me."

Morrison stopped for breath. He looked coldly at me as if wondering if he had said too much.

Prolong the conversation – prolong my life?

"How did you meet Veronica in the first place? You hardly seem to have been people with similar interests. She was a freelance secretary and you a mechanic of sorts. What made you think she would ever be interested in you?"

"Little you know," he said, calmer again. "We did have interests in common." He reached, left-handed into his hip pocket and removed a worn, brown leather wallet. From deep within the centre fold Morrison removed a paper which he unfolded carefully and turned toward me. It was the town 150th anniversary photo from the newspaper; the period costume shot of Morrison with Veronica Graham; the very photo that had started me thinking about him, without actually knowing who he really was in the first place; the one I'd been carrying around showing to damn near everyone in town. He'd been carrying it around for thirty-five odd years.

"You see this? We went to the big party together and got our picture in the paper. Had the two best costumes and we were very happy - you can see that. People said we made a lovely couple." He refolded the paper and carefully replaced it in his wallet.

Not true.

"The fact is, Harold, that you didn't go to the party together; you met there. You did have very good costumes and because of that had your picture taken together. I don't think you even knew her name at that point and you were certainly not a couple. That was when you began stalking her, wasn't it?"

I knew from Connie Osgoode about Veronica's immediate distancing of herself from Morrison after the picture had been taken.

"Didn't stalk her. I tried to get her to go out with me."

"Semantics, Harold. You pestered her relentlessly, followed her, phoned her, wrote her letters. She said she wasn't interested. She told you to leave her alone. She said "no" over and over again, but you persisted. These days, Harold you'd be locked up for that kind of behaviour and she would be able to get on with her life. But this was thirty years ago. People like you weren't recognized as being dangerous. The police heard her complaints and asked her what she'd done to encourage you. They assumed she'd brought the problem on herself. You weren't violent so they left you alone, maybe suggested quietly that you cool it, but that's probably about all."

The cold look was back but the hands were shaking a little.

"No-one was very surprised when it was found that she had run away, packed all her clothes and personal stuff in her old Corvair and hit the road in the middle of the night when there was no-one to see. People believed you had forced her to run away. They shunned you for a while, then it all faded away. She had no real friends in town so there wasn't anyone to raise hell. Her one casual friend got a letter, supposedly from Montreal, saying that she was starting over and not to worry. Veronica Graham was gone."

"If you know she left town why the hell are you after me? Why are you accusing me of killing her? You're crazy."

"Harold, we both know very well that Veronica never left Westport, not until recently when her bones went for a boat ride with the coroner." I didn't let him respond. "Besides, Harold, you told me just a minute ago that you couldn't let her leave. Which is it, Harold? Did she leave or not? You seem to be confused. You said you made a place for her to stay while she decided to accept you."

I paused briefly. Morrison was pacing again, muttering words I couldn't hear, waving his arms. I shouted.

"Harold!"

He stopped pacing and looked at me again. I wished I'd rushed him a moment before. He seemed to have forgotten I was there.

"The truth, Harold. Do you remember the truth after all these years of living this lie? Come on. Let's hear it."

There was that fragrance again. I wondered if it was a figment of my imagination; it came and went so fast. It was almost recognizable. Almost.

Again I refocused, this time to find Morrison back in his chair, leaning back comfortably, alert and with the gun at the ready.

"I think you're a coward, Harold. I think you're afraid to hear the truth come out of your own mouth, afraid to face your own evil."

"She shouldn't have died - could have lived if she'd wanted to." Morrison paused, regrouping.

"I found out she was going to leave town and I couldn't let that happen. She thought it was all a big secret but I found out. Only had a couple of weeks to get everything ready. I went to her house that night, the night she was supposed to go, tricked her into coming outside.

"There was no-one living at the Gilmore Island House then so I took her there. I'd already prepared the attic room with everything she'd need. I tied her to the bed – she'd have tried to run away otherwise - went back to the house she rented - put the last of her clothes and other stuff into her suitcases. There wasn't much left to pack - she was already planning on leaving that night. Put it all in her car 'n' drove it out to my cabin in the woods on Foley Mountain - hid it there for a while. Took me most of the night to walk back to town and get back out to the island.

"As I got close to the house I could hear her screaming. I told her that she would have to be quieter or I'd have to gag her when I left.

"I untied her, gave her the food I'd brought but she wouldn't eat. I *told* her all she had to do was say she loved me and everything would be okay. She said I was a beast; a kidnapper, a vile inhuman thing and that she would not *ever* change that opinion. She would hate me to her dying day. I knew she was just teasing me though. In time she would give up the game and admit she loved me."

His eyes became unfocused as he stared at the wall – remembering.

"I'd never been alone with her before and now had a new problem. I wanted to have sex with her like people who are in love. When I told her this she cried and said "no, please no." I said I wouldn't rush her.

"I left her - locked the attic hatch - left her with candles and water and a chamber pot. Told her I'd be back the next day to see if she'd changed her mind.

"I came back the next day, and the next and the one after that. Every time I asked the same questions and got the same answers - same unkindness. Each day I brought hot water up for her to bathe but she refused. Finally I had to insist - made her get undressed and put her in the tub. After that it wasn't a problem. Just needed to be shown who was in charge.

"Each time I came I brought food but she wouldn't eat. Didn't know what to do about that. Thought she'd eventually get hungry enough to eat.

"I was wrong about that. In a very short time - couple of weeks, she became so weak that I had to carry her to the bath and wash her as well. She got stupid - couldn't concentrate - hardly talked at all.

"One day, I knew she would come around eventually, after her bath, I asked if she was ready to have sex with me. She didn't say no. We enjoyed it greatly and later I bathed her again and put her back in bed."

Morrison started to cry. Huge tears rolled down his face and he wiped them away with the back of his hand. He sniffed loudly.

I have to say I was too shocked and appalled to say a word. Eventually Morrison went on with his horrific story.

"Next day when I arrived she was dead. She shouldn't have died. All she had to do was. . ."

I found my voice. "Stop saying that. You're the one responsible for her death; no-one else. You're the one who put her in that position, made her make the choice of death rather than submission. You killed her as sure as if you'd shot her with that gun."

Now it was his turn to be, or appear to be, shocked. I suppose it's possible that he'd never thought of the thing in those terms before. Probably he still wouldn't admit the truth of it. That didn't change anything.

"We coulda been happy. All those people in town turned her against me – made her afraid of me. I'll go and pay some more of'm a visit when I'm done with you. You ruined everything. Used to be able to go and visit her 'til you showed up. You didn't even notice the attic hatch was still open when you first went through the place with that real estate person. I covered it over before you moved in but you found her anyway - they took her away and I'll never see her again and it's all – your - fault." He was up again and raving, swinging the gun back and forth at his side, pacing.

"Get up. You're gonna pay for ruinin' my life." He pointed the gun squarely at me for the first time. "Get up. We're goin' for a little boat ride. I hear you're not much of a swimmer. Let's go find out." He waved the gun in the direction of the workshop area where there was direct access to the water. As I turned to go my eye caught a glimpse of some of the cars stored there. Most of the vehicles were covered by old, worn tarps but what little I could see was instantly recognizable. There was part of the front scoop of an E type Jag., a bit of wheel cover of an old Citroen and the back quarter panel – hood corner, tail lights and bumper – of a turquoise, Chevy Corvair. Now I knew what was prodding my memory. I'd seen Veronica Graham's car here months ago.

"You collect cars do you, Harold?"

"Yes. Now shut up and move." He waved the gun again but kept his distance.

I stood and turned toward the workshop area, wondering if I could make a break and duck behind some of the mountain of junk that filled the place. Not likely. He was too close. Even if he wasn't much of a shot he could hardly miss from this distance. And he had six shots to get the job done. I reached a decision suddenly and acted on it. I stopped walking and turned to face Morrison.

"You know what, Harold. I'm not going to let you drown me. Surely that's how our little boat ride and swimming lesson is going to end."

"Shut up and get moving." He waved the gun at me again.

"No. You seem to have a thing for slow painful deaths don't you, you crazy bastard. Well, I'm not going to play along. You're going to have to shoot me. Can you do that, Harold?"

There was that scent again. This time I recognized what it was and where it was probably coming from. How, I didn't know, but there it was. I pushed a little harder.

"Come on, Harry, don't you have the guts to kill someone face to face? Or maybe you only kill women?"

"No. Stop it. I'll show you."

He pointed the gun unsteadily at me and thumbed back the hammer. I turned my back on him, then collapsed as fast as I could to the floor.

A figure materialized from the shadows. "Harold Morrison. This is the police. Stop where you are and put down the gun. Now."

Mike Grant stood four metres away, his Glock levelled at his target. OPP to the rescue. Mike was really going to be pissed at me for this stunt.

Chapter 26

People say that these kinds of surreal situations seem to play out in slow motion. Not for me. I rolled twice, into a partial shadow and watched.

No more words. Three seconds of silence, then three shots from the Glock.

I guess Morrison decided that he had to eliminate the more significant threat before taking care of me. He turned his head at the sound of Grant's voice, instantly assessed the situation and made his decision. The gun had been held outstretched and aimed at me on the floor. Now with a visible twist of his upper body Morrison swung the heavy weapon toward Grant.

It never reached the target.

Grant's aim was sure and steady and all three shots found their mark, sending Morrison reeling backward over an upturned canoe and crashing in a heap on the ancient wood floor. The big, old Webley revolver fell where Morrison had stood, spinning round like a bottle in a drinking game.

Out in the open gunshots from a handgun are not actually very loud but in that confined space the effect was deafening.

My ears rang and cordite fumes filled my nose. Grant was already on his cell. He approached rapidly, pocketing his phone with his left hand as he came, gun still at the ready in his right. He passed by me without looking and skirted the canoe where he knelt and checked for any sign of life in his would-be killer, then rose slowly and stood staring down at the body on the floor, holstering his gun.

Less than twenty seconds had passed.

I began to hoist myself up and my movement drew his attention. He came back around the canoe; took hold of my arm and helped me to straighten up the rest of the way.

"You all right?"

I could hardly hear him. "Yes. A couple of new bumps and bruises but nothing serious." I hesitated briefly then added, "Thanks for that. I'm sorry you had to do it but I have to say I'd rather it was him lying there than me."

Grant only nodded. A small movement caught both of us at once and we looked toward the canoe. A thin trickle of blood had found a deep groove in the scarred, uneven floor and lengthened slowly until, finding a small rise, it began to pool.

"You know, it's weird. Most cops in this country never even have to aim their weapon at another person, let alone shoot to kill. And I've done it twice. Doesn't get any easier the second time around."

"No. I don't suppose it does."

"I think we had this conversation before, didn't we?"

We were quiet for a minute then Grant continued. "I'll be doing paperwork for a month. Last time was bad enough but this will be worse. When the cavalry arrives they'll separate us and take statements and ask several million questions."

"So we need to get our story straight before they get here." I thought a moment then added, "I think it's best if we agree not to mention our mutual cooperation with the investigation. That's the thing that will get you the most grief, even more than the shooting. If it comes out we'll deal with it somehow. We'll say that you warned me off but I didn't listen. We each arrived at Morrison as a suspect separately, from talking to Wil Bascome, Constance Osgoode and Mrs. Samuelson."

Grant waited then said, "I went to check out the cabin up on Foley Mountain after I got the address from MTO and left you at Mrs. Samuelson's and what I found there led me to decide to have a look at the nephew's boat shop."

"I blundered in on him on my own at the boat shop and you arrived in time to hear his confession and save my ass," I added.

I waited for a response. None. Sometimes these strong silent types are not much help at all.

"We leave out our joint conversation with Mrs. Samuelson entirely," I said.

"Unless we're forced to do otherwise. She's the only one who actually saw us working together," added Mike finally.

"Most of what we've laid out is true. All of it could be if you don't look too closely." I waited. "Anything else?"

After a moment Grant responded.

"We won't have an easy time of it, and depending who comes to do the interviews, it could be very rough. But, your version of the story fits the facts, and that will be the most important thing. You ready for some heat?"

"Yes. I've had heat before. Besides, what can they do to me for being nosey and stupid, getting myself into a situation like this? Not much really. I didn't break any laws that I know of, no misrepresentation or breaking and entering or anything like that. They may not be happy with me but, well, it won't be the first time I've had people unhappy with me. Speaking of which, I figured you'd be mad as hell at me over this whole thing."

"I'll be mad later. Right now I'm too relieved that it's not you or me lying here dead."

In the silence that followed I realized that my hearing was returning to normal. From far in the distance, for the second time that day, came the sound of sirens; several of them, again.

We began to walk toward the office area where we would meet the new arrivals and on the way I paused.

"How long were you there before you made your move?"

"You were sitting up on the floor when I got to the storage area. I heard voices as soon as I got inside so I was very quiet. I had a bead on him with the Glock every second from then on. I figured I'd let you work him for a while, until it got too dangerous to let it go on any longer. You did good."

I let that go.

"I noticed a change in your demeanour near the end there, like you knew I was there."

"I'd been getting whiffs of a familiar scent on and off for a few minutes. I finally figured out what it was. Your aftershave. I knew you were there. You can always tell when there's an Aqua Velva man around."

"Polo, wise guy."

"Right. Like I'd know the difference."

He let that go.

"I finally figured out what's been poking at me for the last day or so," I said. "You didn't find Veronica Graham's car at the cabin on the mountain did you?"

"No. Why?"

"I didn't think you would have." I reached down and grabbed a handful of tarp and pulled until it fell away revealing the rest of the turquoise Corvair. "He said he hid it at the Foley Mountain place originally so he must have brought it here later. Looks like it's been here for years. Maybe her belongings are still inside. I must have seen it – or part of it - when I was first here looking at my boats. Ever since I talked to Constance Osgoode something has been nudging the edges of my memory, just out of reach. Now I know what it was."

Noises of doors banging and voices calling invaded our reverie and we knew the marines had landed.

Let the fun begin.

Chapter 27

It turned out to be not very much fun at all. Mike had been right. We were not given an easy ride. As it should be.

There was the shooting review team, the crime scene investigators and the detectives, all of whom came from outside the region. They asked their millions of questions, then asked them again in a different order. They reviewed all the evidence and dug up more. They went everywhere Harold Morrison had ever been or might ever have been.

The last phone call Grant had received as he was leaving me at Mrs. Samuelson's house that day, gave him Harold Morrison's address on Foley Mountain.

Once there was something to compare to, it was found that Morrison's fingerprints were all over the attic at Gilmore House, not just the structure, which would have maybe been explainable, but also on the artefacts found with the body, which was not explainable. His prints were also found to match those lifted after a suspicious fire at the local museum, a fire which was believed to have destroyed some furniture and clothing items displayed there. Turns out that they were not burned after all. Morrison had removed them and set fire to some scrap wood and fabric. The museum director later identified the pieces found in the Gilmore House attic as being those lost at the time of the fire.

I buttermilk-drenched and coconut-coated another shrimp and made a mental note to tell Kim that the museum was sending a crew to remove the last of the bits and pieces from the attic.

Morrison's cabin did not yield much in the way of evidence but his room at the Morrison Boatworks was a goldmine. A closet had been converted to a shrine of sorts. Old photos of Veronica Graham, taken on the sly, covered one wall. There was a blow up of the picture from the newspaper. There was a scrapbook of newspaper clippings from the time of the 150th anniversary. There were thirty-year-old un-mailed letters telling of Morrison's warped fixation with Veronica Graham; his stalking, pleading, demands and threats. There were several early drafts of the letter he had written to Constance Osgoode and mailed from Montreal, the letter which purported to be from Veronica and which attempted to explain her sudden departure from Westport.

One find of significant importance were several volumes of irregularly used diaries, some bound, some just spiral notebooks. They spanned most of Morrison's life, annotating his often erratic thought patterns. It occasionally skipped years and even decades, but, at times, entries were daily and even hourly. The highs and lows of Harold Morrison's life were there, including the famous Costume Ball, Veronica's rejections, her imprisonment in the attic, her death. Also included, the fire which had added physical damage to the emotional already present in Morrison and which caused his almost total retreat from society to his cabin on Foley Mountain, with only occasional visits to the Gilmore house. That isolation would end when I arrived at Westport.

Some years had passed in the diary before the entry which detailed events surrounding the fifth and, for him, final refit of the Gilmore house.

I became the focus of his life after my discovery of the lady in the attic.

Whole pages described his time spent watching me. A detailed description was included of the bent tree booby- trap which almost sent me flying off the cliff onto the rocks of Loon Point. He told of his many trips to the stony beach - only some of which I had been aware of - the last time with a rifle which he hadn't been able to use right then - and of his earlier invasion of my suite at the Inn and his removal of the rock with the green paint and the rope fragment. He was quite sure at this point that I was on to him. He seemed to have been following me around during the daytime and watching the Inn at night. He wasn't sleeping. The last week his pursuit had become relentless, culminating in his attack on Wil Bascome, Frankie's near miss, the attempt to kill the person he thought was me in the street, and his truck attack on Josée and me on the morning of the day when it all came to an end. He was in process of writing about that event when I showed up at Morrison's Boatworks.

Such was his focus on me that he never, except in passing, mentioned Grant, with whom I had spent most of those last two or three days, or, except briefly, Josée Allard whom he had almost killed trying to get to me.

This, more than anything else I think, seemed to convince the investigators that our story was true. Grant's name was never mentioned in connection with mine in Morrison's diary. He was alluded to on several occasions but only as a peripheral annoyance. I still think that the investigators had their suspicions that we were somehow working together but there was no evidence and we held firm to our version of events.

Mrs. Samuelson and Constance Osgoode, once they realized that the focus of the new investigation was more on Grant and me than on Veronica Graham, each reverted to individual versions of ditzy-old-woman mode and the investigators soon gave up trying to get any good information from them.

I also found out why no-one had realized that Veronica was not the 100 year old run-away, Victoria. There had been a serious motel fire some way away and almost all local resources had been diverted to dealing with the aftermath. After the backlog had been cleared and the forensics people and the medical examiner had a chance to breathe, they somehow did not follow up on the body from the Gilmore House. Other cases came and went. It was not forgotten exactly, but since it was thought to be so very old it was not anyone's priority. It became so after the revelations of Jeremy Greenwood.

The skeleton was not lost exactly but was well hidden, though not deliberately.

Once someone was able to properly look at the Gilmore case it was determined that nothing special had been done to the body of Veronica Graham to have her end up looking the way we found her. Time, roughly thirty-five years, and weather, season after season of freezing and roasting, had done their worst. That, combined with the period clothing, had led us all astray temporarily.

Dental records and DNA, from a sample of hair from a hairbrush taken from the attic and others from her car, were used to finally confirm Veronica Graham's identity. No-one rushed the examination or report writing, not realizing how wound-up the investigation had become in Westport. The report was on Grant's desk when he returned to duty after the shooting inquiry. If not for the delay caused by the motel fire the Medical Examiner could have saved us all a lot of trouble. Better late than never. We still wouldn't have known who she was initially but at least we'd have been looking for someone from the right half of the century.

The medallion Veronica was wearing remained a mystery until someone compared notes with those of the Harold

Morrison autopsy. He was wearing an identical medallion. Notes in his diary showed that he'd forced her to wear it after he put her in the attic.

Throughout the investigation they had given Grant a harder time than they had given me but eventually they concluded that he had done only what had been necessary to save the life of a citizen, albeit, in their opinion, a foolish one.

When it was over they all went away and we were tired, rattled and happy to see them go. We were also, somehow, off the hook. Grant had been cleared in the shooting and I'd been lectured sternly and at great length, by an old Detective Sergeant, about the folly of what I'd involved myself in.

Josée made a good recovery and has taken a promotion to north western Ontario, starting after her recuperation from a concussion. Other than that her injuries were relatively minor. We had a little send-off party for her at the Inn but we never did get together again privately.

I did get a call from Jeremy Greenwood soon after the whole business was wrapped up. He had related the entire incident to his mother. She said Jeremy's grandmother had written a lengthy letter to her parents explaining that she was going to go away with Albert Greenwood, of whom they were not especially fond it seemed. She planned to leave it for them to find after the pair had departed by boat for Westport. At the last moment her defiant streak re-emerged and she had a change of mind and decided it would be appropriate to let them stew about her for a while. She tore up the letter. They left the fragments burning in the kitchen stove as they went out the door.

Grant never did get angry with me over the whole business and we have become what you might call casual friends. We're going golfing next week, weather and schedules permitting.

"RJ." The voice was a sharp whisper. Bud. "RJ, do you want me to finish prepping those shrimps?"

"No, Bud. Thanks. I've got it. I was just thinking about all that's happened in a very short time."

Bud looked around to be sure no-one was overhearing. Jeany was at the prep sink and Frankie at the dishwasher. "RJ, I know you're the boss and all but I have to say something. Isn't it time you started thinking less about the body in the attic and more about the bodies in the dining room, the ones we're supposed to be feeding in a little while?"

I realized Bud was making sense. Bud always makes sense – very annoying sometimes. I'd be a while getting over recent events but this was not the time or place for reliving them.

"You're right, Bud. Swat me with something if I drift off again will you please."

"Sure thing, boss. Whatever you say."

Readers:

Thanks for looking at the story.

What follows is a copy of the Gilmore House Inn Dinner Menu for one of the days of opening week – that week is quite a blur so I'm not exactly sure which day it was.

Also appearing are a few of the recipes used at the Inn during that week and the weeks following. Try them out and see what you think. Some are original to the Inn, either Bud's or mine usually, and others are adaptations of meals I've had and enjoyed. I'm not always sure where they came from, but I wouldn't be using them at the Inn if I hadn't thought they were really good. Bud and I put our own little spin on everything we cook at the Inn but we try to be consistent, always using the same spin. These recipes are as close as possible to what we actually serve, scaled down for home use. I hope you enjoy them and that they bring back pleasant memories of your time with us. We will be publishing a Gilmore House Inn Cookbook in the near future.

I've also included some floor plans and a topographical map. I believe the map was made by Alexander Gilmore. The floor plans don't seem to be professional but were among the papers stored at the Barrhaven real estate office.

We hope to see you again.

R.J.Harison

The Gilmore House Inn

Gilmore Island, Westport, Ontario, Canada.

Dinner Menu

Starters (changed daily)

Soup du Jour - Please ask your server to tell you about our soups of the day. Each is made right here, using fresh, local and organic ingredients wherever possible.

Escargots - Six large Escargots prepared in our own blend of garlic butter and seasonings and served with lots of garlic toast.
Caesar Salad - Made to order – just for you, with our own Caesar dressing.

Mains (changed daily)

International Salmon - An 8 ounce salmon fillet, marinated in Bourbon, maple syrup, pineapple juice, soy sauce and seasonings, seared on the grill then finished in the oven, Served with fresh, local asparagus and our own blend of multigrain rice.

Crispy Parmesan Chicken Breast - Chicken breasts marinated in our house made Italian dressing, then rolled in a combination of seasoned bread crumbs and Parmesan cheese and baked to a golden brown. Served with home fried potatoes and sugar snap peas.

New York Strip Steak - A 12 ounce striploin steak grilled to your specifications. Served with your choice of potato and vegetable.

Layered Vegetable and Potato Bake - Very thin slices of tomato, zucchini, mushroom, red onion, red pepper and potato layered together with a creamy sauce. Served with garlic toast.

Please note that salads and breads are available at no additional charge with all mains.

Desserts (changed daily)

Cheesecake - Please ask your server to tell you about our cheesecake style and flavour of the day.

Crème Caramel - Home made at Gilmore House with a hint of maple syrup.

Freshly Baked Pie - We have a couple of types of pie available every day. Please ask your server for today's selections.

We provide bag lunches upon request, These include a sandwich, fruit and a Great Canadian Fruit and Nut Cookie. Canned soft drinks and bottled water are also available. Please arrange for this with your server tonight if you would like one tomorrow.

a recipe from

The Gilmore House Inn
Westport, Ontario, Canada.

Gilmore's Chicken Cordon Bleu

Ingredients : yield: 2 servings

2 skinless / boneless chicken breasts
2 slices Swiss or Ementhal cheese (each slice slightly smaller than the chicken breast)
2 slices black forest ham thinly sliced or shaved
1 egg 1 oz. water
1 c dry bread crumbs
1/4 c flour
2 tbsp shredded cheddar cheese (good quality old cheddar)
1 tsp dried parsley
1/2 tsp granulated onion
1/2 tsp granulated garlic
1/2 tsp black pepper – ground 1/4 tsp sea salt
2 tbsp water

Pre-heat the oven to 325° Centre the rack

You'll need a cutting board, three shallow bowls or pie plates just large enough to take the chicken breasts, and a baking pan, preferably with a rack. Line the pan with foil. Spray the rack with a non-stick cooking spray.

Rinse the chicken and pat dry with paper towel. Place one chicken breast on the board and hold it gently but firmly in place. With a sharp knife, cut sideways into the thickest side of the meat to open a flap. Be careful not to cut all the way through. The chicken breast should open like a book.

Season both the top and bottom of the flap lightly with salt and pepper.

Lay one slice of Swiss cheese, one slice of ham and 1 tbsp of cheddar onto the bottom flap.

Fold the top flap over and repeat with the other breast(s).

Mix the last 5 ingredients with the bread crumbs in one of the bowls.

Beat the egg and water into the second bowl.

Spread the flour over the bottom of the third bowl.

Holding the chicken breast closed firmly, push any stray ham or cheese inside. Roll the breast carefully in the flour until it is coated on all surfaces.

Next roll the breast in the egg wash to coat.

Last, roll the breast in the seasoned crumbs until all surfaces are covered and place directly on the baking rack.

Sprinkle extra crumbs on any thin spots and repeat.

Discard all the coating leftovers - none can be kept or reused

Bake for 45-50 minutes. Let stand for five minutes, tented with foil, before serving.

Enjoy

a recipe from

The Gilmore House Inn
Westport, Ontario, Canada.

Crisp Parmesan Chicken Breast

Ingredients: Yield: 4-6 servings

4-6 chicken breasts – skinless and boneless
2 c herb vinaigrette
(or Italian salad dressing - any variety will do)
1 c dry bread crumbs with your choice of dry seasonings.
(my choices are *)
1 c grated Parmesan cheese
1 tsp granulated onion (*)
1 tsp granulated garlic (*)
1 tsp dried parsley (*)
1/2 tsp ground black pepper
1/4 tsp sea salt

Preheat the oven to 350°. Centre the rack.

In a deep, narrow bowl or a sealable bag toss the breasts and the salad dressing to coat well. (cover and) Refrigerate for at least 1 hour, or up to 4 hours.

Drain the breasts and <u>discard the dressing.</u> Do not rinse the chicken.

Mix the last 7 ingredients in a bowl.

Coat each breast thoroughly, one at a time, with the cheese and crumb mixture. Place each on a rack over a flat shallow pan covered with foil or parchment paper (these are not a necessity but make clean up easier). If you don't have an open rack use a flat pan, with foil or parchment paper.
Spray the rack, paper, foil.

Bake for 45 minutes until the crumb coating has browned. Let stand for five minutes, tented with foil, before serving.

(if you want to change it up a bit, substitute a balsamic based dressing or add oregano or basil in place of the parsley or both)

Enjoy *RJH*

a recipe from

The Gilmore House Inn
Westport, Ontario, Canada.

Not Your Everyday Scrambled Eggs yield 2 servings

Ingredients

1-2 c potatoes - cooked, diced and cooled firm – don't overcook
4 slices back bacon thick cut cooked and diced keep warm
4 large eggs
2-3 green onions chopped 1/2 cm.
1-2 cloves of garlic chopped very fine
1/4 c red or Spanish onion minced fine
1/4 c roasted red pepper chopped
1/4 c milk or cream
1/4 c old cheddar cheese grated
2 + 1 tbsp olive oil
1 tbsp fresh parsley chopped fine

In a large, heavy fry pan heat 2 tbsp of oil and fry the potatoes over medium/high heat until they start to turn golden. About 5 minutes stirring frequently.

Add the red or Spanish onion and cook 2-3 minutes stirring frequently

In a bowl, beat the eggs with the milk or cream. Preheat a second fry pan to medium heat with 1 tbsp of oil.

Add the bacon pieces and the garlic to the first pan. Add half the green onions to the second pan and stir and cook each 2 min.

Pour the egg mixture into the second pan and add the roasted red pepper.

Continue stirring both pans until the egg mixture has solidified. Remove from heat and stir in the cheese and the parsley

Divide the potato mixture onto two plates and cover each with half the egg mixture. Sprinkle with remaining green onions.

Serve with toast or toasted English muffins

Enjoy *RJH*

a recipe from

The Gilmore House Inn
Westport, Ontario, Canada.

RJ's Salmon Salad yield 4 good sized sandwiches

1 can red salmon drained
(or leftover salmon from a previous meal)
1/4 c red onion chopped fine
1/4 c celery chopped fine
1/4 c red pepper chopped fine
1/4 c carrot grated chopped
1 tsp green relish
1/4 tsp horseradish
1/4 c mayonnaise
1 tbsp Ranch dressing
1/8 tsp salt
1/4 tsp black pepper

In a large bowl break up the salmon roughly with a fork.

Add the vegetables and the salt and pepper and stir thoroughly

Add the horseradish, relish, dressing and mayo. Stir until well mixed. Use as much mayonnaise as you like to get the desired creaminess

Serve this on a bed of lettuce with some tomato slices or use it as a sandwich filling. I like mine toasted lightly with some cucumber slices and a thin slice of Gouda on it.

Change it up a bit. Use tuna and finely chop some green olives with pimiento instead of the relish.

Enjoy *RJH*

a recipe from

The Gilmore House Inn
Westport, Ontario, Canada.

International Salmon

Ingredients : Yield: 2 servings

2 8 ounce salmon fillets (skinned)
1 c amber or dark Ontario maple syrup
1/2 c pineapple juice
1/2 c vegetable oil
1/4 c Kentucky whiskey
2 tbsp soy sauce
1 tbsp garlic purée (or very finely chopped or grated garlic)
1/2 tsp black pepper (cracked) 1/4 tsp sea salt

Whisk together the pineapple juice, soy sauce, maple syrup, whiskey, salt, pepper, garlic and vegetable oil.

Rinse the salmon and pat dry.

Place the salmon in a 1 quart sealable bag. Pour the marinade into the bag with the salmon. Marinate for a minimum of 1 hour, or up to 4 hours, laying flat in a single layer.

Remove the salmon from the bag and discard the marinade. Grill or broil the salmon for approximately six minutes on each side, until the center of the fish just starts to look opaque when flaked. Let stand 5 minutes, tented with foil, before serving.

(for a thicker sauce, purée a small can of pineapple tidbits instead of using just the juice)

Enjoy *RJH*

I called this International Salmon because it has noticeable flavours of Ontario, Kentucky, and the tropics.

a recipe from

The Gilmore House Inn
Westport, Ontario, Canada.

Buds All Canadian Fruit Cookies

Ingredients:

1 c whole wheat flour
1 1/4 c quick oats
1 tbsp wheat germ
1/2 tsp salt
1/2 tsp baking powder
1/2 tsp baking soda
1/2 c dried apple
1/2 c dried strawberries
1/2 c dried cherries
1/2 c dried cranberries
1/2 c dried blueberries

4 tbsp butter or margarine
4 tbsp apple sauce (unsweetened)
1 c maple sugar
1/4 c maple syrup
2 eggs
1/4 c milk

(Spelt or Kamut flour can be used if you like - to eliminate gluten use a non-wheat flour or flour blend and lose the wheat germ)

Preheat the oven to 350°. Raise the rack to one level above centre position.

Chop all the fruit into small pieces.

Mix the first six - dry - ingredients.

In a separate bowl mix the chopped fruit.

In a mixer bowl mix the butter, sugar and apple sauce until thoroughly blended.
Add the eggs one at a time with the mixer running then add the milk and then the syrup.
Reduce the speed to low and add the dry ingredients and mix well.
Add the fruit and mix well with a spoon or spatula.

Refrigerate the mixture for 1 hour.

Using a small scoop or spoon place the dough on a cookie sheet spacing well.

Bake for about 18 minutes, let cool slightly then remove from pan to a cooling rack.

Enjoy *Bud*

About the Author

Brian Lindsay has recently retired after ten years of operating a personal chef service. He spent numerous years in food service, as a food and beverage manager and a kitchen manager. Before that he was, for a few years, in retail security. He has now turned his focus to writing crime fiction with an epicurean twist.

He has two grown children, a son and a daughter, and lives with his wife in Kitchener, Ontario.

This book, *Old Bones* – A Gilmore House Mystery, was short-listed as a finalist for the 2016 **ARTHUR ELLIS AWARD** for Best First (Crime) Novel.

To contact the author please visit www.brlindsayimagist.com